Anne turned her head in his direction, her gaze meeting his. He heard her breath catch in her throat as he slid one hand over the smooth wood of the bench and slipped it around her.

This was dangerous.

Tor knew it was dangerous. But he could no more have stopped himself from kissing her than he could have kept from falling after leaping off a mountain cliff.

She made no attempt to move away, as he half expected, half hoped. She did not close her eyes either as he leaned over her, lost in her blue-eyed gaze. Her mouth was soft, her lips slightly parted. He barely touched his mouth to hers, yet his head swam with the scent of her bright hair, the feel of her lips against his, the quiver of her hand as she slid it onto his knee.

When he pulled back, her eyes were half shut. She just sat there, exhaling softly. She was so beautiful. Her cheeks were flushed from the sun and wind on the beach. She smelled of the salt sea and dreams he never knew he had.

He could not resist a chuckle as she sat beside him, utterly still. "What are you doing?" he finally breathed, lifting his fingers to her chin so that she would open those lovely eyes and gaze at him.

Slowly her lashes lifted and he was again lost to her.

"I want to savor it. My first kiss." She laid her hand on his cheek. "I let ye kiss me because 'tis what I have wanted since I first set eyes on ye. . . ."

Books by Colleen Faulkner

FORBIDDEN CARESS
RAGING DESIRE
SNOW FIRE
TRAITOR'S CARESS
PASSION'S SAVAGE MOON
TEMPTATION'S TENDER KISS
LOVE'S SWEET BOUNTY
PATRIOT'S PASSION
SAVAGE SURRENDER
SWEET DECEPTION
FLAMES OF LOVE
FOREVER HIS
CAPTIVE
O'BRIAN'S BRIDE
DESTINED TO BE MINE
TO LOVE A DARK STRANGER
FIRE DANCER
ANGEL IN MY ARMS
ONCE MORE
IF YOU WERE MINE
HIGHLAND BRIDE
HIGHLAND LADY
HIGHLAND LORD

Published by Zebra Books

HIGHLAND LORD

COLLEEN FAULKNER

ZEBRA BOOKS
KENSINGTON PUBLISHING CORP.
http://www.zebrabooks.com

ZEBRA BOOKS are published by

Kensington Publishing Corp.
850 Third Avenue
New York, NY 10022

All Kensington titles, imprints and distributed lines are available at special quantity discounts for bulk purchases for sales promotion, premiums, fund-raising, educational or institutional use.

Special book excerpts or customized printings can also be created to fit specific needs. For details, write or phone the office of the Kensington Special Sales Manager: Kensington Publishing Corp., 850 Third Avenue, New York, NY 10022. Attn. Special Sales Department. Phone: 1-800-221-2647.

Zebra and the Z logo Reg. U.S. Pat. & TM Off.

First Printing: January 2002
10 9 8 7 6 5 4 3 2 1

Printed in the United States of America

PROLOGUE

January 1323
North coast of Scotland

"*Hun krever De.* She calls for you," Tor's eldest half-brother snapped in their mother's Norwegian tongue from the curtained doorway between the main room of the cottage and his mother's room. He made no attempt to hide his bitterness toward his brother born out of wedlock as he shouldered by him. "She wants only you."

Tor met his brother's blue-eyed gaze, but neither spoke again. The reason why Henne called for Tor was obvious on his brother's windburned face. She was dying.

Tor shoved the curtain aside and ducked through the doorway. His mother's chamber was barely larger than her bed. The room was dark save for the flicker of a single tallow candle and the glow of coals on the brazier. The room smelled of peat smoke, wool, his mother's fragrant hair . . . and death.

For a moment, Tor hovered in the doorway, struggling with a sense of loss that already weighed heavily on his heart. Well known among the Norsemen for his strength and his formidability, he did not like this feeling of helplessness. And though the ceiling brushed the top of his head when he stood full upright in the room, he felt small. Insignificant.

Henne lay on the narrow bed, pale as the winter moonlight, her eyes closed. Her blond hair, sprinkled with gray, was parted in the center. Two long plaits rested on her chest, which rose and fell so laboriously. When she exhaled, she sounded as if an ill wind whistled through her body.

His mother's eyelids flickered and she lifted her hand from beneath the heavy woolen blanket. *"Mengmin sønn . . .* Tor,'' she murmured.

He went to her, down on one knee beside the bed. The floorboards were rough and uneven, and he felt the cold of them even through the leather of his pants. *"Mor,"* he responded tenderly in her native tongue. "Mother."

She smiled and let her eyes drift shut because it seemed to take too much from her to speak and keep them open at the same time. "My time grows near," she whispered.

He gripped her tiny hand tightly between his massive ones and spoke firmly. *"Ingen!* You were better this morning. You said so yourself."

She inhaled sharply and her breath rattled in her chest, making Tor feel guilty for upsetting her, for making the difficult task of breathing even more difficult for her.

"I am sorry, *mengmin mor,*" he whispered, bowing his head. "Say what you will."

She pressed her dry lips tightly together, and Tor saw that she was still a strikingly beautiful woman. Even pale and thin and on her last breath, she would still turn men's heads, both Norse and Scot.

"I want to make a request," she murmured. "And I want you to vow to grant me my wish so that I may see my glory in heaven."

Tor gazed down at his mother's hand clasped between his. He did not know if he believed in her Jesus Christ. He did not know what he believed in beyond strength, beyond fortitude. Beyond himself and the power of the sword and ax. "I am listening," he soothed, rubbing her cold hand between his.

"Lov meg." She coughed a dry, hacking cough that turned her pale skin even more pasty. "Promise me."

Tor lowered his cheek to her hand and waited patiently until the coughing spell passed.

"Promise me," she rasped.

"Promise you what?" He could not hide the tremble of emotion in his voice. He only hoped that she was too ill to detect it.

Slowly Henne opened her eyes, and the warmth of their blue depths overwhelmed Tor. He never failed to be shocked by the love she felt for him, reflected in those eyes that so resembled his own.

"Promise me that you will leave this place."

Tor clenched his mouth until his teeth ached, but he said nothing. She had spoken of this matter before and the conversations had never gone well.

"Promise me that when I am gone, you will leave this place and ride south to your father. To the Highlands. To the place called Rancoff." She spoke the last word with the same reverence as she used when saying "heaven."

"I have no father." Though he tried for her sake, he could not keep the bitterness from his voice.

"Remember, I am a child born of a human mother and a Norse God."

She smiled sadly. It was a tale he had made up as a young child to fight the teasing that came with being a bastard. Later he had learned to use his fists, which were far more effective.

"You must promise me you will go to your father and let him lay claim to you, my son." She closed her eyes.

Tor shook his head. "I cannot." His words were soft, calm, but inside his gut twisted in turmoil. His mother did not know how much he hated the man who had sired him.

Again Henne opened her eyes. It was obvious that it took almost more effort than she could afford, yet the strength of her voice was surprisingly strong. One last rally. It was so like her.

"You must promise your mother on her deathbed that you will go to your father, the Scottish lord, and lay claim to what is rightfully yours." She took a rattling breath. "There is nothing here for you, Tor. Our way of life has decayed, rotted from the inside out."

He could feel her life's blood growing cooler with every word she spoke. Her breath was shallower now. He had to lean closer to hear her.

"Promise me," she croaked.

Tor was painfully torn between wanting to grant his mother her last wish, and the hatred he felt for the Scottish lord who had abandoned his pregnant mother so many years ago.

Once more, her eyes flickered open. "Promise me," she said fiercely, "or I will haunt you the rest of your days, my son. I swear I will."

Tor did not want to utter the words, and yet he

heard them slip from his mouth, foreign and metallic-tasting. *"Jeg lover.* I promise."

"Say it again," she insisted, lifting her head from the bed. "Say it."

"I promise." Tor felt as if she were gutting him with each word she demanded from him. "I promise to seek my Scot father and lay my claim to him as his son."

Henne fell back on the bed, beyond exhaustion now. Her hand went limp in his.

"Mor?" Tor leaned forward, panic fluttering in his chest. "Mother?"

With the last strength she possessed, Henne opened her eyes. "I always loved you best," she whispered, smiling sadly. "I knew it was wrong, but I always loved you best."

Tor felt his lower lip tremble, and he feared that a tear gathered in one eye. Tor had never cried, his mother had once told him. Not even as a babe in swaddling cloth.

"Your father, Munro, tell . . . tell him I . . ."

"What?" Tor had to lean even closer to hear his mother's words. Her lashes brushed his cheek. The smell of death was strong in the room now, heady and cloying. "What do you say, my dear mother?"

"Tell . . . tell him," she breathed, "that I'm sorry for wanting to keep you to myself. Tell him . . ."

She expelled her last words as a sigh, and her chest did not rise again.

Tor stared in disbelief for a moment at his mother's peaceful face. That was it? A woman of such strength, such greatness, dies quietly in the darkness of night?

Tor pressed a kiss to her cheek and tucked her cool hand beneath the blanket as he fought the knot of nausea in his stomach. The lump in his throat. He rose and walked away from the bed.

"Hun er død! She is dead!" he cried as he stepped through the curtained doorway. "My mother is dead." And then, in rage, he swung his fist at the nearest object and shattered his mother's precious glass window.

CHAPTER ONE

Three months later, April 1323
South of Aberdeen, Highlands of Scotland

'Twas surely Beelzebub himself bearing down upon the castle, Robert thought as he stared down from the rampart walk at the three horsemen approaching the open gate of Lord Rancoff's castle.

"The two men who rode abreast were hulking creatures with massive forearms and broad chests, but the beast who led them . . ." Perhaps he was the Antichrist. Rob's grandmother had always warned him that Beelzebub would not come with a forked tail, breathing fire, but in human form—as a strikingly handsome man on a dark steed. Rob had always imagined that Satan's hair was black, his skin ruddy.

The blonde who approached the castle changed his mind.

The man rode a black horse that dwarfed every Scottish pony in Rancoff's garrison stables. Rob had never seen a man like the leader: a giant, taller and broader of shoulder than even the lord of this keep. He had long, wild blond hair that blew in the wind, and a body of muscle and sinew that bulged at the seams of his leather tunic and trousers and fur mantle. Even from this distance, Rob could tell that the intruder was a foreigner and not of Scottish blood. But a foreigner from where? The tar pits of hell?

Rob spotted the glimmer of a broadsword nearly as long as he was tall strapped to the steed's side, and immediately shouted an alarm to the clansmen below. "Lift the drawbridge! Lift the bridge!"

"What ye say, lad?" someone called from the bailey.

Rob hated being called a lad. He was more than twenty years old—old enough to wed. To be a father. The man of his own cottage. But as long as his father, Rancoff Castle's steward, lived, he knew he would just be a lad. "Lift the damned, blessed bridge, I say! Lift it or your head will roll," he barked.

There were many things on God's earth that Rob loved: cool ale; his mother's hearth on a winter night; Mary, the smith's daughter. But what he loved most was this land. This castle. He would die for his master, the Lord of Rancoff. He would die for the men and women who lived within and beyond these walls. It was this love, his father told him, that would one day make him the keep's steward.

Rob gazed down at the blond men pressing toward the castle walls, trying to suppress the sick fear he felt in his stomach. At long last, he heard the screeching sound of iron against iron as the drawbridge swung upward.

The leader of the foreigners reined in his mount and the horse rose up on its hind legs, not because it had lost control of its footing and might fall into the moat, but as a show of the strength and power of the man who rode it.

A part of Rob wanted to run and not stop until he had reached the safety of the warm kitchen and his mother's arms. But a part of him was fascinated by the blond foreigners.

Rob peered over the edge of the stone rampart just as the leader peered up.

"You! Boy!" He spoke English, but with a strange accent that Rob could not place.

Rob straightened his posture, hoping to appear broader of shoulder than he was, gathering the courage to reply. "What be your business?"

He eyed the broadswords and battle axes strapped to the men's horses, the leather and metal shields and conical-shaped helmets with nasals. They were strange weapons with embossed leather handles and fur-and-leather straps—implements made in some foreign land. But they were *sheathed* swords, Robert reminded himself as he tried to remain calm. "I say again, what is your business?"

The giant blond man gathered his reins in his gloved hands and glanced up again. His wolfskin mantle flapped in the salt breeze that blew in with the coming tide. "I come in peace," he ground out, the anger in his tone that of a man not accustomed to closed gates.

"Ye carry swords," Robert answered boldly.

The foreigner's gaze did not stray from Robert's. "What man does not ride armed these days?"

He had a good point, but Robert would not concede that aloud.

"I have business with the lord of this castle, Munro Forrest of Rancoff," the giant called up. "I will speak to none but him."

Robert gazed out over the meadow just to be certain no other men accompanied the strangers. Naught was there but the sway of brittle grasses, a dusting of snow, and the call of a solitary gull. The tide was changing, and he could smell the salt air of the ocean nearby.

"And who do I say calls?" Robert questioned.

The stranger's eyes narrowed dangerously. His features hardened. "You do not."

Robert swallowed hard. The leader's sword was not unsheathed. He was two stories below and offered no threat, and yet Rob felt a fresh flutter of fear in the pit of his stomach.

"I will see if m'lord is receiving," Not waiting for an answer, Rob fled to the ladder that led below stairs.

It was fortunate his lordship was here at the castle today, for often he was not. Eight years ago Munro Forrest, Lord of Rancoff Castle, had married Elen of Dunblane, and it was there that he resided. With the castles only a short riding distance apart, his lordship, with the help of loyal men like Rob's own father, was able to run both households with amazing ease. Of course, gossip had it that it was her ladyship who truly ran both castles, and ran them well.

"My lord! M'lord Rancoff!" Rob burst into the paneled hall to find his master seated at the great table, studying a ledger.

Munro Forrest, Earl of Rancoff, glanced up with a smile of amusement. Though his lordship had fought with the Bruce at Bannockburn, married, and sired children, he was still a powerful man in his prime, despite having seen forty and eight winters.

"Rob. What is it?" He gestured. "Calm down, lad."

"The gates!" Rob fought for breath. "Men."

His lordship's brow furrowed as he half rose from his carved high-backed chair. "Englishmen?"

Rob shook his head fervently. "Nay, I think not. But I nae know who or what they are." He gulped in a great mouthful of air; he was feeling light-headed. "Foreigners, m'lord. I ordered the drawbridge lifted. There are only three, but they look to be barbarians."

"Barbarians?" Rancoff harrumphed as he lowered himself into his chair again.

"Long, wild blond hair, m'lord. Strange broadswords and axes. I swear by all that's holy, the blades look to be as long as ye are tall."

"They simply rode up to our gates?"

"And demanded to see you. The leader says— nay, *demands*—he will speak only to Munro Forrest himself."

"And what did ye say?"

Rob stiffened his spine. "I told him I would give ye the message, naught more."

Rancoff arched an eyebrow. "And he called me by name?"

Rob nodded.

"And who do they say they are?"

Rob was still breathing heavily from the sprint down the stairs. "He willnae say."

"Such kindly manners," the Lord Rancoff remarked. He glanced down at his papers, then back at Rob. "Ye say the gates are closed and no others approach?"

"No more, m'lord."

Rancoff picked up his quill and dipped it in an ink bottle. "Take a couple of men with ye, Rob. Stand guard on the wall."

"What . . . what shall I say to the foreigners?" Rob felt calmer now that he was in the presence of his lordship. He trusted this man as utterly as he trusted his own father.

"Tell them . . ." He scribbled a figure. "Tell them

your lord is presently occupied. I will see him when I am finished.''

"Occupied?'' Tor shouted upward to the stone wall. He was still on horseback, his half-brothers beside him.

"M'lord says he will see ye when he is done with his task,'' the young man called down, bolder now than he had been before he sought his master.

"How long?'' Tor demanded of the young man, who seemed to be of the age of his brother Olave. Tor did not like to be put off. This was not part of his plan. He had intended to ride straight through Rancoff's gates and demand audience with the man who had seeded his birth.

The boy shrugged. "He doesnae say.''

Tor scowled as he glanced back at his brothers. They had ridden hard since sunup to reach the castle. They were all tired, hungry, thirsty. Tor turned back to the lad on the rampart wall. "Are we not to at least be admitted beyond your outer walls? My brothers and my horses thirst.''

"I cannae open the gate without Rancoff's word.''

Tor gritted his teeth, twisting the reins in his gloved hands. "Can ye at least send out a bit of bread, ale, water?''

'' 'Tis a stream through the meadow.'' The smug young man pointed. "Ye are welcome to drink.''

Tor wheeled his mount around angrily and took off across the meadow. His brothers followed wordlessly.

"You think he will make us sit out here all night?'' Tor's youngest brother, Olave, asked in Norwegian.

He lay stretched beside the stream, chewing on a piece of dried haddock from his saddlebag.

Olave was a simple young man with simple needs, simple pleasures. There were some at his mother's village who had called Olave addle-witted as a child. Those children had received a fist in the mouth from Tor. It was not said often. Olave was neither as bright nor as capable as Finn, and perhaps he was a little slow-minded, but he was a good man, a loyal man.

Finn was handsome, tall like Tor, but slimmer. He had the face of an angel and the scheming, conniving mind of one of hell's demons. Though he still had not wed, Finn was said to have more children scattered across the continent than any other Norseman born of man.

Tor glanced at Olave as he rose from the rock where he had perched beside the stream. He gazed first at the setting sun, then back at the castle wall. It would be dark soon. Hours. It had been hours since he and his brothers had arrived, and still Rancoff would not admit him.

"I said," Olave repeated in his mother's tongue.

"I heard what you said," Tor answered quietly in English. Unlike Finn, he rarely lost his patience with Olave. He accepted Olave for who he was and accepted his limitations with it. "I do not know if we will sleep here tonight."

"Dumb way for a man to treat his son." Olave chewed thoughtfully on the smelly fish. "If Olave had a son like Tor, I would—"

"Olave, shut up," Finn piped up from where he stood leaning against a tree trunk.

Tor flashed Finn a look of warning.

"Olave is right," Finn said. "He ought not treat you this way. You didn't ride this far to be turned away at the gatehouse."

"He does not yet know it is me." Tor paced along the streambed, glancing occasionally at the castle wall that was losing its shape in the settling darkness. "I wish to tell him face to face," he ground out. "To see the look in his eyes when I ask him why he left our mother."

Finished with his fish, Olave wiped his hands on his leather breeches. "Olave hopes they have meat and bread inside. And a bed. I want to sleep on a bed tonight."

Tor ran his fingers through his hair, wishing he could promise Olave that bed tonight. But of course, he could not. What if his father did not see him tonight? What if he turned Tor away?

Tor wore the Forrest family brooch pinned to his leather-and-fur cloak. His mother had given it to him, the only gift she had received from the Scotsman. It would bear proof that Tor was who he said he was. That still did not mean that Munro Forrest had to take Tor in.

But Tor was determined, not only to force Munro Forrest to admit the mistake he had made in leaving Henne pregnant and alone, but to take a rightful part of his father's wealth. For it was obvious from the look of the castle that the man was beyond wealthy. He would take the man's coin, and then he would ride north again. Home, home to Ny Landsby, his mother's village, where Norse long houses and Scottish cottages lay side by side.

His mother had meant well when she had said she wanted Tor to become a part of his father's world. But she didn't understand that Tor would never fit in here in the Highlands. Half Scot or not, his only home would ever be among the Norsemen. On the open sea. At the foot of a campfire on a cold, dark night.

Tor turned as movement on the castle wall caught his eye. It was the young man, waving. Signaling.

Slowly the castle's drawbridge swung down.

"Olave! Finn!" Tor strode toward his ground-tied mount, who grazed on the tiny green sprouts of grass just popping up from the ground.

"It looks as if we will finally be admitted to my father's abode," Tor said sarcastically.

Mounted, the brothers rode over the lowered drawbridge. Inside the muddy bailey, the redhead from the rampart wall met them.

Tor dismounted, eyeing him.

"My name is Rob. My father is his lordship's steward."

"Near six hours," Tor spat. "Your *lordship* has kept me waiting near six hours."

"This way," Rob said, leading them toward a doorway that opened into the castle's main structure. "My lord says ye have to make it quick because he is wanted at home for supper. M'lady doesnae take kindly to his lordship coming late to supper."

Tor turned back to eye his brothers, who were grinning with amusement. What kind of a man was his father, Tor wondered, to be so controlled by a mere woman?

Tor followed Rob from the walled yard of the keep through an arched doorway with a formidable iron-and-wood door. Inside the small paved entryway, they took a steep staircase upward. The plastered walls of the cylindrical staircase within the walls of the tower were close and the stair treads narrow and triangular, forcing Tor to take each step carefully so that he would not tumble backward onto his brothers.

They entered a great hall richly paneled in a dark wood. Stags' heads lined the walls high overhead, and a small balcony jutted out from one corner of the room. A fire blazed in a great stone hearth at the far end of the rectangular room. A pitcher of ale sat on a large dining table in the middle of the room, and Tor's mouth watered for the taste of it.

There was no man to be seen.

"He says he comes in a moment." Rob backed out of the hall.

Tor turned on him. "If Rancoff thinks I will wait longer—"

A door opened at the far end of the room, a paneled door that Tor had not even detected in the wall when he'd first entered the impressive room.

"Are you Rancoff?" Tor demanded in English, taking a broad stance, his gaze riveted on the man on the far side of the room.

His father bristled with annoyance, opened his mouth to speak, then shut it. A look of recognition crossed his face. "Do I know ye, sir?"

"Do you?"

"Henne," his father murmured in disbelief as his face paled. "God in heaven. Are ye Henne's get?"

For a moment, Tor was taken back. Another unforeseen event; he had not expected Rancoff to make any connection. He had not even expected a man like this to remember a Norwegian widow from so many years ago.

"Ye *are* her son." The lord of Rancoff took a step closer, a strange, bittersweet smile of welcome on his face.

"Aye," Tor said, speaking clipped English. "I am the son of Henne . . . and also yours."

CHAPTER TWO

Tor stared into Rancoff's startling blue eyes that were so similar to his own. He had to wonder now if it was his father's eyes he had inherited, and not his mother's as he had always assumed.

"My son?" Rancoff said, his slight Scottish accent sounding strange to Tor's ear.

Tor locked his jaw. "I am Henne's son, Tor Henneson. My father was a Scot who passed through my mother's village more than three decades ago. My mother called him Munro Forrest." He spat Rancoff's name as if the words pained him.

"Henne's son? My son?"

Tor expected the Scot to deny him, or to demand proof at the very least, but instead he just stared. Perhaps he had seen the brooch on Tor's shoulder and recognized it.

"I nae knew," he said quietly.

Munro Forrest was a tall man, though not as tall as Tor, and he was handsome as looks went for a

Scotsman. He had an air about him that spoke of education, good breeding, and all the other characteristics that made a man lord of a castle and lands. Had this man been Norse, Tor thought, he would have been a leader in his village as well.

Tor's gaze did not waver from his father's face, though his resolve did, if only for an instant. The look on the man's face told him he truly did not know Henne had been pregnant. His face was awash with sorrow, regret, and bittersweet memories.

Tor glanced back toward his brothers, who stood behind him. He did not care for the emotion that curled in his stomach. Emotion was useless to a Norseman such as he. Emotion was for women. It only got in the way of action.

"My half-brothers," Tor introduced gruffly. "Olave and Finn."

The two younger men nodded.

Rancoff stood a moment longer at the door, obviously still attempting to adjust to the idea of having a bastard son. He waved a hand. "Come in. Let me call for ale and bread."

"Ah, now you offer hospitality," Tor accused, "After we have waited hours beyond your walls."

His father frowned. "I nae knew who ye were. Only that ye rode up frightening my servants and demanding to see me without speaking your name or your purpose." He pulled out a stool from the table. "Sit and I will call for something to eat. I havenae much here. I live through the woods with my family. I only came today to take care of business."

Tor made no move to take the seat offered, but he lifted a shoulder. "I did not come for your hospitality, nor your apologies."

A strange look came across the Scot's face. "Apologies? I made no apologies." He took a step closer.

"So that is what's got ye so bristled? Ye blame me for—"

"I blame you for abandoning my mother. Leaving a boy to be raised by a brutal—"

"I nae knew," his father repeated as loudly as Tor.

His tone surprised Tor. Not many men dared raise their voice to him. "It does not matter, now," he spat.

Munro crossed his arms over his chest, studying Tor, calm again. "Nay, I suppose it doesnae. Nae now. Nae when ye are full grown and a head taller than your father."

"That is it?" Tor asked incredulously. "You accept that I am your son? How do you know I do not come in carrying tales of untruth?"

Munro Forrest smiled sadly. "It has been many years, but I see her in your eyes." He pointed. "And the brooch. I gave it to Henne."

Tor did not know what to say. He was unsure how to proceed next. Before he could speak, his father moved past him.

"And now I have explaining to do. My wife is going to run me through when she sees you." He motioned to the door. "If ye willnae take ale and bread here, let's go and see to m'lady at Dunblane."

Feeling off balance by Munro's calm invitation, Tor watched as his father walked toward the door they had entered. Finn and Olave moved as if to follow. Tor could not move. Munro Forrest wanted to announce his grown bastard son to his wife? It smacked of more than mere acceptance, more than acknowledgment of responsibility. It smacked of being taken into a family.

Never. He wanted nothing but his birthright from this man, and that only because he had promised his

mother. He had lived without his sire's family for
more than thirty years and would continue to do so.

"I will not leave this place," Tor said firmly. "Nor
will my brothers."

Finn and Olave looked to Tor. He knew they were
both thinking of their stomachs and not the principle
of the matter here.

"Ye will nae go to my home?" Munro Forrest asked.

Tor gestured. "I thought this was your family home.
Rancoff Castle."

"This was my father's home and his father's before
him. It is still mine, but I live in my wife's home a
short ride from here. The story is long and best told
over ale by a warm hearth." He gave a wave and
smiled kindly. "Once ye meet her, ye will better
understand."

But Tor wanted neither kindness nor hospitality
from his father's woman. He grabbed a stool from
the table and dragged it toward the low-burning fire.
"I will not leave this place until I have settled with
you, Munro Forrest."

The Scot stood for a moment in indecision. Tor
ignored him.

"Ye willnae accept the hospitality I offer ye?"
Munro asked haltingly. He was obviously growing
angry.

Let him be angry, Tor thought. I've been angry
since the day I was born.

"I came to speak with Munro Forrest of Rancoff.
I see no reason to go farther."

Rancoff thought a moment and then spoke as if
Tor were a child. "Well, sir, I am expected to sup
with my wife. Should ye and your brothers wish to
join me, ye would be most welcome. Otherwise," he
lifted his hands. "Then ye may stay here the night
and we will speak on the morrow."

"Olave wants to go," Olave piped up in English. "Olave is hungry."

Tor shot his youngest brother a look that silenced the young man.

"Ye are welcome to come," Munro said to Finn and Olave. With or without . . . Tor."

Tor turned away, another rush of emotion washing over him. It was the first time he had ever heard his father speak his name.

"My brothers remain with me," Tor snapped.

"A good night to ye all, then," the Scott said and closed the door quietly behind him.

Tor sat before the fire, staring into the glowing coals, feeling more like a chastised child than the formidable man he'd worked so hard to be. His brothers approached slowly.

"I do not see the harm it would have done to eat with him," Finn complained.

"Olave's stomach growls," Olave said to no one in particular, dragging a stool to the hearth to sit beside Tor.

Tor reached out and patted Olave's knee. "I will find you something to quench your thirst and ease your hunger," he said quietly. "Just give me a moment."

Finn walked around the large paneled room, gazing up at the mounted stags' heads and assorted paintings that surrounded them. "He seems like a good man."

"He left my mother," Tor ground out.

Finn sighed, but knew better than to push the issue further.

Tor stared into the fire, trying to decide what his next move should be. He should find something to eat in the kitchen, he supposed, and then bed down here for the night to wait for the Scot. What other choices did he have? The decision made, he rose. "Stay here, both of you. I will see our horses cared for and bring back food."

"We sleep here tonight? In here?" Olave asked, his broad, shovel face filled with innocence.

Tor strode toward the door. When they had entered the castle, he had smelled bread baking from the direction of another stair, one that led below. He guessed that was where the kitchen lay. "Better than on the ground, isn't it?"

Olave propped his chin on the heel of his hand. "I suppose. But would you try to find a sweet?" He smacked his lips. "I miss Mor's sweets."

Tor eyed Finn. "Keep him here." And then he set out to find his brothers a meal in their strange surroundings.

Munro entered Castle Dunblane's great hall to find his wife, his children, and the children's maid, Anne, waiting for him at the high table. Below table were the men who served him and his wife, Elen: her steward, his bailiff, men of the Clan Forrest, men of the Clan Burnard, and vassals from both families. Once upon a time, they had been separated by a land dispute, but with Munro and Elen's marriage eight years past, all that had come to an end.

"So there ye are." Elen smiled but did not rise to greet him. "And I thought I would eat your venison as well as mine."

He walked behind the table and leaned over to brush his lips against his wife's. "I beg your pardon, my love, for my tardiness. I vow I will make it up to ye later."

She kissed him back. "Aye, later. Is that before or after the snoring begins?"

He chuckled and leaned to kiss the curly heads of his two daughters, Leah, who was seven, and Judith, a precocious five. "And how be my sweets this evening?"

"Papa." Leah beamed.

Judith ignored him, too busy attempting to sop up gravy with a heel of bread.

"And how are ye this evening, Anne?" Munro questioned, taking his seat beside his wife as she heaped venison onto his plate.

Anne glanced up from her place at Munro's left side. She was the illegitimate daughter of King Robert the Bruce himself, sent eight years ago to the household to be kept safe until her father could find her a suitable husband. Anne, with her long red hair and angelic face, looked so much like his wife that she could have been Elen's younger sister.

"Business kept ye late?" She sipped ale from a handled cup.

Munro had to force himself to keep his expression passive. He needed to tell Elen about Tor, but he wasn't quite certain how. He considered waiting until after the evening meal, when they could be alone in their chamber, but to delay the topic even an hour would be dishonesty.

Munro slipped his knife from the belt he wore at his waist and stabbed a succulent piece of meat. During the ride home to Dunblane he had repeated the words "a son" over and over in his head. He had a son.

He would have been no less shocked if a winged dragon had entered Rancoff's hall, but the moment he had laid eyes on Tor, he had known he was somehow connected to Henne. He looked just like her. But it was not until Tor had spoken the words that he had realized Tor was his son as well.

The son he never knew he had.

Munro had been barely sixteen the summer he and a troop of Scots had marched through a tiny Viking town on the far coast in the northland called Ny Landsby. When a fever had fallen upon the soldiers, they had camped there for a fortnight. Munro had not caught the fever, but what he had caught was the eye of a young widow woman named Henne.

Henne had been his first love, the first woman he had ever made love to. He had fancied himself in love with her those two weeks, and for a good year after. But when the soldiers had marched, he had dutifully marched with them. It had never occurred to him that he might have left his seed behind. With Henne being a widow and already the mother of two, he had simply assumed that she had something to prevent pregnancy.

A son, Munro mouthed, taking another bite of meat.

"What did ye say?" Elen poured wine into his cup and then into her own horned cup that had once been her father's.

"I . . ." Munro looked down at his charger and then up at Elen. She gazed into his eyes, waiting. He set down his knife.

"I've something to tell ye," he said quietly. The room was filled with the sound of the men eating dinner and the crackle of the massive fire in the stone fireplace. Leah was giggling about something. "An important matter," Munro added.

"Important enough that it cannot wait until after we've supped and put these minxes to bed?" She indicated their daughters.

Anne had turned her head to listen. Munro didn't mind. She was family. He loved her as a daughter. And it was not as if he could keep Tor a secret. By morning every man, woman, and child under the care of Rancoff and Dunblane would know. By morning next, the gossip would have spread to Aberdeen.

"Important enough," he said, suddenly feeling a wee bit dizzy. A son. He had a son. "I nae know how to say this, so I will just tell you."

Elen set down her cup, giving him her full attention.

"Go on."

"I had a visitor to Rancoff today and he turned out . . . he turned out to be my son," Munro said, suddenly dry-mouthed.

Elen did not take her gaze from his but slowly rose straight up from her seat to stand over him. "*Your* son?" she said in a dangerously soft voice. Several of the men sitting just beyond the head table glanced their way. Munro wanted to ask Elen to sit, but he knew better than to suggest the idea. She was not a woman to be controlled, and certainly not a woman to take news such as this meekly.

"My son by a Norse woman. I was just sixteen, Elen, I—" He gestured lamely.

"A *son?*" she said, her voice rising with her eyebrows.

Now she had the attention of the entire great hall.

Elen gestured to the men who served her and him so loyally. "He has a son." She gazed down at him, her green eyes narrow with anger. "And why did ye not think to tell me of this son these last eight *years* we have been wed?"

"I nae knew." He reached for her hand but she jerked from his grasp. "His mother, she was a passing . . . a first love."

"A son?" Elen repeated. "Ye are certain he is yours and not another man's by-blow in search of a better inheritance?"

Munro reached for his knife, thinking he would need nourishment for the knock-down, drag-out fight he could smell coming. He loved his wife dearly, but this was the way between them. They had loved each other from first sight, and still after eight years and two babies, they could not let a week go by without shouting at each other about something. Sometimes he thought it her strong will that was responsible for these fights; other times he wondered if she was not sent by the spirit of his father to keep him alert.

Munro chewed on a bit of venison, though he was not really hungry anymore. "He is mine," he said louder than he intended. Then, more softly: "He has my eyes. His mother's forehead. And a brooch with the Forrest crest I gave her," he added.

Munro saw a mixture of emotions cross her face: pain, jealousy. Anger. He wished he could spare her these things, but he could not. The truth was that Tor was his son; he knew it as well as he knew that Leah and Judith were his daughters, and he would not deny him to anyone. Still standing, Elen gazed out over the room.

The hall was abuzz with conversation and bawdy laughter. Though comments of the lord's virility were not loud enough to reach the dais, Munro knew what they were saying. Elen knew, too.

"Enough," she said to the men and women in the room, who all gawked at the head table with interest.

Munro knew he was not the first Highland lord to claim a by-blow, but it was the first for him and his father before him. Accepted or not, he did not like the feeling in the pit of his stomach that this easy embrace from the room produced. He was not other men. Never once since he and Elen had wed had he taken another woman to his bed.

"Go back to your meals. I am certain ye will all learn the sordid details in time."

Realizing they could have offended their mistress, or at the very least hurt her feelings, the room quieted awkwardly. Suddenly, there was great emphasis on passing more bread, calling for more ale.

Elen pressed the heels of her hands to the table and looked at Munro. "Where is he?"

"He waits at Rancoff."

Elen turned and stepped away.

"Where are ye going?"

"Where do ye think?" his wife hollered back. "To get your son and feed him properly."

"I tried. He refused me. He is angry."

Elen lowered her hands to her hips, and Munro could not help but notice what shapely hips they were, even dressed as she was in a man's tunic and shirt.

"For what?"

"I nae know. Leaving his mother. Not returning for him. For all the ills of the world, I suspect."

"I will return with him," Elen said, striding away.

Any other husband might have attempted to stop any other wife. It had already gone dark, and the wind whistled outside, but Munro knew he was wasting his breath to protest. Long ago, he had accepted Elen as his equal and enjoyed the freedom it gave him to share the burdens of their domains. Anne popped up beside him.

Munro glanced up. "And where are ye going?" he demanded, exasperated.

Anne tossed her lap cloth onto her plate and called over her shoulder as she passed him. "Where do ye think? To fetch your son."

* * *

"You couldn't find anything else?" Olave asked, staring down at the dry, curled crusts of bread on the table.

" 'Tis nourishment," Tor snapped, tossing another log on the hearth. A log he'd had to haul from a pile in the kitchen's yard.

"But we smelled bread when we came in."

"I cannot find it. The servants took it, I suppose. Now eat what I give you and be thankful it is not moldy."

"A little jam would have been nice," Finn groused, cramming a piece of hard bread into his mouth.

"I told you, the larder was locked and no one was to be found." Tor paced in a circle around the table. The opulence of the room made him uncomfortable. Though he had been inside castles such as Rancoff a few times—when pillaging long ago or trading more recently—he did not feel as if he belonged here. It further upset his balance that Rancoff seemed to think he did belong.

"Locked?" Finn handed Olave another heel of dark bread. "And no servant to unlock the larder?"

"What is your complaint?" Tor growled, losing his temper. "You have a warm fire to bed down before and a roof over your head. That is more than we have most nights."

In truth, Tor, too, was angry that he could not find more food. Even angrier that his father must have left word with the servants to leave the kitchen locked up and return to their homes.

None of this was going the way he had expected. He had anticipated more of a confrontation with his father. He had been prepared for denial, shouting, the shaking of fists. He liked shouting, and like most Norsemen, he was good at it.

Munro Forrest had taken him completely by surprise. The man had not been willing to take any of the initial blame for Tor's situation. He had instead turned the whole matter around and behaved as if Tor had no right to be angry. And then he'd just taken off to have supper with his wife. What man was so browbeaten that he would leave the firstborn son he had just met to sup with a woman?

The great hall's door opened, and a woman dressed in men's clothing walked in. "Good even," she said smiling.

The woman was beautiful despite her mannish dress, red-haired with green eyes that met Tor's without the slightest apprehension. "I am Lady Rancoff, Munro's wife." She walked toward him, offering her hand in welcome.

Behind her, another woman appeared. Younger. A striking woman with spun golden-red hair, bright blue eyes and a look of determination that seemed to match that of his father's wife. Tor lifted his hand to Lady Rancoff's but could not tear his gaze from the other woman staring brazenly at him.

As Lady Rancoff's hand met Tor's, she glanced back over her shoulder, apparently realizing that his attention lay elsewhere. "Ah, I see." She stepped aside. "And this would be our Anne."

Anne dipped a slight curtsy, still not taking her gaze from his. Tor was fascinated. Most women found him frightening. Even the ones who were attracted to him kept their eyes averted and stood well away from his reach.

"My father's daughter?" Tor heard himself say. He had never been so mesmerized in his life. Yet, if she was the Scot's daughter, he had no right to look at her this way. A part of him prayed she was not his half-sister.

Lady Rancoff laughed. "God's teeth, nay. She is a family friend and cares for our daughters."

Tor took a step closer to Anne and answered her curtsy with a slight nod.

"We've come to ask ye to sup with us," Anne said, smiling as if she knew she had already cast a spell over him. "Will ye join us?"

CHAPTER THREE

Anne waited calmly for the man to respond, but inside she was anything but calm. Her heart was stumbling, her palms were damp, and she felt as if she couldn't quite get a full breath. Never in her life had she experienced such an overwhelming attraction to a man. Until this moment, she had thought herself invincible to male charms.

And what a man Munro's son was! Tor looked to be close to Anne in age, and he was a giant. She barely came to his mid-chest, though she was taller than average for a woman. And he had the wildest, most beautiful hair Anne had ever seen: long and yellow, windblown and tangled so that it looked like a lion's mane. And his eyes . . . They were icy blue, full of anger and a certain vulnerability that fascinated her.

Anne heard herself speak but barely understood her own words. Something about supper.

Elen stood between them, a look of bemusement

on her face. She wasn't fooled. Many a man had accused Elen Burnard Forrest of behaving in a masculine manner, but she had the sharp instincts of a woman.

The giant, Tor, stared at Anne and she stared back. A Norseman, that's what he was. What else could he be with his leather clothing, wild hair, and bare, bulging biceps? He was a Viking, a wolf from the north that struck terror in the hearts of men and women alike.

Anne was utterly enthralled. She didn't want to be, but she was.

Elen cleared her throat. "So what say ye?" She scrutinized him, not intimidated by his size or wild appearance. "What are ye called? Tor, is it?"

The Norseman turned his head slightly toward Elen. "I am called Tor Henneson, son of Henne."

"Well, son of Henne and Munro, will ye ride to my keep and dine with us?" She glanced at the two men who stood near the hearth, eagerly looking on. "Your friends are welcome, as well. I've a stag roasting on my hearth at this very moment. Pickled quails' eggs, herring soup, bread, and plenty of ale," she tempted.

"Brothers," Tor rasped in his stiff, strangely accented English. "These are my brothers, Olave and Finn."

Both men nodded, the first, Finn, so handsome that some might call him beautiful. He was nearly as tall as Tor with a more slender, less muscular build, but with the same enchanting blue eyes as his brother. Olave was much shorter than the other two, his build stocky with a thick neck and big, soft forearms and slack jowls. He had the look of a man that was not entirely of his senses, but he had a warm smile that made Anne smile back.

"Aye, do come," Anne said to Tor. "I know ye must be fatigued from your long journey." Though from where he had come, she didn't know. "But the ride is short."

"I nae know what ails my husband," Elen went on. "To have ye declare who you were, and then he rides off to take his supper." She gestured, then shrugged and smiled warmly. "But what can I say? There is hell to pay when he does not arrive on time to sup with us." She met his gaze. "And he did say ye were unwilling to join him."

Tor seemed to take a moment to find his tongue. He was still staring at Anne and making her feel deliciously warm. She had never before given a man much consideration. She had not met many who deserved it, but this man somehow seemed different. She just couldn't put her finger on why.

The few men she had known in her lifetime were not as bright as she, and certainly did not possess the common sense she did. She had grown up ducking the shadow of her maternal grandfather, who was not only stupid but also cruel. And she had never met her father, the great king of Scotland. Munro Forrest was truly the only man she had ever met whom she found in the least bit dependable or likeable. As far as she was concerned, he was a freak of the nature of men.

When she'd traveled over the Grampian Mountains years ago to come to Dunblane, she had known that her father was merely depositing her here until he found her a husband. A politically advantageous one. She would have no say in whom she married, so to cast her intentions in any direction was a waste of breath. Not that many men passed through Dunblane who would interest her—at least until now.

Elen waited for Tor's reply to her invitation.

"I . . . I told him I would wait here," he said vaguely.

"Aye, I ken what ye told him. But 'tis foolish for ye and your brothers to stay here the night in this drafty tomb when we've a meal and warm beds at Dunblane."

Anne knew he was debating. It was a manly notion. When a woman offered the only logical choice, a man often balked simply because it was a female's suggestion. The fact that it was the best choice seemed to matter little.

Anne crossed her arms impatiently. She wanted Tor to come to Dunblane to sup with them because he was the most exciting thing that had happened here in ages, maybe ever. But she wanted him to be sensible, too. She wanted him to be different from other men. "I said I would wait here," he repeated in his strangely accented English.

Anne lifted a brow. "Aye, we've already established that. But Munro is at Dunblane. Come. Eat with us and then ye can talk. That is why ye came from wherever it is ye live, is it not?"

Tor glanced over his shoulder at his brothers.

Anne sighed loudly. "Munro says ye are angry with him. Ye can most certainly eat at our hearth and remain angry. Elen and Munro do it all the time." She glanced at Elen with a smile of jest.

Elen smiled back. Her relationship with Munro fascinated Anne. They loved each other greatly; it was obvious to even the casual bystander. But it amazed Anne that Elen had retained her own identity when she had wed. She had even retained her power over her father's keep, lands, and men, something unheard of in the Highlands. Elen and Munro did not see eye to eye and often fought quite publicly. But when the day came to an end, they always climbed the tower stairs together. If Anne could make one wish, it would be to love and be loved that fiercely.

" 'Tis only meat and bread," Anne said, raising her voice. She didn't want to beg the beast, but she really wanted him to come home with them. " 'Tis no concession of any sort."

Again he looked to his brothers. They obviously wanted to come along. They were both practically salivating at the mention of meat and bread.

"It has been a long journey," Tor said carefully. "And there was not much in the kitchen I could find to eat."

"We nae live here," Elen explained. "So the kitchen is nae well stocked. Meals are cooked mid-day for the men who work here."

"A warm meal would set well just now," the brother Finn said in the same accented English.

"Olave wants to eat food," Olave said excitedly, rubbing his belly.

Tor glanced back to Anne.

"I am nae going to beg ye," she finally said, turning on her heel. "Come or dinnae come. I am going home for apple tarts." She opened the hall door and Elen followed.

As often happened, both women were in unspoken agreement. They would make no further attempts to persuade the man. If he wanted to spend the night on the floor of the draughty hall (for none of the other rooms was heated save for the servant's quarters), he was free to do so. Munro had offered to provide food and shelter, as had they. Anne and Elen could do no more.

"It is my responsibility to see my brothers fed," he called as Anne stepped into the hall. "We will come."

Anne kept walking, headed for the stairs, her heart

hammering with an excitement she dared not reveal
in her expression.

Tor rode beside the women in silence. He had no
idea what had possessed him to agree to go with them
to where his father waited, but it was too late to
go back now. He told himself he had done it for
practicality's sake. There was little to eat at his father's
castle, and apparently, a great feast lay beyond. He
told himself he did it for his brothers, but he had a
nagging feeling that it was the young Anne who lured
him southward in the darkness.

As they rode, Anne bantered with his father's wife.
The women laughed and talked of trivial things. He
paid little attention to their words, but watched their
actions and the manner in which they spoke to the
men who had escorted them to Rancoff Castle. He
found the women and their apparent positions baf-
fling. Women riding without husbands or guardians?
Women ordering men about, and men obeying?

Tor was also confused by this entire idea of his
father owning one castle, yet residing in another. He
had understood the man to say that Dunblane castle,
to which they were headed, belonged to his wife's
family. But why reside there? A man belonged in his
own home, his women at his beck and call. Didn't
he? He glanced up at the sound of Anne's laughter.
She was silhouetted by the torches the men carried
to light the way. She was small but not overly so. And
strong. In the bailey, he had seen her leap into her
saddle without waiting for the assistance of a servant.
She was beautiful—he could see that even in the
darkness—yet it was not so much the curves of her
breasts and hips or the slight upturn at the end of
her nose that interested him, but her eyes and the

way she had considered him. No woman had ever looked him in the eye the way Anne had back in his father's great hall. There had been a bewitching challenge in that green-eyed gaze that he did not quite understand.

"Ye see. There ahead lies the outer walls of Dunblane," Anne said, turning in her saddle. She addressed Tor and his brothers, but her gaze was on him. "I told ye 'twas nae far."

They rode over a drawbridge and beneath the gatehouse into the enclosed bailey, where young boys ran out to meet the party and take the horses. Tor gazed up at the castle, lit by burning torches. Dunblane Castle was not shaped like a single tower as Rancoff was. She was larger and more sprawling, with an obvious original tower, and a larger addition added later. Lamps blazed in many windows, giving a certain enchantment to the Scottish keep.

"This way, sirs." Elen led them through a door into a small paved chamber.

Tor glanced down as his boots sounded on a metal grate. "The oubliette," Anne explained. "A dungeon. Ask your father some day of the time he spent below."

Tor lifted a brow in question, but Anne only laughed, pushing her heavy woolen mantle over her shoulders and skipping up the steps ahead of him. They entered a great hall that was more than twice the size of the one at Rancoff. Brightly lit with torches, the room smelled of roasted venison, and hickory smoke, and the fresh rushes that covered the floor. It had a vaulted ceiling and on the far wall were windows tall enough to ride a steed through had they not been on the second story. A fire burned in a great stone hearth on one wall, and long tables were scattered here and there. Men who had finished dining played at games of chance and drank ale from horn-and-leather tankards. The clansmen glanced up with interest as the three Norsemen passed. Finn and Olave gawked back, but Tor lifted his chin high, threw his shoulders back, and kept his gaze fixed on his father.

Munro Forrest sat at a raised dais table beneath the darkened windows. He did not seem surprised by Tor's arrival, and Tor did not like the idea that his father assumed the women would bring him back. Did his father think Tor to be as weak and easily beguiled by women as he was?

Munro rose as Tor approached the table, led by Elen. "So I see ye changed your mind. Excellent. Please, sit." He motioned toward a bench.

At the sight of a charger of steaming venison and another plate heaped with fresh bread, Finn and Olave hurried around the table to follow their host's bidding. Tor remained standing before the table, his gaze locked with his father's. "You did not even ask me of her health," he said in careful English.

The Scotsman looked down and then up again. "Nay. I am sorry. In my shock . . ." He let his words drift into silence.

Tor had never met a man who apologized so easily. So genuinely. Munro Forrest was not at all what he had imagined he was. What Tor wanted him to be.

"How is Henne?" his father asked quietly.

"Not good." Tor stared stoically. "She is *døde*— dead."

His father's eyes crinkled at the corners, and Tor thought he saw pain cross his face. It was Tor who looked away this time, uncomfortable with such obvious emotion.

"She was kind to me. A good woman," Tor heard

his father say. The words were genuine, and he didn't know if that pleased or displeased him. "I am sorry."

Tor stared at the table laden with food. He could hear Olave eating heartily. "So am I."

Silence yawned between the two men.

"I am glad ye came," Munro said, breaching the chasm. "I mean that. Now come, join us in our meal. We've much to talk of, but nae tonight. Did ye come all the way from Ny Landsby?"

Tor ground his teeth. He did not like the kindness in his father's tone. It took the edge off his anger, and Tor needed his anger. It was what had kept him alive all these years. "Let me make it clear, Munro Forrest. I came to fulfill my *mor's* dying wish. Not because I wished to."

The Scotsman said nothing until finally, when the silence was too much for Tor to bear, he lifted his gaze to meet his father's. The man had the slightest hint of a smile on his face, a smile Tor ached to wipe clean.

"Fair enough," Munro said. "Now sit. Eat."

Munro's lack of anger or defense left Tor with nowhere to go but where he was directed. Begrudgingly, he walked around and took a seat on the bench beside his brothers.

Anne leaned around him to pour ale into a cup. She said nothing, but he could feel the warmth of her body as her woolen sleeve brushed his shoulder. He could hear her breath in his ear. Smell the fragrance of her hair. The woman was as intoxicating as a heavy mead.

"Bread?" she asked, a playful tone in her voice.

Was she mocking him somehow? Why? He glanced sideways at her as he took a great hunk of venison on the end of his eating dagger and stabbed it into his mouth. "You eat well here," he said, wanting to say something. The moment the words were out of his mouth, he realized what an idiotic comment it was. It sounded like something Olave would say.

Again the smile played on her lips. She poured herself some ale and sat beside him. Tor was fascinated by the way this woman, who was not even a family member, came and went as she pleased. Said what she pleased. And sat with men?

At the center of the table, his father and Elen sat beside each other talking, heads bowed. Their voices were soft so that he could not hear what they said, though she was obviously not pleased with him. Tor could hear his father defending himself, then becoming angry in return.

"Pay no attention to them," Anne said, sipping her ale. "I have come to look at their fighting as a love dance of some sort." She laughed and her voice was not the high-pitched tinkle of laughter of most women, but deep, throaty. Sensual in an innocent way.

"You are not of the Forrest clan?" he asked, passing the bowl of bread to Finn at his brother's request.

"Nay." She rested her elbow on the table, and her chin on the heel of her hand. "I am here for safekeeping until my father finds me a husband. My father is the king."

She said it so unpretentiously that at first Tor thought he had heard wrong, or misunderstood in the translation. He spoke English fluently, but his first words had been Norwegian, the tongue of his mother's homeland, and in their home they had always spoken Norwegian.

Tor ceased chewing the large hunk of bread in his mouth. "The Scottish king's daughter?" He lifted a brow quizzically.

"His merry-begotten child. His bastard," she spat.

Tor immediately felt a connection with Anne. He could tell by the way she had spoken the word *bastard* that she had surely suffered for her parents' trespass, just as he had. The affiliation gave him a strange feeling, one almost of tenderness.

"And Munro Forrest is your guardian." Tor could not yet refer to him as his father aloud. "That is good of him to give you shelter."

"I suppose, though he is surely well compensated." She struck the table angrily with her cup, then gave a sigh. "I am sorry; that is unfair," she said more quietly, seeming to mentally chastise herself. She met Tor's gaze, unaffected by his size or appearance. "Munro and Elen have been good to me. Munro has been more of a father to me than mine ever has."

Tor concentrated on his plate again. He did not want to hear good things of his father. Didn't want to consider that Munro really might not have known he had a son, or that if he had known, things might have been different. He was also not ready yet to consider that if it was not Munro's fault he had never known, then it had to be Henne's. That meant Henne had lied to him all those years ago when she'd said that Tor's Scottish father wanted no part of Tor's life.

"More bread?" Anne asked Finn as she rose from the bench. Finn sat on the other side of Tor. "I can call for more, if ye like."

Finn flashed his handsome grin that had been known to make ladies swoon. "A bit of bread and a bit of you would please me."

She lifted the empty bread trencher, speaking casually. "I have sheathed my dirk, sir, but I am not prohibited from taking it from my belt and lifting it to your throat." She flashed an equally attractive smile and Finn burst into hearty laughter.

Tor wanted to laugh, too, but managed to remain stoic.

Anne passed the trencher to a serving girl, who hurried off to refill it.

Elen rose from her place beside her husband. Tor had been so caught up in his conversation with Anne that he had not followed that of his father and his lady. He could not tell whether or not the matter they had argued over had been settled. These Scots and their ways were an oddity. He honestly could not imagine a man and wife arguing over anything. In his village, there was never an argument between man and wife, because what a man said or did was the final answer. There was no room for disagreement.

Elen approached to stand behind Tor and Finn. "I will order beds to be made for ye in the tower. Ye must be exhausted after your journey. My husband says ye came from far in the north on the western coast."

The thought was tempting. His appetite satisfied, Tor was now feeling the weariness of his journey. The idea of climbing into a warm bed was as close to Valhalla as any he could imagine. He rose. *"Ingen.* No. We came to eat, but we will return to Munro Forrest's castle."

"We will?" Finn asked as he sopped gravy with fresh bread from the kitchen.

Tor eyed him warningly.

Elen lifted a brow, looking as if Tor had said something absurd. "Ye want to ride back?"

"I came to speak with Munro Forrest. My mother asked that I go to Rancoff Castle and speak with the Scotsman. I will wait there to speak with him."

Elen glanced at Munro, who now stood before the table. "Tor, 'tis silly to ride back in the cold and darkness. Stay here the night, and in the morn' ye and I will—''

Tor bolted out of his seat, anger again filling his chest. He met his father's gaze with challenge. "I will wait at Rancoff.''

Munro's face was just as unrelenting. "Fine. Then I will meet with ye on the morrow.''

"Munro," Elen said.

Husband and wife locked gazes. "I cannae force him to stay, Elen," Munro said tightly.

She threw up her hands, muttering something about men, and headed across the hall.

"Finn, Olave," Tor called. "Let us go.''

"But I am not done," Olave protested childishly, stuffing more bread sopped in gravy into his already full mouth.

"Olave!" Tor rounded the table, anxious to get out of the warmth and comfort of Dunblane Castle. Away from his father. And away from a king's daughter who made him feel too soft inside.

CHAPTER FOUR

As Tor and his brothers took their hurried leave of Dunblane's hall, Munro turned to Anne with concern. "Have I done the right thing in letting him go off this way?"

Anne thought carefully. She liked it when Munro or Elen asked her opinion. She was pleased that her opinion mattered. That they respected what she thought, even when they didn't agree with her.

"Aye, let him go," she answered, her tone equally somber. " 'Tis a shock for him to find ye here settled and happy and nae the fork-tailed sea monster I imagine he thought ye were . . . hoped ye were."

Munro's blue eyes crinkled with surprise. "What did he say that makes ye think so?"

She watched as Tor's broad back disappeared through the arched doorway, and heard his heavy tread down the stairs. "He said little. I am nae privy to your son's thoughts, m'lord. But it was the way he said it." She considered her words carefully because she felt she had become Tor's confidante in some small way and did not want to betray that confidence. "Perhaps 'twas my imagination, but I think he has led a difficult life, and I think he has enjoyed having someone to blame for it."

"Me."

She smiled, but it was not happiness that tugged at her heart. It was sadness—sadness for the woeful boy she imagined Tor must have been. She glanced away from the man who had become like a father to her. "I know a wee bit of the business of being a bastard."

Munro sighed and reached out to squeeze her hand, but knew better than to engage her in conversation about her father. The Bruce was Munro's friend, and she and Munro had long ago agreed to disagree about his responsibility to a daughter born on the wrong side of the bedlinens.

"Well," Munro said, continuing their conversation, "he thinks 'tis a shock to see me. How does he think I feel? Christ's brittle bones, Anne!" Munro ran his fingers through his hair, making it stand on end. "When I woke this morning I was the father of two delightful daughters. I nae knew I had a son until he walked into Rancoff's hall only a few hours ago."

He began to walk, and she kept pace at his side.

"But I knew he was Henne's son. I knew it the moment I laid eyes on the big gawk. Knew he was Henne's," he repeated softly. Proudly.

"And she didnae tell ye she was with child? Never sent word to ye or your family?"

Again he looked at her. "Of course not. What kind of mon do ye think me, Anne?" They went down the steps over the oubliette that covered the cell in which he had once spent more than a fortnight. "I am nae saying I would have married her. My father would have never allowed that, but I wouldnae have abandoned the lad. Nor would my father have expected me to."

Anne thought of her own situation. Her mother had not told her father of her birth, not until she had sickened. But all those years Anne had hated her father anyway. And even now that he did know of her existence, he paid her no mind. Yes, he had found her a place to live when her mother had died. And he no doubt sent the coin that paid for her gowns, but that was not being a father. That was simply being a good steward of a man's possessions.

Anne gave a little laugh, thinking about what Munro had said. "A mon with a conscience, were ye? A mon who would have seen his responsibility in the seed he had sown? Ye'd have been lucky if ye'd nae been tossed in an asylum."

He gave her a wry smile.

"So tell me," she prodded, "Forgive my curiosity, but what would ye have done if ye had known she carried your son?"

"I would have brought him to Rancoff, of course, raised him as a Forrest. Which side of the sheets he was born upon would nae have mattered then."

"Does it now?"

Their gazes met; he hesitated, then opened the door for her. She could see that he was not yet ready to answer that difficult question.

They stepped out into the cold and crossed the bailey to the tower house, where the bedchambers were located. "A son," he murmured, letting her question drift away from them with the peat smoke that clouded the air.

"And ye are certain he is your son?" she questioned. She was not necessarily dubious of Tor's claim, but it would not have been the first time a

man had ridden out from the mountains claiming
to be a rich man's long-lost son.

"Aye, he's mine, all right." Munro opened the
tower door for her and they both stepped into the
warmth. "Ye heard that sharp tongue. His mother
was as sweet as summer honey. Nay, he's Forrest, all
right."

Anne leaned against the wood-and-iron door, mus-
ing over the evening's events. She could not explain
the emotions tumbling inside her. She did not know
the significance of Munro's son's arrival, but somehow she sensed she was at some crossroads in her
life. And after all these years, she knew well to heed
her intuition.

"So what do ye think he wants?" she asked Munro.

He frowned and rubbed his temple with his thumb
and forefinger, as if the day had given him a terrible
headache. "Recognition, I suppose. A roof over his
head. My head on a platter? Honestly, I nae know."

"I suppose the morning will tell." Anne, ever prac-
tical, passed him in the small, dark hallway and started
up the steps. "I will see to your lasses. Ye'd better go
to your wife. My guess is that she is nae in the best
of moods." She flashed him a grin over her shoulder.

They both loved Elen, but they also well knew her
temperament. Elen may have been accepting of Tor
in the great hall because she had no choice but to
be gracious. But that did not mean the matter would
be so easily settled. Anne knew full well that Elen
would not be pleased with the thought that Munro
had fathered a child elsewhere. No woman wanted
to be reminded that her husband had slept with other
women before meeting her.

"God keep ye in your sleep, Anne. And thank ye,"
he called up.

Again she glanced over her shoulder. "For what?"

"Elen said it was ye who persuaded my son to sup with us. She said it 'twas your enchanting eyes."

Anne laughed, and turned away, feeling a strange warmth come over her. Munro thought her eyes enchanting. Did Tor, as well?

Munro entered the bedchamber he had shared with his wife for the past eight years. He closed the door quietly and leaned against it. Elen stood at one of the windows, gazing out into the night, her reflection wavy in the dark glass. Absently she pulled a brush through her waist-length red hair.

"I am sorry," he said simply.

She did not turn to him. "Sorry ye conceived him or sorry he has come?"

Munro exhaled. Elen was never the typical female. But then, that was why he had fallen in love with her, wasn't it? What other female in the Highlands would have dared take him prisoner and toss him in her oubliette until she gained what she wanted?

"That is an unfair question," Munro returned. "To say I wish I had not conceived him would be to say I wished a soul did not exist upon this earth. And to say I wished he had not come . . ."

She turned. "Ye are right. 'Twas unfair. I'm sorry." She held his gaze. "But that doesnae mean I am nae still angry with ye."

"Angry for what?" Annoyance made his tone sharp. Why was nothing ever easy with this woman? "That I was foolish and unthinking at sixteen? That I was lonely and missed my family? That I accepted the comfort a woman older than I offered?"

She tossed the hairbrush onto a small table and began to undress. "Aye."

He crossed his arms over his chest, still leaning

against the door. He could not resist a little laugh. At least she was honest. "Elen, Henne was a long time ago. Before my first wife. I—"

"Ye loved her?"

"Loved her?" He lifted one hand. "For Christ's bones, I was barely sixteen summers. I was far from home. Afraid and lonely. She took me in when the others were sick. She fed me and she . . ."

Elen stepped out of her woolen skirts and pulled the man's shirt she wore over her head. "Took ye to her bed."

He exhaled, going to her to help her with the shirt. "Aye, she took me to her bed and I went willingly." He tossed the shirt onto a chair.

Man and wife studied each other face to face. He did not understand how Elen could be jealous of a woman he had barely known more than thirty years ago.

"I love ye, Elen; ye know that. And she's dead. Henne is dead."

"That's why he's come?" She walked away from him and perched on the edge of the bed to kick off her shoes.

Munro went down on one knee in front of her and rolled down one of her stockings. "I nae know why he's come. We didnae get that far in the conversation."

She lay back on the bed. "He is angry with ye."

"That much I have gathered."

"I would be, too, I suppose."

He removed the second stocking, enjoying the warmth and smoothness of his wife's skin. "Anne is certainly angry enough with Robert."

"Aye, we've discussed that matter before. I can see both sides of the coin there. Robert has his business of being a king, and Anne is just a female."

"But as ye have said, she is his flesh and blood," Munro said, climbing across the bed to lie beside Elen.

"As is Tor yours." She turned her head to look at him, their noses nearly touching.

"This changes naught between us, Elen. Naught between my daughters and me."

She gazed upward at the bed hangings. "Some would say he is firstborn and should come before his half-sisters."

Munro rolled onto his side on the great bed where he and Elen had conceived their beloved daughters. He brushed a stray hair from her face. She looked tired. "Ah, so 'tis that, my love? Ye fear for your babes?"

"He is a son. They are daughters." Her mouth was slack as she waited for him to respond.

"Daughters of my body and yours. *Our* daughters. Surely ye know me better than that." He wrapped one arm around her waist. "Ten sons, a hundred, a legion, could not move Leah and Judith from the place they hold in my heart."

She smiled. Munro knew he was not yet out of the boiling water, but getting closer.

"My love for ye and for our daughters will never wane," he said as kissed her gently on the mouth. "Know that always."

"Poetic words, husband, but that doesnae change the fact that a man sits in your hall at this moment claiming to be your son." Her brow creased and she sat up. "Are ye certain he is your son?"

Munro tucked his hands beneath his head. "Anne asked the same thing. Women are so suspicious."

She climbed off the bed and tugged off his boots. "And men are so gullible."

"Aye, he is my son."

"How do you know?" She rolled off his stockings.

"How did ye know that Judith was yours, or Leah?"

She slapped him on his calf. "Because I saw them spring forth the same as ye did. I felt the pain of bearing them."

He laughed and then sobered. "Did ye nae see the clasp brooch he wears? I gave it to Henne."

"Could be a ruse," she offered hopefully.

He shook his head slowly, wishing he had not hurt her this way. "Nay. He's mine, Elen. I felt it the moment he spoke the words." He laid his hand over the Clan Forrest green-and-burgundy plaid draped across his chest. "Here."

She sighed. "Perhaps he wants naught. Perhaps he is just passing through and—"

"Elen, Elen." Munro sat up, grabbed her hand, and pulled her onto the bed again. "Let us wait and see what the morrow brings. I will ride to Rancoff and speak with my son."

She lay beside him again, resting her head on his shoulder. Munro loved his life here at Dunblane with his wife and daughters. He loved the hustle and bustle of the castles. The excitement of the occasional reiver, but his favorite part of life was lying here in the evening, with Elen in his arms. Sometimes they made love, not as often as they once did, but this, this was where he felt the most loved.

She closed her eyes and snuggled against him. "Tomorrow willnae be easy. He is very angry, your Viking son."

He kissed her brow as he reached over to draw a woolen coverlet over them. "I am nae worried, wife. I survived telling ye I have a bastard son. Tomorrow will be a walk on the beach."

* * *

"I do not want your excuses," Tor boomed. He had had all night to stew over his father's behavior yesterday, and this morning his anger was so great he could taste it.

Munro sat back in his chair before the fireplace in Rancoff's hall and tossed a chip of wood into the blaze. "Must ye shout every word ye speak?" He covered his ears with his hands. "God's teeth, ye be giving a headache and 'tis nae yet noonday."

Tor sucked in his breath and held it until he thought his lungs would burst. Today was going no better than yesterday. He had not rested well all night, and when he had fallen asleep, he had slept so deeply that the fire had gone out and they'd woken to a frigid Highland morning. Again, no servants could be found, and he and his brothers had broken their fast with cups of hot water, stale bread, and dried fish from their own packs.

Munro Forrest had not arrived until midmorning, long after Tor had grown impatient. Instead of remaining at his side, his brothers had abandoned him to see the castle's vast stables. And now Munro was stretching his legs before the fire, as if ready to sit down and have a casual conversation. Obviously, he did not understand why Tor was here. He did not understand how furious Tor was with him. How resentful.

Tor exhaled slowly. "I have come a long way," he said stiffly.

"That ye have. But that does not give ye the right to be rude. To ignore my offers of hospitality. To shout in my home."

Tor stared at the back of his father's head and

toyed with the thought of how easy it would be to kill this man. What kind of fool was he to present his back to his enemy?

Tor turned away in disgust, not sure if it was with his father or with himself. Of course, he would not kill an unarmed man. And no matter how tempted he was, he could not kill the man who had spawned him.

"I can forgive your past behavior, owing it to your long ride, the misunderstanding upon your arrival, but"—Munro lifted a finger in the air, not bothering to turn and face Tor—"I will not tolerate rudeness again."

Tor stomped across the floor, coming around to face his father, putting himself between the man and the fireplace. Now Munro had no choice but to look him in the face. "You speak to me as if I am a child."

The older man looked Tor in the face. "Because ye are acting like one."

Tor swore and stalked away. He circled the table that was larger than the bed his mother had died in. It angered him that his father lived amid such vast wealth while his mother's life had been so hard. Surely, it was the cold winds and difficult work that had brought her early death.

"Now," Munro said, clapping his hands together as he rose from his stool, "that said, tell me why ye have come."

Tor met his father's gaze across the table, his tongue suddenly thick in his mouth. All the way across the frozen meadows, through the snowy mountains, he had practiced what he would say. How he would make his demands. Only now, those words would not come to him.

"My . . . my mother asked that I come," Tor said carefully. "She made me promise." He opened his arms wide. "And now I have come. I have fulfilled her dying wish."

"Ye didnae come these hundreds of miles to tell your mother in heaven ye did as she asked," Munro said, narrowing his eyes shrewdly. "Why have ye come? Tell me what ye want of me. If 'tis to be your fath—"

"You are not my father," Tor ground out. "You are the man who got my mother with child and left me."

Munro's eyes almost sparkled with amusement, making Tor even angrier, if that was possible.

"Methinks we should move beyond that now," Munro said. "I have already told you that I was barely a man yet. And I nae knew. She never told me. Never sent word, though I told her my family name and she knew where Rancoff lay."

Tor thought back to the days when he was a lad going head to head with his stepfather. When he had begged his mother to send him south to live with his father, the Scot. Henne had told him that she'd sent word again and again to Rancoff, yet had received nothing in response. Tor had accepted his father's lack of response as abandonment. Worse—as denial. Now the Scot was saying he had never received word of Tor's birth. Could Henne have lied?

"Money." Tor bore his gaze into the Scotsman's. "Coin and lots of it. That is what I want."

Munro lifted one eyebrow, still not seeming to take Tor seriously enough. "Coin, is it?"

"You are a wealthy man," Tor said, waving one hand wildly. "Give me what I want, and you will never set eyes upon me until we meet again in the fires of hell—which surely we will."

"How much is this we speak of?"—Munro pressed

the heels of his hands to the table and leaned forward—"out of curiosity?"

Tor took half a step back. These Scots were strange people, always wanting to get in other people's faces. He named an amount. An exorbitant amount. More money than he could hope to see in his lifetime. It was not the original amount of money he had told his brothers he would ask for. Tor did not know what had made him say it.

Munro did not blanch.

Nor did he speak.

Tor waited, and as he waited, he felt the back of his neck grow warm. Then warmer. The large room seemed to close in on him. His father's gaze seemed to bore into him. The men in the portraits overhead watched.

"And what have ye done for this coin?" Munro asked finally.

"What have *I* done?" Tor used this opportunity to look away. "It is not what I have done, but what *you* have done. What you have *not* done."

"And for that ye think ye are due a portion of my property? A large portion of my property?" Munro demanded.

"Yes."

Munro turned away. "All right."

Tor blinked, thinking he had not heard correctly. "What?"

"I said all right." Munro poured himself ale from a pitcher on the table. "I will give ye that sum, in coin . . . or in land should ye wish it."

"I do not want your land," Tor spat, taken off balance by the tone in Munro's voice. Not anger, as he'd first thought, but something else. Something like disappointment.

Somehow, that bothered him far more than anger would have, or even denial.

Munro raised a finger. "Ye may take your pick, but . . ."

"But?"

"But first ye must show yourself worthy. Ye must show yourself a mon of the clan Forrest, for only a true Forrest has a right to this land and to what it has yielded over the centuries. I will not hand over one copper to a mon who is nae worthy, sprung from my loins or not."

"That is preposterous," Tor shouted so loudly that his voice echoed off the high, plastered ceiling.

The door to the outside hallway opened and Anne strolled in as if she had been expected. "Ah, there ye two are. I knew where to find ye, for I could hear the Viking bellowing."

CHAPTER FIVE

Tor's concentration was suddenly shattered, and he tightened his balled fists at his side. Couldn't this woman, this Anne, tell that he and Munro were in serious conversation? Serious *male* conversation? What right did she think she had to strut in and interrupt?

Tor's father glanced up at her and smiled as if she was not an interruption at all. "Anne, what brings ye here?"

Tor watched as Munro exchanged words with her, still fascinated by the way he treated her. As if she were an equal. No, more than that. He liked her. He adored her.

Tor turned away from them both, wondering what kind of land this was. This Scottish castle, his father and his family, all were as foreign to him as if he had walked into a Venetian shop.

"The lasses are busy with their stitching. Elen is overseeing whilst she hears complaints from the kitchen staff. Ye know, her weekly court.'' Anne grinned, not seeming the least bit uncomfortable in this room that was taut with the static of anger between father and son.

"I wanted to ask Tor if he and his brothers would like to dine with us tonight. I ran into Olave and Finn." She lifted a feathery brow. "He's quite the charmer, that Finn. They say they'll come to dine with or without their brother." With those last words, she turned toward Tor.

Tor prickled at the mention of his brother. Women adored Finn and his handsome, grinning ways. Why should Anne be any different? Yet still it rankled that she might not be different from other women. For some reason he wanted her to be.

Tor had not intended to meet Anne's gaze, or even acknowledge her if he could help it. Having a woman here—*that* woman—was unsettling, and he had come not to be unsettled, but to settle with his father.

"I have no time to think of where I will eat tonight," Tor snapped.

Her enchanting mouth tugged back in a slight smile—or a sneer; he could not tell which. "Well, then, sir, we've a problem, ye and I, because I havenae time to guess how many will sup with us tonight. I've orders to give the kitchen, and then I must move to other duties." She placed her hands on her hips, hips whose curves could not be hidden, not even beneath woolen skirts and a mantle. "So eat or nae eat, but have the common courtesy to say which."

Tor heard Munro chuckle, and he knew his own face reddened as anger twisted in the pit in his stomach. He did not like this red-haired, sharp-tongued witch. He liked her immensely . . .

The look she gave him demanded a reply.

"I . . ." He swallowed. He felt completely off balance. Lost. How could he think of supper when he and his father were arguing over his birthright? "No."

"Ye willnae eat?" She lifted her shoulders in a shrug of disregard. "Suit yourself, sir." She turned back to her protector, dismissing Tor as if he were some lowly servant.

"Elen says to tell ye that Jod has broken his arm and ye need to stop by his cottage on your ride home. She wrapped it and sent him home with a draught for his pain. She also says she knows ye've much to speak of with your son, but if ye know where your bread is buttered, ye'd best be home to sup with her."

Munro rose from his chair. "Actually, I ride for Dunblane now. We have finished here. We can ride home together. I thought I might go by way of the sea."

"Finished here?" Tor came out of his stupor enough to turn toward the Scotsman. "We have not finished here."

"I believe we have, Tor." Munro met his son's gaze. "Ye have told me what ye seek, and I have told ye what ye must do to get it. 'Tis simple enough."

"I know nothing of farming! Of fishing! I know nothing of running a place like this." Tor swung his arms, gesturing in disbelief. "What is it that I could possibly do here to prove to you that I am worthy of being your son?"

" 'Tis nae a matter of whether or not ye are my son, Tor. That has been established. But the question remains, are ye worthy of being a Forrest?"

Munro closed the door behind him and Anne before Tor could speak another word.

* * *

Anne rode astride one of Dunblane's short-legged, shaggy Highland ponies, comfortable with the silence between her and Munro. She had not liked Munro in their early days together. At her father's request, he had crossed the Grampian Mountains to fetch her from her mother's family after her mother died. In those early days, she and Munro had not gotten along well. She had only recently found out who her father was, and she simply saw Munro as another example of her father's hand sweeping down to alter her life without his ever making a personal appearance.

But as the days passed at Dunblane, after the children came, Anne and Munro settled into a comfortable relationship. Once she finally allowed herself to get to know him, she discovered that against her will, she liked him. She admired him. She had come to love him like a father, an uncle . . . a friend.

A gull called overhead, and Anne gazed upward. Sunlight sparkled on the water like jewels drifting toward the craggy shore. She and Munro rode side by side along the ocean's edge, just out of reach of the ebbing tide. The wind was cold, but the combination of the chill and the smell of the pungent salt sea were invigorating. Spring was upon them, and Anne loved spring in the Highlands.

"So," she said, looking at Munro, "your talk with your son didnae go well, I take it."

"As well as to be expected, I suppose."

"What does he want?" Anne had no qualms about asking Munro anything. If she stepped over the line, he would tell her so.

"What do ye think?"

She glanced ahead, staring between her mount's

ears at a rock formation on the beach. "Coin," she sighed. "And ye are disappointed?"

"Nay . . ." He exhaled, fingering the reins in his gloved hands. Paused. "Aye, I suppose I am."

"Ye thought he had come to be your son."

"Nay," he argued. " 'Twould be ridiculous. I only thought—" He hesitated again. "I suppose a small part of me hoped he had come for me and nae my gold."

Anne thought about her own relationship with her estranged father. She certainly wanted no part of him, so she could surmise what Tor must be feeling. But she would never go to Robert and ask for money. Not if she was alone and destitute. What kind of man was Tor to ride these miles through the treacherous mountains only to get money from his long-lost father? She knew Munro must have been thinking the same. She knew he must be disappointed. Hurt. She could only imagine how it must feel to gain a son one day only to lose him the next.

To conclude that all Tor truly wanted was money was logical, and yet Anne hesitated to believe it. There was something about the man, something in his blue eyes that told her there was more to him than his blustering.

Anne reached between herself and Munro and rubbed his arm. "Nae be so quick to judge."

"I make no judgement." Munro gestured. "The lad said himself that he wants coin and naught more. He intends to return to his mother's land. I daresay he likes the occupation of marauder."

"Lad? I fear he is beyond a lad." She chuckled. "And ye know he's a marauder?"

"What else do men like him do, Anne?" He shook his head. "Ye havenae seen the world I have seen. Those Norsemen, they thieve; they pillage; they rape."

"Some are traders, ye said so yourself once. Fishermen. And it was ye who said the Vikings were no longer marauders. Perhaps he was a mercenary."

He made a derogatory sound in his throat. "Ye can look at that big oaf and guess he doesnae trade fish to earn his keep. Did ye see his hands? He makes his way wielding an ax."

Anne had taken notice of his hands, but she feared it was not weapons she had thought of when she had seen them. "Perhaps ye are right. I only hope that ye would nae jump to conclusions too quickly. To be a bastard is a difficult matter to deal with."

He glanced at her and smiled with understanding. "Methinks ye are taken with my son born to the wrong side of the sheets."

She looked away. "Methinks ye drank too heavily last night, m'lord, and are now feeling the effect." She tightened her legs around the pony's barrel and urged him forward faster, pulling away from Munro.

Her guardian's laughter echoed off the sheer rock of the beach and was lost in the crash of the waves.

Anne only half listened as Finn told the tale of a night he and his brothers were in a boat that nearly capsized off some island. She toyed with her poached haddock, pushing it around her bread plate with the tip of her knife. Finn was handsome, and entertaining, but it was not this Norse brother she thought of as she watched a servant add another log to the fireplace in Dunblane's hall.

Instead, she thought of Tor. He had remained true to his word and had not come to Dunblane to dine tonight. She wondered what he was doing right now. Rancoff was cold and drafty on a night like tonight. With no family members living there, only the sleeping rooms being occupied by vassals who came to serve their lord were heated.

Somehow, Anne doubted Tor would bring himself to join those men simply for the warmth of their fire. He was too much of a loner.

There was little food at Rancoff, because most nights the Clan Forrest vassals came to Dunblane to dine. Elen liked the boisterous roar of men eating and gaming, and always welcomed members of her husband's clan to her supper table.

Anne could not eat her own meal for wondering if Tor was hungry. She knew it was ridiculous to care. Munro's son or not, he was a stranger to her. And he was a man full grown. He could go out and bring down a stag and eat it whole if he so wished.

But when she thought of Tor, she did not see the hulking blond giant of a man she knew others saw. In her mind's eye, she saw a young man who was hurting. It was a hurt she knew all too well. She knew that no matter what Tor said, he had grown up wishing for Munro Forrest, just as she had grown up secretly wishing her unknown father would come and rescue her. Anne had loved her mother well enough, but at times, living with her grandparents and listening to her grandfather's berating of her mother had been almost too much to bear. As a girl, she had dreamed that her father would ride in one day on a silver horse, sweep her into his arms, and carry her away to live in some great castle.

There had been no rescue. Her mother had never admitted who Anne's father was, nor contacted him until she was dying. The great Robert the Bruce had not come to her mother's bedside. And when her mother had died, he had not come to the likewake. All the Bruce had done was send Munro to fetch her. Not a word of contact. Not a word of his sorrow.

Bastard.

Anne smiled at her choice of words. Giving up on the thought of eating, she wiped the blade of her dirk clean and slipped it into the little sheath she wore at her waist. She rose from the dinner table. Not wanting to disturb Finn's tale of adventure, she leaned between Elen and Munro. "If ye nae mind, m'lord, I think I will ride to Rancoff. My guess is that your son's bravado isnae so great now that his belly hungers."

Munro glanced up at her. "Ye need nae go. He is a big lad. If he doesnae choose to dine with us, 'tis his choice. Besides, there are flurries. May be a storm moving in."

Anne looked to Elen. Although Robert the Bruce had placed her in Munro's care, it was Elen who made all final decisions concerning his charge. Anne would not disobey a direct order from Munro because she respected him too much. Owed too much to him. But until this moment, that had never been an issue.

Elen studied Anne's eyes. "Ye want to take him supper?"

Anne pressed her lips together, hoping Elen did not read more into her intentions. She hoped there was no more to her intentions than hospitality toward Munro's son.

Elen slid her hand across the table to Munro's. "Let her go."

" 'Tis well dark," Munro argued. "And what of the snow? I dinnae like her traveling alone this time of night. Our king has enemies everywhere."

"Ye only wish to make your son go hungry in punishment for nae joining us," Elen teased good-naturedly.

"At least send them home with her." He motioned to Tor's brothers. "They'll soon eat us out of larder and barrel if ye dinnae pull the plate from beneath them.''

"Nae be such a crank. Let them eat. The girls adore Finn. I will send Alexi with her." She turned back to Anne. "Have the kitchen pack a hearty supper and enough food for tomorrow as well. Take Alexi with ye and should the storm roll in, stay the night. Send someone to let us know ye are safe, though."

Anne nodded. "I'll nae be gone long."

Munro grumbled something else into his plate, but gave a wave to her and with it his blessing. Anne impulsively kissed Elen's cheek.

"Dress warmly," Elen called after her as Anne hurried from the dais.

Finn continued his tale of his high-sea adventure as Leah and Judith listened, wide-eyed and utterly enchanted by their foreign visitor.

Anne began to question her impulsive decision to take Munro's son poached fish. Though it was almost spring, the Highland mountains followed no rules of the calendar, and the dusting of snow had turned to biting sleet.

Anne rode the mare with her head tucked down, the hood of her mantle pulled down over her forehead to protect her eyes from the blinding wind and stinging snow. On occasion, she looked to be certain she still followed in Alexi's tracks.

"Ye want to turn back, m'lady?" Alexi called, cupping his hand to his mouth.

She shook her head. They were in the middle of the north wood, more than halfway to Rancoff now. What was the sense in turning back? Besides, they were riding with the wind to their backs. To turn around now, they would have to ride into the wind.

Of course, once at Rancoff it would be foolish for her to ride home again if the sleet did not let up. Anne pushed that thought aside. She would cross that drawbridge when she came to it.

The journey between the two properties was no more than six miles, and yet time seemed to stand still as they pushed forward in the cold. As they rode, Anne muttered to herself, listing all the reasons why Munro had been right. Why she should not have come. By the time they reached the walls of Rancoff and Alexi called for the gates to be thrown open, Anne was bitterly cold and not in as fine a mood as she had been when she left the warm hall of Dunblane.

Without waiting for Alexi to help her, she dismounted. "See to the ponies," she hollered in the wind.

A stable boy with a wool blanket thrown over his head and pinned beneath his chin nodded.

She motioned for Alexi to unload the saddlebags of food and ale and follow her.

Anne sent no one with the announcement of her arrival, but climbed the stairs directly to the great hall, where she guessed she would find Tor. Sure enough, when she opened the door, she discovered him perched on a stool before the fireplace, sulking like a boy left behind on a hunting trip.

Tor shot up off the stool as she entered the hall, shaking the snow from her cloak as she walked. "Some plates, cups, then heat the wine in the kitchen," she told Alexi. "Make yourself a draught, too. 'Twill warm your bones."

The young man nodded and left through the door on the far side of the room.

Tor glared at her across the long table in the center of the room. "What are you doing here?"

"I am pleased to see ye as well." She slipped off

her green-and-blue plaid mantle and threw it over Munro's chair at the head of the table.

"Where are my brothers?" He looked beyond her as if she carried them behind her skirts.

"At Dunblane, where anyone sensible would be this night." She walked to the fire and lifted a heavy log to toss it into the flames. As she leaned to lift a second, he reached out to take it from her. She pulled away. "I was tossing logs on a fire long before ye came, sir, and will be doing so long after ye go." She heaved it into the burning pile and sparks flew up.

"You did not say why you came," Tor said, standing back from her.

"Nay. I didnae." She walked around him and began to set out the battered wooden trenchers that Alexi had just set on the corner of the table.

Tor watched her set out the eating ware and then begin to unpack the basket that Alexi had carried in. She heaped poached fish and roasted venison and bread and thick white cheese onto his plate. She gave herself a smaller sample of each.

"This is for me?" he asked, staring at the plates.

"For us both." She slid onto the stool to the right of Munro's at the head of the table. "Sit. Eat."

Tor looked at his father's chair and then at her.

"What? Dinnae say ye are not hungry, because ye would be a liar." She sawed off a piece of venison with the dirk from her belt and popped it into her mouth.

Tor slowly came around the table to take his seat beside her. "Ye brought me this?" he said quietly, still staring at the plate. He lifted his serious blue-eyed gaze to hers.

For once Anne saw no anger.

"Why?" he pushed.

She lifted a shoulder. "I like your brother, Finn,

well enough, but he monopolizes the supper conversation.'' She chewed a bit of fish. "Has he really done all those things he says he's done, or is he a teller of tall tales?"

Tor was still watching her, and she was surprised to find that she liked it. She liked the feel of his gaze as it swept over her, contemplated her. He didn't look at her the way other men did, summing up the curves of her body and the upturn of her nose. He looked at her as if he were looking within.

"A little of both," he said slowly.

She chuckled. "He is amusing, I will give him that. Leah and Judith are fascinated by him."

Tor wielded a wide-bladed knife with a handle carved in the form of a fish tail. It was a beautiful piece that moved fluidly within his hand. "Munro's daughters?"

"Aye. Elen's and Munro's daughters. Your half-sisters." She reached across the table for a horned cup that Alexi had brought from the kitchen. She poured some ale from a skin she'd brought with her, took a sip, and slid it toward Tor. "Of your flesh, of your blood. Of the Clan Forrest, like ye."

He chewed slowly. "You do not have to do this," he said, gesturing toward his trencher. "I do not want you to."

She had a feeling she knew what he meant. He felt an attraction to her, too. An attraction neither wanted. But she pretended not to understand. "I dinnae have to do what? Be hospitable to my guardian's son and bring ye some cold fish?"

Again, he met her gaze, this time holding it. "You know what I mean. I am not staying. I am taking what is rightfully mine and I am returning to my mother's home."

She worked over his words as she carefully stabbed

at another piece of meat. "So all ye came for was coin?"

"That is what I told him."

"Then I feel sorry for ye. He has a lot more to offer ye than just gold."

"I do not want your pity." Anger crackled in his voice. It seemed to be the only emotion he knew, or at least could accept. "Ye know nothing of what it is like."

She laughed, though she was not amused. "I nae know what it is to be a man who is a bastard? Nay, I do not know. I do not know what it is like to come and go as I please. To make what friends I wish. To choose my own destiny." She met his gaze with her own anger. "I only know what it is like to be controlled every waking hour of the day. To be sent here and there. To be told what to wear, what to say, and when I may say it." She lifted her knife and sank its tip into the wooden table between their two wooden trenchers. "I only know what 'tis like to be a bastard's *daughter.*"

CHAPTER SIX

Tor stared at the knife stuck in the table. It vibrated, the hilt moving back and forth. He looked at Anne. No woman in the world he had lived in would have ever behaved so aggressively.

Nor stated her opinion so well . . .

Tor slowly reached out and plucked the slender-bladed knife from the table and laid it on the edge of her plate. She was watching him. Watching him with a penetrating blue-eyed gaze that seemed to reach to the very heart of his being.

"So you and I are alike, then," he said. The room was quiet save for the crackle of damp wood in the fireplace, and the sound of his own breathing, which was not as regular as it should have been.

"I didnae say we are alike." Anne snatched up her knife and sawed off another piece of venison. "I only say that ye are not the only one who has ever suffered. I only say that it isnae an excuse."

He frowned, his brow creasing heavily. "An excuse for what? I give no excuses!"

" 'Tis nae an excuse for your rude behavior. For being so stubborn that ye cannot see the mon your father is."

Tor sopped up the drippings from the meat with a slice of nutty bread. "You make this all sound so simple when it is not."

She leaned forward toward him, pressing her forearms on the table. "And ye make everything so difficult when it doesnae have to be."

He shrank back, not knowing if he was intimidated or offended by her assertive behavior. "Where did you learn to speak this way to men?" he demanded.

Her blue eyes narrowed. "We all learn to survive the best way we can. Ye survive by raping women and pillaging churches. I survive by being as tough, tougher, than those around me."

It was his turn to press his arms to the table, leaning so close to her that he could feel her breath on his face. "I have never raped a woman in my life. What I have taken was given freely."

To his surprise, she leaned back in the chair and laughed.

If he had thought to shock her with such insinuations, it had not worked. She seemed neither shocked nor impressed.

And he liked her for it. Liked her entirely too much. "And I am nae a thief. I made my coin trading, or by fighting other men's battles, but never by thievery."

As Tor reached out to pour himself more ale, the door opened and the servant she had brought with her entered.

"Your wine, m'lady." Alexi placed a bowl-like cup

of mulled wine before her. "I was wondering if ye'd return this night."

Her eyes twinkled. "Find something or someone of interest in the kitchen?"

The young man blushed and averted his gaze, grinding the toe of his boot on the floorboards. "The weather has worsened, m'lady. Would ye have me fetch the ponies?"

"How much worse?" She sipped her warm wine, its aroma filling the air.

"Snowing now. Cannae see a blessed thing."

She sighed. "I suppose we had best stay the night. Send a lad to Dunblane with word and tell him to stay there the night. If Tor's brothers have any sense, they will remain at Dunblane until morn. Ye and I will dig up some bedclothes and sleep here on the floor tonight with our friend."

"Aye, m'lady. I'll see to it."

Tor stared at Anne. "You will what?"

"Sleep here tonight. Elen allowed me to come, but she made me promise that if the weather worsened, I would stay the night and return in the morning."

He lunged out of his chair; the thought of spending the night alone with this woman was nearly intolerable. He could not have her here. He could not have her so near. "You cannot stay, woman."

She gave a laugh. "And why not? I have Lord Rancoff's permission—nay, his order—to stay."

"But you . . . you have no . . ." He rolled his eyes, trying to think of the English word. "No one to vouch for your . . . your honor."

She made a face, taking another sip of wine. Her tongue darted out to catch the wine from her lip. "I have Alexi. He'll sleep here between us."

"That . . . that . . ." he stammered, unable to take

his gaze from her mouth. "It is not right. What will people say of you? Of me?"

Again she chuckled. "What will they say? They will say naught save that the weather grew bad and I stayed the night in my guardian's home. I nae know how those ye live among speak, but we speak the truth."

He began to circle the table like a caged wolf-hound. "You should at least stay in another room. I sleep here on the floor."

"It would take a day to warm one of the other chambers, and this one is already perfectly warm. Of course, if ye wish to sleep in a cold room, ye are certainly welcome. I, however, am bedding here." She waved a small, delicate hand to indicate the paneled room.

Tor grabbed the wolfskin bedroll he had left in the corner of the room and shook it out. Without glancing her way, he dropped it to the floor in the far corner of the room from the hearth. "Put out the light when you go to sleep," he mumbled as he climbed, fully clothed with boots and all, into the bed.

"As ye wish, sir."

It was not long before the servant returned with blankets for his mistress. The two spoke briefly, and after cleaning up the supper plates, they bedded down in front of the hearth.

His belly pleasantly full, his bed warm, Tor thought he would easily drift off to sleep, but he did not. Instead, he lay wide-awake, trying not to move or breathe irregularly and give himself away. He wanted her to think he was asleep. Carefully he turned on his side so that he faced the hearth at the far end of the room. With the candles out, there was no light save for the golden glow of the fireplace, but he could make out Anne's form. He could hear her soft breathing as she fell to sleep easily. She lay on her side, her arm cradling her head. Her red-blond hair spilled onto the woolen blanket and onto the floor.

It was with that image in his mind that Tor finally slept.

"Ye are certain ye nae wish me to ride to Rancoff?" Munro questioned as he slipped naked into bed beside his wife.

She sat up, leaning against the carved headboard, and brushed out her glorious red hair. "She will be fine."

Munro chuckled. "It wasnae Anne I thought of. 'Twas my son. Ye think he's safe without the protection of his brothers? They both lie snoring on our hall floor."

Elen laughed with him. Tossing the tortoiseshell brush onto the table beside the bed, she began to wind her hair into a long plait. "She is taken with him, nay?"

"Taken with him?" He studied his wife's face. "What do ye mean? She only went to take him a meal because he was too stubborn to sit to the table with me. She rode in the snow only as a favor to me."

Elen smiled that all-knowing female smile of hers that still utterly perplexed him, even after these years of marriage. "Methinks she likes your handsome Viking son."

"Well, she cannae 'like' him. She is the king's daughter."

"And that prevents her from falling in love?"

He dropped back onto the bed, his head falling to a goose down pillow. "That prevents her from falling in love with my illegitimate son. Elen, he intends to get what he can from me and ride away. He intends to go back to his village, set sail on one of his dragon-headed ships, and go back to the marauding life he led. He isnae a mon fit for the king's daughter."

"Nae a mon fit for a king's daughter or nae a mon fit to be your son? Which do ye mean?"

He crossed his arms over his chest, staring at the dark ceiling. "That isnae fair."

Elen rolled onto her side, propping her head up with her hand. "Methinks ye need to give the lad a chance."

"He isnae a lad! He is a mon full grown."

"A mon who grew up without a father." She smoothed the graying hair at his temple. "A mon mayhap in need of a father now?"

"Ye misread him."

"Now ye sound like him," she teased. "Or is it the son sounds like the father?"

"I nae ken what ye speak of, wife." He closed his eyes, settling on his pillow. "Put out the light. I am tired."

"There, there 'tis again. Same tone. He grumbles just like ye." She leaned over to blow out the candle, taking the blanket with her.

The chilly air hit Munro's bare leg and he snatched back the woolen cover.

"A pity neither of ye are more like Finn," she continued. "I doubt *he* ever says a cross word."

"I doubt he ever says a cross word," Munro mimicked into his pillow. Tonight, listening to Finn tell his tall tales of adventure, listening to his daughters' laughter, his wife's entertaining questions, made Munro feel his age. His days of traveling the world were over. He was settled now with a wife and children. He was a happy man, but it was still hard to listen to young Finn and not at least consider what it would like to be so young and off to adventure again.

"Good night, love," Elen said, brushing her lips against his turned cheek. "I love ye."

She rolled onto her side and turned her back to him. For a moment, they lay back to back, but finally Munro gave in and rolled to face her, wrapping his arm around her bare waist. He was a fool to envy Finn and his great adventures. He kissed his wife's bare shoulder and she sighed, already drifting off to sleep. Munro had the best life a man could ask for. And now, with his son come home, it could only be better. If only he could convince the angry Tor indeed to be his son.

Anne woke to the sound of wood being added to the fireplace and the feel of the warmth as the flames flared. She opened her eyes to see Alexi fueling the fire. She stretched her hands over her head. She had slept surprisingly well last night, despite the hardness of the floor and the presence of the Viking. "Good morning, Alexi."

He smiled, his face reddening. " 'Morning, m'lady."

Anne rolled onto her side in the direction of where Tor had slept the night before. His bedding was rolled up and placed neatly in the corner of the hall. She and Alexi were alone.

She sat up, running one hand through her tangled hair. "Where's he gone?"

"Lord Rancoff's son?" Alexi asked. "To the kitchen. He told me to let him know when ye awoke."

"Did he, now?" She couldn't resist a smile. "And why is that?"

He shrugged comically. "Why do any foreigners do what they do?"

She rose and began to fold up the bedlinens she'd slept on. "Ye return these to their place, and I will go see what the Viking is up to."

Nodding, Alexi grabbed up the bundle of bedding and headed for the door.

"Alexi?" she called after him.

He turned.

She ran both hands over her head, trying to smooth the tangled mess. "Do I look too bad?"

Alexi blushed, dropping his gaze to the floor. "No, m'lady. Ye look right bonnie this morning."

She smiled. "Thank ye, Alexi. See to our mounts and we will soon return to Dunblane. The girls will be looking for me if we dinnae go directly."

Anne went in search of Tor. Downstairs, she was surprised by the smell of frying pork that wafted down the passageway leading to the kitchen. He must have found some poor serving lass to make him a meal to break his fast.

She found no serving girl in the warm kitchen, only Tor hunched over a bed of coals on the hearth, pushing pieces of frying meat around a flat iron pan. She couldn't resist a smile.

"What are ye doing?"

He glanced up, hurriedly getting to his feet as if he'd been caught doing something he shouldn't have. "Cooking meat," mumbled, hooking a thumb in the direction of the hearth. "I—I thought you might be hungry."

Anne was touched in a strange way, for her guess was that Tor Henneson had never made a meal for a woman, not even for his mother. " 'Struth, I think I am famished," she said, patting her abdomen. "Where did ye get the pork? Smells heavenly."

His back remained turned to her. "Killed a pig."

She laughed and walked to the large table in the center of the low-ceilinged room. She liked Tor's sense of humor; it was much like her own. "I think we've still some bread from last night. Dried apples, too." She opened the cloth bag brought from Dunblane and dug around inside.

Tor was silent as he finished frying the meat and brought it to the table where Anne set out two wooden plates. He slid equal portions onto them and set the hot pan aside.

Anne added bread and dried fruit to the plates and pulled up a tall three-legged stool for herself, leaving him to find his own. "So what will ye do today, your father and ye? Ride the land, see what Rancoff has to offer?"

He scowled, stuffing bread and pork into his mouth. "I do not wish to see what Rancoff has to offer. I do not care about this land. I do not care about these people. I want what is mine and then I want to go."

She lifted a brow. "I understand that ye want coin from your father, but ye've come so far. Munro showed me on a map where ye live. Do ye not think ye might as well stay a time before ye head back to your land of sweet dreams and honey?"

He eyed her across the table, which had a light dusting of flour on it. "Do ye always talk so much?"

She chewed a piece of the hot, spicy pork. "When I've something of import to say, aye."

He reached for another slice of bread from the cloth bag left on the table. "My brothers did not return last night."

"With the snow, they probably chose wisely to make their bed at Dunblane's hearth."

"They will grow soft, eating and sleeping like this."

"And having fun?" she teased. "Will that make them soft, too? Enjoying themselves?"

"You do not understand me. Us. You do not know what you speak of."

She laid her eating knife across her wooden plate. "So tell me. Make me understand ye, Tor."

He seemed to squirm under her scrutiny. "Why are you like this?" he mumbled.

She leaned closer, refusing to back off. "What did ye say?"

He lifted his gaze from his plate to her face. "Why do you go on like this, woman?" he growled. "Why do you push me? Why do you twist like a blade beneath my skin?"

"I nae know," she said softly. "I've a soft place in my heart for bastards, I think. For ye."

She caught him by surprise with her honesty, and his facial expression softened.

So, he was not made of stone and steel, after all.

His gaze held hers and she felt her stomach flutter. There was something here between them at this moment. It wasn't anything Anne could see or hear, but she could feel it. Smell it, taste it on the tip of her tongue.

Her breath caught in her throat. Suddenly her mouth was dry, her palms damp.

"Anne," he said so quietly that it seemed a whisper on the wind in the warm morning kitchen. "You—I—"

The kitchen's back door flew open with a bang and Anne jumped, the moment between her and Tor shattered as if it were Venetian glass.

"M'lady! M'lady!" Alexi shouted. "Fire! 'Tis fire in the village."

Anne leaped off the stool, running toward Alexi. She grabbed a motheaten wool cloak from a peg at the door. "Where?" she demanded, giving him a push to follow after him.

"A barn shed, m'lady. And there's bairns trapped above!"

Anne's chest tightened in fear. Of course the children were not hers, not her sweet Judith and Leah, but it didn't matter. They were children—helpless and in danger. She didn't know what she could do for them, but she knew she had to do something. As she raced down the hall, neck and neck with Alexi, she heard Tor's heavy footfalls behind her.

CHAPTER SEVEN

By the time Anne reached the bailey, Tor was running beside her. "Where are ye going?" he demanded.

She glanced at him as she tried to keep her footing in the icy bailey. "Where do ye think I go? To the fire."

His feet pounded beside hers as he reached out to grab her arm and steady her. "Let the men—"

She jerked her elbow from him as they clambered over the drawbridge. "This is my home, do ye nae understand?" she shouted into the wind. "These are my people now. My family."

Behind them, a wagon drawn by a pony rolled over the drawbridge. The rear of the cart was filled with odd-sized buckets and containers of sloshing water. As it passed them, Tor grasped Anne by the waist and lifted her in his arms.

She struggled as he raised her muddy feet off the ground. "Let me go! I willnae stay behind, I tell ye."

Ignoring her protests and flailing arms, Tor ran behind the wagon and deposited her roughly onto its open gate. "We can go faster this way," he told her, their gazes locking.

Anne's first impulse was to jump off the back of the wagon, but Tor was right. He could run faster than she could, and they were now closing in on the small village that lay to the west of the castle.

Dark smoke billowed in the distance, and Anne could smell the acrid scent of fear and burning wood. She struggled to turn where she sat, to spot the fire. Her hands were cold and she rubbed them together for warmth, wishing the distance were shorter between the village and the keep. The wagon, driven by one of Munro's clansmen, hit a rut and rocked on its two wheels, sloshing water down the back of her borrowed mantle.

Tor's arms flew up to keep her from being thrown off the back of the cart. He was barely breathing hard, and yet he had run more than half a mile. As he struggled to balance her and slide her back farther on the gate, his hand caught her lower lip.

It stung with pain.

"Are you all right?" He reached out to touch her face where he had struck her, but she ducked and rubbed her mouth with the back of her hand.

"I'm all right," she cried over the rumble of the wheels on the frozen ground and the shouting of men and women running for the burning barn. She could smell the smoke stronger now, thick and acrid as the thatch roof burned.

"Me bairns," a woman cried, running toward the wagon. "Please, sweet Christ in heaven! Save me bairns."

Anne leaped off the back of the cart as it pulled

as close to the burning barn as the driver dared. She grabbed the woman's arm. "Where are they?"

"Me bairns! Me bairns!" the woman shrieked, flapping her arms. "Save me wee bairns!"

Anne grasped the woman's flailing arms and forced her to look her in the eye. "We cannae help ye if ye nae calm down," she said sharply. "Now, where are they?"

The teary-eyed woman gasped and tried to focus on Anne's words. "In the loft above. They willnae come to me. They be too scared. Oh, God, m'lady, please save me bairns."

Anne grabbed the nearest woman to her; she did not know her name, but she had a kind face and seemed to be relatively calm. "What is your name?" she asked the mother of the children.

"Beck, m'lady."

Anne turned back to the woman whose arm she grasped. "Stay here with Beck," she ordered. "Keep her here, out of the way."

The other woman nodded fervently, taking the mother into her arms. "We'll stay right here, m'lady, and wait for the lad and lassie."

Anne took off for the barn, tossing orders over her shoulder. "Get her a blanket, a mantle—anything to keep her warm."

At the front of the barn, the heat of the fire struck Anne full in the face. She drew back. Men and women alike had already formed a line and were passing the buckets of water to splash on the barn. The scene was pandemonium. People were running back and forth, shouting orders. A frightened pony that had apparently broken free from the barn slipped and slid in the mud as two lads tried to capture her.

Anne gazed upward, spotting orange-yellow flames

that licked up the far side of the barn. "Where are they?" she screamed to no one in particular.

A sooty-faced teen with a shock of orange hair pointed upward. "We cannae reach the loft ladder. The smoke . . ."

Anne stood a moment in indecision. The air was so thick with smoke from the damp thatch roof that it was difficult to breathe and becoming more difficult to see. In the midst of the chaos, she spotted Tor. She could not miss his hulking frame, even in the clouds of noxious smoke. She ran to him, grabbing his leather sleeve. "We have to get them out," she cried, close to tears. "Can we get inside?"

"I do not know. I will try." He gazed upward at the burning building, evaluating his options. "Get blankets. I will bring them to you. Do not come inside."

She nodded as his hand shot out to catch hers.

"Did you hear me?" he shouted. "Do not come after me, woman."

Anne took off without answering him. She bobbed and wove through the line of people passing along water buckets. Near the wagon, she found a woman carrying an armful of blankets.

"For the bairns," she said.

Anne grabbed them from her arms and ran back toward the barn. Several men, women, and children had gathered in a cluster near the ragged, burning entrance to the barn. "Where is the foreigner?" she called to them. "The blonde?" She raised a hand to mean the tall man.

A woman clutching a toddler to her breast pointed into the burning barnshed.

Without thinking, Anne thrust the armful of blankets into someone else's hands, took a deep breath, and ducked in through the opening of the shed.

The barn was so filled with smoke that Anne had to drop immediately to her knees. The roar of the flames seemed to consume her. She had never heard a sound so hideous and knew this must be the sounds of hell.

On her hands and knees, she crawled forward. "Hallo," she shouted. "Hallo! Tor! Where are ye?"

She thought she heard a high-pitched voice and she halted, pressing her face to the hard-packed dirt floor. "Hallo," she hollered again.

This time she was sure she heard a response, a high-pitched cry of fear. "Get down," she shouted to the voice, thinking the sounds came from in front of her and upward. "Get down on the floor. I'm coming for ye."

Anne scrambled forward and struck something hard right in front of her. She gave a gasp of surprise when it moved.

"What are you doing in here?" Tor growled, turning around to grab at her. Even though she could not see him, there was no mistaking who it was. She knew his voice as well as she knew her own.

They both rose on their knees, facing each other. The smoke stung Anne's eyes so that they watered and she could barely see.

"I hear them," Anne told him, resting her hands on his broad shoulders so that she could get close enough for him to hear her. "Ahead, I think. Up. They must still be in the loft."

His face was smeared with black soot, his mouth drawn back in a tight frown. "Get out." He brought his face so close to hers that she could see his nostrils flare.

Anne had to lower herself flat to the floor again to escape the unbearable heat. "They willnae come to ye! A giant man," she explained. "Ye'll frighten the wits out of them.'' Without waiting for his response, she pushed past him on all fours.

He caught one of her feet and she wiggled it free, nearly losing her slipper. "I'm coming," she cried. "Do ye see me?"

"Help," came a croaky little voice. "Help me and my sister, will ye, m'lady?"

Anne reached blindly with her hands. The voice was directly overhead. She had to be near the ladder to the loft.

"Come back here," Tor growled, crawling up behind her.

Anne sat back on her haunches and pointed upward. "There," she choked. "There they are."

Tor leaped up and reached out, grasping the rung of the ladder out of nowhere. He climbed upward. "Here," he shouted to the children. "Come here and I will take you out."

There was a shrill scream of a little girl from above.

"Come here!" Tor boomed, balancing on the ladder above Anne and reaching up with both hands. "Drop down to me and I swear I will catch you, boy."

More shrill screaming.

"She's afraid of ye," Anne choked. She was feeling light-headed now. Her thoughts were no longer racing, but dragging slowly through her head, as if through mud.

She grabbed Tor's leg and pulled herself up. "Get down and let me see if they will come to me.

Standing, Anne was blinded by the smoke, deafened by the roar of the fire and the pounding of her own heartbeat. As she tried to pull Tor off the ladder, it occurred to her that she could die in this shed, trying to save two runny-nosed children she did not know.

She did not care.

"Tor! We haven't time to argue," she cried, her voice sounding scratchy in her ears. Bits of smoldering straw and wood were falling down like rain now. "The roof is going to cave in!"

Tor made some sound that was half shout, half cry, and he leaped off the ladder. Anne scrambled upward, closing her eyes. She could no longer see anything, anyway. Three quarters of the way up she opened her eyes and thrust out her arms. "Come to me."

Through the thick smoke, her watery eyes saw a boy and a girl four or five years old huddled together in the loft. "Come with me," she said, trying to sound calm. "Your mum waits for ye outside."

The little boy held his sister in his arms. They were both covered in soot and shaking.

"Come with me," Anne pleaded, trying to keep her balance on the ladder. "That's right," she soothed as they crept closer.

The moment they were within reach, Anne snatched the little boy and handed him down. Her muscles burned as she lowered the weight into Tor's waiting arms. The little girl came willingly.

"Pass her down," Tor shouted.

But the little girl clung so tightly to Anne that she could not pull her away enough to lower her. With one arm around the child's waist, she stumbled down the ladder.

"Go! Go!" Anne shouted, shoving Tor forward.

Out of the darkness and smoke came his hand, reaching behind him, and Anne latched onto it. She squeezed her burning eyes shut and ran in his wake, holding dearly to the lass, trusting Tor not only with her life, but with those of the children.

They burst out of the heat and smoke into the morning air. There were shouts of exuberance as they appeared from the burning barn. Someone reached for the little girl and took her from Anne's arms. Through a cloud of hazy smoke, her eyes burning, Anne saw the children's mother run toward them.

Anne bent at the waist, leaning forward to catch her breath. She heard Tor's voice. Felt him at her side.

"Are you mad? That was a senseless thing to do," he shouted at her, grabbing her arm. "Are you all right?"

Anne meant to shout back at him. She meant to tell him she was fine. Just a little dizzy. A little disoriented. But as she tried to focus on his handsome, soot-streaked face, the ground seemed to tilt. She opened her dry mouth that tasted of ashes, but no words sprang forth. Her legs went weak and she felt herself slip downward, the voices of those around her fading.

Tor closed his strong arms around her, and then there was nothing but darkness and silence.

"She will be all right, I tell ye," Anne heard Elen say.

She felt a cool rag on her face. She was lying in a bed somewhere. Elen was at her side. Anne wanted to open her eyes, but she was too tired. Too weak. She gave herself a moment.

"Why is she not awake by now?" came a rough male voice.

Anne knew that voice. She smiled inside. It was Tor.

She heard his heavy footsteps on the floor as he paced, and she wondered if that was the only way the man knew to walk. To stomp.

"I tell ye, she is fine. She breathes easily now. She has no burns, just a little singed hair."

Anne felt Elen's mothering hand caress the top of her head.

It felt strange to lie here, half-awake and half-asleep, listening to Elen and Tor speak of her. She felt as if she were drifting, but it was a comfortable drifting. She was warm and unafraid. She could still smell the burning barn, but the scent was faint now.

"I went into the same barn. Breathed the same smoke," he argued. "I did not faint away."

Faint, Anne thought. *I didn't faint.* The thought was embarrassing. She had never fainted in her life. Not even the time she had thrust an awl through the palm of her hand. She tried to open her eyes, to move out of the dreamlike state, but she just couldn't quite manage. Her eyelids were so heavy, her tongue so thick.

"Have ye any brain a'tall?" Elen argued. "Look at her. She's half your size. Has half the lung of ye."

Again Anne felt the cool cloth on her face. "Just give her a little time. She'll be fine."

A door opened in the room.

"M'lady," Anne heard someone say, "the master wishes ye to come look at the burn on a mon's leg. Got hit with a falling timber, he did."

Anne felt Elen remove the cold cloth.

"I . . . she's not awakened yet," Elen said, her voice edged with worry. I nae know that I should leave her."

Anne heard Tor's footsteps as he drew closer. "Go. I will sit here with her."

A chair scraped as Elen moved away from where Anne lay. "Are ye sure?"

"I am no good with a burn," Tor said stiffly. "But I can sit on a chair and put a cloth to her head."

"I'll be back directly," Elen said, hurrying out of the room. "Come for me if ye need me."

The door closed and Anne knew she was alone in the room with Tor. The idea made her uncomfortable, but at the same time, it made her warm in the pit of her stomach. They had made a good team today, once he had seen the matter her way. They worked well together, and she liked the thought of that.

The chair beside the bed scraped, wood against wood, and she heard Tor settle into it. She heard water run into a metal pan and then felt the coolness of the rag on her head again.

She could feel him close. Hear his breath. He made a sound in his throat. A groan.

"Anne," he said in a soft voice that made her feel silky inside. "Anne, it's time for you to wake now."

Again he groaned. Shifted in the chair.

She probably could have opened her eyes then.

She kept them shut.

"Anne," he whispered.

She felt the weight on the bed and then his large hand, engulfing hers.

"It was a brave thing you did there," he continued softly. "I have never known a woman to be so brave. And few men." He exhaled. "God of my mother, please wake up. . . ."

He sounded so hurt, so desperate, that she could not hold back any longer. She squeezed his hand that was wrapped around hers, surprised at how much strength it took. How little she had left.

"Anne?" He leaned closer. She could feel his breath on her cheek.

Slowly she lifted her heavy lids and smiled. "I'm awake." Her voice was thick and raspy and her throat hurt when she spoke.

"You are awake," he breathed. This time he caressed her forehead with his bare hand rather than the rag. It was a simple enough gesture, and yet it somehow seemed intensely intimate.

"You are all right?" he questioned.

Her words came forth sluggishly. She felt so sleepy, still woozy, and her chest hurt. "I am all right. Just winded I think. I feel as if I've run half way across the Highlands." Her laugh turned to a choke and she sucked in a great breath of the sweet, clean air of the bedchamber.

He smiled, and it was the handsomest smile Anne had ever seen.

"I think you could do it—run across the Highlands," he teased.

She smiled back and let her eyes close again. She liked the feel of his hand on hers. "Dinnae leave," she whispered, feeling herself drift off to sleep again.

"I will not leave you," he answered firmly. "I swear by my mother's grave."

CHAPTER EIGHT

"How is she?"

Tor glanced up, realizing that his father stood watching him pace in front of Rancoff's keep door. It was late in the afternoon. Tor had stayed with Anne until Elen had returned from the village and shooed him out.

"She's well enough, says your wife," Tor answered tersely. "She says it was just the smoke." Still pacing, he hooked his thumb in the direction of the upper tower. "She sleeps again. Elen . . ." He paused, not liking the familiarity he was feeling with these people. "Your wife says she hopes Anne will be willing to stay the night and return home tomorrow when she is rested."

Munro stood perfectly still, watching him, which made Tor even more uncomfortable. How could he be so calm? The foolish girl could have died in that barn.

He rubbed his burning eyes with his forefinger and

thumb. He just couldn't get the image out his mind. When Anne had crumpled into his arms, he had been so afraid she was dead that he had not been able to react. He'd just stood there for a moment, staring into her beautiful, soot-smudged face. And even now, when Elen insisted she would recover, he could not stop thinking that she could have died saving those children. And somehow the idea was incomprehensible. He had known her only two days, and he could not imagine the world without her.

" 'Twas a brave thing ye did in the village," Munro said quietly.

Tor halted, facing the stable barns. "I did not think of it as bravery. The girl—Anne—she went running off. I followed her as much as anything else." He scowled. "Had it not been for her, I would have finished my breakfast and left the fire to the Scots."

Tor hoped Munro would go away after that declaration, but he wouldn't. He kept pressing. "My clansmen saw what happened. They saw ye enter the burning barn, my son."

Tor ground his teeth. The wind had picked up and it blew from the west into his face, carrying the last of the scent of the burning barn. "Do not call me that."

Munro was silent for a moment. "I just wanted ye to know that I was proud of ye. Proud of what ye did. No mon could have said a word if ye'd just let those bairns die. No mon in his right mind would have gone into that barn for those children."

Tor could not bring himself to face his father. "But you," he said, with a hostility in his voice that he could not understand. "You would have gone."

"Aye, I suppose I would have." Munro spoke slowly, considering each word—a trait that grated on Tor's nerves. "But these people are my people. The Forrests have been protecting these families for generations. They are my responsibility, as they were my grandsire's."

"Do not make what I did more than it was," Tor grumbled and walked away. He headed directly for the barn, expecting his father to stop him. Half hoping he would.

Munro did not.

"Ye certain ye can travel?" Elen questioned, peering into Anne's eyes.

Anne sat on the edge of the bed and slid her feet into her slippers. She was in one of Rancoff's bedchambers. "I want to go home." Anne sniffed her shoulder. She stank of peat smoke. "I swear this gown is ruined." She looked up at Elen. "I just want a bath and my own bed."

"Ye certain ye nae wish to spend the night? I would stay with ye and we could travel home tomorrow."

"And what would Judith and Leah think? Will they nae be frightened if we do not return home?" Anne questioned. "Heavens, 'twas just a little smoke. Ye've been run through with a sword." She stood up and the room spun.

Elen slipped her arm around Anne's shoulders and steadied her. " 'Twas a flesh wound while playing in my aunt's courtyard with my cousin. Nae a wound of battle."

Anne met Elen's gaze. "I just want to go home," she whispered, feeling teary-eyed and not knowing why.

Elen hugged her. "All right. Home to Dunblane we shall go, but then to bed with ye. Will ye at least promise me that?"

Anne nodded, holding Elen tightly for a moment. Then she allowed Elen to help her across the room.

Downstairs, Elen found Anne's mantle for her. By the time they reached the bailey, the sun was beginning to set. Elen called for mounts, and as they waited, Munro crossed over the drawbridge. His clothing was dirty and covered in smears of black soot. His plaid bonnet rested on his head cockeyed.

"Where are ye going?" he called to them.

"She wants to go home," Elen explained.

His forehead creased in thin lines. "I thought we were going to spend the night. I promised the widow I'd come by and see how the bairns are doing."

Elen reached out to adjust his hat. "We were going to stay, but she wants to go home. And the lasses are there with Meggy. Anne fears they'll worry if we nae return home."

Munro glanced toward the drawbridge and the village. "Well enough. I'll escort ye home and just come back in the morn."

"That is ridiculous," Elen said. "Have I suddenly become too addlepated to make my own way across my own north woods?"

"*My* north woods," Munro corrected.

Anne rolled her eyes as she released Elen's arm to stand alone. The two had been arguing over those woods since Anne had come to live with them. Apparently, it was the fight over that property that had ultimately taken them to the altar.

"We willnae need an escort, Munro," Anne quipped. "I breathed a little smoke, naught more. Please dinnae make me feel any sillier than I already do."

"I will escort the ladies back," came a male voice out of nowhere.

Anne turned around sharply to see Tor standing behind her. Where had he come from?

Munro glanced at his son. "I would appreciate that, Tor. I do want to return to the village and check on Beck and the bairns. Then I will come to Dunblane directly."

"We willnae need an escort," Anne complained, her temper flaring. She briefly recalled the conversations she and Tor had shared earlier in the bedchamber. She remembered the gentleness of his voice. She remembered his touch. But now, in broad daylight, with her full wits about her, she didn't know that she wanted him around. He scared her. She scared herself when she was near him. And the idea that he thought she was unable to take care of herself long enough to get home to Dunblane only raised her ire.

A boy from the stable brought a pony around for her, and she allowed him to boost her up into the saddle.

"Anne, Elen," Munro said. "For once, will ye ladies humor me and let my son take ye home?"

Anne shrugged as Elen climbed on horseback unaided. "He can suit himself. If he wishes to ride to Dunblane, I cannae stop him."

"Wait a minute and I will get my mount," Tor said, hurrying across the bailey toward the barn.

"Ye'll have to catch up," Anne hollered over her shoulder as she urged her pony over the drawbridge in front of Elen.

"I'll see ye at home soon," Munro called after them.

Side by side, Elen and Anne cut across the meadow and headed toward the north woods that separated the two properties. If they hurried, they could make it back to Dunblane before nightfall.

"Ye should nae be so hard on him," Elen chastised gently.

"Who?" Anne was feeling better now that she was out in the cold, clean air. Her light-headedness had passed, and though her throat was still scratchy, she knew she'd be fine in a day or so.

"Ye know who. Tor. He is obviously smitten with ye," Elen teased.

Anne glanced at her, then ahead again. "The mon irritates the life right out of me. He thinks women are chattels to run at the beck and call of a mon."

"Mm-hmm," Elen intoned.

"He thinks a woman's place is at the hearth, babe in hand." She flashed her eyes angrily. "Or beneath the sheets, I suppose."

"I see."

"He doesnae think I have enough of a head to make up my own mind about anything."

"Does he, now?"

Anne looked to Elen. "Ye make fun of me."

Elen laughed. "Nay. Nae at ye, but just . . ." She hesitated. "Seems to be the way between men and women."

"The way?" Anne shifted in the saddle, not certain she liked Elen's tone of voice. Was she insinuating that there was something between her and Tor?

"At odds. When first Munro and I met, there was no question who was at whose mercy." She laughed. "But, I must say we were certainly at odds. Everything the mon said and did annoyed me and yet . . . intrigued me in the same breath."

"At odds, ye and Munro?" Anne teased, ignoring the suggestion that perhaps Tor *intrigued* her. "I cannae imagine."

Elen laughed with her but then sobered. "The only thing I will say, Anne dearest, is to take care."

She held both reins in one hand so that she could tighten the mantle at her neck. Though the trees blocked much of the wind, it was still cold. "Whatever do ye mean?"

"I mean the Viking. Ye are young—"

"I am nae young. Some already say I am too old to be wed."

"Ye are young," Elen repeated, "and an innocent in the ways of men and women, Anne; and he is greatly experienced, I should guess."

"I nae ken what ye speak of." She stared straight ahead, knowing she did know what she meant. Were these inklings of hers so obvious that others could see it? And if Elen could see it, could Tor?

Elen reached between the horses to touch Anne's gloved hand. "Ye know your father will choose a husband for ye soon. He has already put it off too long. And though I nae know our king well, methinks his choice willnae be a long-lost Viking son. I just dinnae want to see your heart broken. 'Tis all I am saying."

Anne wanted to retort, but could think of nothing to say. Fortunately, she was rescued by the sound of hoofbeats behind them. Riders were coming up fast.

Tor, accompanied by both brothers, rode up as if he meant to surround and attack the two women. Riding at a full gallop, leather-and-fur mantles whipping in the breeze, they stirred up a cloud of dirt with their arrival.

Both women ignored them.

"I told ye to wait," Tor said, riding his towering black horse in a tight circle around Anne and Elen.

Anne urged her little pony forward, not bothering to turn his way. "And I said ye would have to catch up."

" 'Twas good of ye to accompany us," Elen said

diplomatically. "With the coming of spring always come reivers. I wouldnae want to be caught poorly armed out here and dressed in this fluff." She flapped the skirt of the gown she wore.

One of the first adjustments Anne had had to make when she came to Dunblane was to the Lady Rancoff's attire. Elen had gowns aplenty, but most often she wore an interesting combination of male and female dress. Anne had neither the audacity nor the desire to dress as Elen did, but on occasion she was envious. Riding astride or fishing on the beach had to be easier in a man's tunic and leggings than in cumbersome skirts.

Tor, who had seen Elen's male attire the first night he had come, lifted a disapproving eyebrow but seemed to know better than to make a comment.

"The lad and lassie ye saved are right as new grass," Elen told Tor as he edged his mount up to ride in front of the women. His brothers remained to the rear in a protective formation. "Your father is proud of ye." She looked to Anne. "He's proud of both of ye. Heroes, ye are."

Anne frowned. "I certainly thought naught of being a hero and I am sure Tor didnae either. The barn was on fire. Children were inside and we knew they had to get out. 'Twas little more than that."

"I understand." Elen lifted the woolen hood of her mantle to cover her head. "Because if ye'd had time to use that head God gave ye, ye would have realized how insane the idea was." Her tone softened. "But we are proud of ye both the same. Beck swears the next babe born will be named after one of ye."

Anne laughed. "A Scottish lad called Tor. Imagine that."

Tor glanced over his shoulder. "And what is wrong with the name Tor? It was my *farfar's* . . . my grandfather's name."

"Oh, 'tis a fine enough name." Anne continued to laugh, not really knowing why she was laughing. It wasn't *that* funny. "I just find it hard to picture a Scottish lad called Tor."

Tor faced forward again, making it obvious he no longer wished to participate in the conversation. The remainder of the way home, Anne and Elen conversed and Tor ignored them.

In Dunblane's bailey, Tor helped Elen to dismount. Anne tried to dismount on her own before he reached her pony's side, but her skirt hung up in the saddle.

"Let me help you," he said in his deep voice that made Anne feel strange inside.

"I'll go to the hall to find the girls. To bed with ye," Elen called as she hurried off, with two servants talking to her at the same time. "I'll be up directly to bring ye a wine caudle."

Anne's gaze met Tor's as he caught her around the waist and lifted her down. She was embarrassed by his touch, and she didn't know why. Men assisted women down from their mounts every day. She looked away.

"I smell of soot," she mumbled as his hands lingered at her waist, even after her feet had touched the ground.

"You should go to bed. Rest."

"Should I? And what if I have other duties?"

He stepped back. "Makes no difference to me," he answered gruffly. "I only—"

His brothers were dismounting. Talking to each other.

"Ye only what?" Anne crossed her arms over her chest, demanding a reply.

Tor was an astounding specimen of man with his long blond hair, thick arms, and wolf's pelt mantle thrown over his shoulders; and she could not stop herself from thinking about what Elen had said about her being an innocent and his being experienced with women. Anne knew what rutting creatures men could be, and knew better than to think a man reached Tor's age and remained celibate, but a part of her wished it was not so. She was shocked at her own jealousy of all the women he must have known.

"I only spoke out of concern for you."

"Well, dinnae be *concerned*."

His wide brow furrowed. "Why do you speak to me this way?" Tor said, moving in closer. "First you are nothing but honey, and then you snap at me. I have done nothing to you."

"Done nothing to me?" she flared. "Done nothing to me? Ye've walked into our lives and set them upside down. Ye have altered Munro's and Elen's lives forever and therefore altered mine, so nae tell me ye have done naught to me."

He slowly lowered his gaze to his booted feet, which had sunk into the mud, and pulled one out with a sucking sound. The sun at midday had warmed the bailey and melted most of the snow. With so many men and women and animals coming, the bailey always became muddy this time of year.

"I did not mean to upset your lives."

Anne was surprised by the change in tone of his voice. He was suddenly apologetic, almost forlorn.

His quiet voice released the wind in her sails. She lowered her voice so that his brothers could not hear them. "I didnae say it was a bad thing. Only that your coming makes everything different. Different forever."

"I came only because I promised my *mor*."

"Your *mor*?"

He reached out to fiddle with her pony's bridle as a stable boy led his mount away. "My mother."

Anne moved closer to him and petted the spotted pony's neck. The warmth of the horse, the nearness of Tor, set her off balance. "Ye can tell yourself and others that," she murmured, "but I know differently. No mon would come so far, take such risk, merely to fill a dying person's wish. Nae even their mother's."

His gloved hand brushed hers as he loosened a strap on the bridle. "I do not know what you speak of, woman."

She looked him in the eye, and he seemed unable to look away, though she knew he wanted to. "Oh, I think ye do, Tor Henneson. I think ye know exactly what I speak of, only ye pretend 'tis nae so. Just like ye pretend ye nae care for others. I nae care what ye say. A mon doesnae risk his life to save two snotty-nosed bairns, and have nae a care for mankind."

Not knowing what made her so bold, she reached out and brushed her gloved hand against his cheek. The look on his face told her he was as surprised by her gesture as she. "But nae worry," she whispered, her voice breathy. "Your secret is safe with me. Ye pretend ye are a selfish brute, and I will pretend right along with ye."

Anne walked away and did not allow herself to look back.

CHAPTER NINE

"I do not know what a man does to find himself a woman here," Finn said, lifting his mug to his brothers.

Tor eyed Finn and realized that his brother's image was a little hazy. He wondered if it was the smoke in the room from the damp wood they were burning, or the amount of ale he had consumed.

Hours before, he and Olave had located a small keg in the cellars of the castle. Most of the foodstuffs were locked in small chambers, against would-be thieves known and unknown. The keg had already been tapped, so Tor surmised a servant had been sent to return it to its locked chamber, and it had simply been forgotten in the dark corridor.

Munro Forrest's loss, the Henneson brothers' gain.

Tor grinned foolishly at the idea that he could have bested his Scottish father, if only in drinking his ale.

"Kvinne." Olave spoke the word as if it represented some foreign deity. He sat on the floor, his back to

a panelled wall of Rancoff's great hall. A portrait of some Clan Forrest ancestor hung high over his head. "Women," he repeated drunkenly and then went back to counting the toes of his bare left foot. *"En, to, tre . . ."*

"Kvinne," Tor said, wrapping one arm around Finn's shoulders. "Why would a man want a woman, brother? I have to ask you this question."

The two brothers stared into the blazing fire on the hearth, enjoying their moment of camaraderie. Tor was not a physical man, and certainly not with other men, even his brothers. But when he drank too much, others told him he got affectionate. It was just the way he was.

"Why?" Finn questioned philosophically, leaning on his big brother for support. "Why does the sun need the stars? The earth the rain?" He gestured with his mug, ale sloshing over the side and onto the planked floor. "Why does the bee need the flower? A hunk of bread need meat?"

Tor choked on a swallow of ale and spat it into the fireplace. The flames protested angrily, snapping and popping. "Bread need meat?" he laughed. He released Finn's shoulder to strike his knee with mirth. "Bread needs meat? Do you say that to all of your women? You certainly know how to sweet-talk."

"What?" Finn grinned crookedly. "It is a great truth of the world. Just as the fact that men need women is a great truth of the world."

"Menneske behøve kvinne. Men need women," Olave muttered from his position on the floor. He had now given up counting his toes and was using a small awl from his bag to drill a hole in the wood floor in front of him.

Finn and Tor looked at Olave spinning the awl

between his beefy palms, looked at each other, and broke into laughter.

"I think the relationship between men and women is far overrated," Tor told Finn. He took his mug to refill it from the tapped keg they had left on Rancoff's dining table. "Far overrated," he repeated, catching a glimpse of the red-haired Scottish lass in his mind's eye. He leaned over and drank directly from the spout on the keg, drowning Anne's image with a long pull of the cool ale.

"And I think your problem is that you have gone too long without a woman." Finn shoved Tor aside and stuck his mug under the running tap, losing only a little ale to the floor.

Tor eyed his brother and waited his turn to refill his own mug. He was definitely hazy. Tor closed one eye while trying to see Finn with the other. Still blurry, he tried the other eye. "And I think you are full of shit."

"And I think you need a tumble with that redhead." Finn jabbed Tor with his mug. Ale sloshed onto Tor's leather tunic.

Tor narrowed his eyes. He had already told Finn once that the subject of Anne de Bruc was off limits. He did not want to discuss her, not with Finn, and he resented the suggestion that anyone thought he needed to talk about her.

"Need a tumble," Tor grumbled, removing Anne from the conversation. "Do you think I need another hole in my head, too? Maybe I could borrow Olave's awl and start one now."

Finn laughed heartily. "Well, if you're saying you're not interested, are you giving me permission to pursue that little bit of sweet meat?"

Tor clamped his jaw shut. One moment he was

happy as a songbird, and now he was suddenly angry. "Leave her alone."

"Aha, so it is not my imagination that you like the way Anne's skirt turns."

Tor threw his mug over his shoulder, and it hit the wall behind him with a resounding clunk just as his other hand met with Finn's jaw.

Finn cried out in surprise. His mug flew out of his hand and the ale sprayed both brothers and the table. Finn fell back against the edge of the dining table, taking down a stool. He came up swinging both balled fists.

"I warned you," Tor boomed, swinging one fist and then the other.

Finn ducked, swung, and caught Tor in the abdomen. "Warned me about what?"

Tor exhaled heavily as he took the blow to his stomach. "I told you not to speak of her. Not to say her name." He kicked another stool out of his way, backing Finn around the table.

Finn clipped Tor's nose and it spurted blood. Tor instinctively reached up to wipe the blood from his face and took another blow, this one sharply in the jaw.

"*Esel!*" Tor cursed.

Finn took another step back as Tor swung wildly. When Finn bumped into Olave's legs, he leaped over them. Tor gingerly stepped over their brother, who was still concentrating on drilling a nice round hole in the floor. He didn't look up as his brothers fought above him and then moved around to the far side of the table.

"You like her," Finn accused. "I see the way you watch her. The way she watches you."

Tor let out a roar of rage and lunged at Finn. Finn fell backward and both men hit the floor hard.

The rear door of the great hall opened and the young man called Rob burst in. "What in God's green hell is going on here?" the redhead demanded.

Olave looked up at Rob and pointed at his brothers. "Fighting." He went back to drilling his hole.

Tor and Finn rolled over and over on the floor, knocking over stools. Tor managed to grab Finn by his tunic. He lifted his head and struck it on one of the legs of the table. Finn's head jarred the table so hard that the ale keg started to roll.

"God's bloody bones," Rob shouted waving his hands. "Please stop! If you kill each other, Lord Rancoff will have my head!"

The keg ceased to roll, dangerously close to the far edge of the table.

Somehow, Finn wiggled out from under Tor and leaped to his feet. Tor scrambled up, ducked his brother's flying fist, and grabbed him again. He swung Finn into the wall, and a large painting of a man with a long nose flew off the wall. Tor ducked as the portrait flew over his head, met with the edge of the table, and fell to the floor.

Rob ran for the portrait, snatching it up just as Tor and Finn, locked arm and arm, fell onto the table.

Rob tried to climb over the men to get to the keg, which had started to roll again, but couldn't protect the portrait and reach for the rolling keg at the same time. The small wooden barrel struck the floor with a deafening splintering of wood and a splash of what was left inside.

Tor took another hard punch to his jaw, which was now vibrating with pain. "Ouch!" he cried. "Don't do that!" He struck Finn so hard that Finn flew back against the table and his head struck the edge.

Finn went down like a stone.

Tor stared at his brother's dazed eyes. His anger

was gone in an instant. The whole room was spinning. "Finn!" Tor dropped to his knees.

"God above. Look." Rob groaned, still clutching the Rancoff family portrait. "Ye've scratched the great granddad of the master's father, and now ye've killed your brother." He shook his head close to tears. "M'lord Rancoff will have my head upon his platter. He told me to look after ye. To see ye had what ye needed."

Tor slid through the ale to lift his brother's head from the floor. Finn was staring, eyes open, but did not seem to see. "Finn, Finn, are you all right?" Tor cried, his heart in his throat. He loved Finn. He would never do anything to harm his brother. "Finn?"

Finn blinked. Once, twice, a third time. "Crap," he moaned, reaching up to stroke the back of his head. "That hurt."

Tor released Finn and fell onto the floor on his back beside his brother. The whole room spun, increasing his nausea. He closed his eyes and wiped at the blood running from his nostrils . "I thought you were dead."

"Not dead."

"Are ye done fighting?" Rob breathed. "Because if ye are, I want to go repair Grandfather here."

Tor opened one eye long enough to see the Scottish man rubbing at the portrait.

"They're done fighting," Olave said cheerfully from the far side of the room. "They always fight when they drink too much. *Mor* wouldn't let them drink too much in her house because they broke things."

"We do not always fight when we drink," Tor protested loudly. It had occurred him that he ought to sit up, but he wasn't sure he could. Both he and Finn were still panting hard, and the room still felt as if it were spinning, even with his eyes closed.

Rob stepped over the Viking brothers' long legs and headed cautiously for the door.

"They always fight," Olave repeated.

"We don't always fight," echoed Finn, good-naturedly. "Shut up, Olave."

"They always fight," Tor heard Olave whisper.

"Well, see they nae tear up any more," Rob told Olave. "I'll be in come morning to clean this mess up."

Tor heard the door close. He was feeling sleepy now. "I did not mean to kill you, brother."

"You didn't kill me." Finn remained flat on the floor beside Tor, their heads under the table.

"It's only that you made me mad."

Finn reached out and patted Tor's arm. "It is all right, brother. A decent fight is good once in a while. Starts the blood flowing."

Tor ached in a hundred places: his jaw, his gut, his left eye, his shoulder. But he was feeling good. "So," he murmured, "you really think she likes me?"

"I nae understand why we had come here," Finley said, riding beside Rosalyn through the woods. "We will be caught."

"We willnae be caught because we are clever." She glanced at him. "Well, *I* am."

"I thought we were going to England. When ye came for me in Inverness, ye said we were going to England."

She looked at him, her gaze narrowing threateningly. "Do ye want to go back to that piss hole?"

Finley stared at his hands wrapped in the stolen pony's mane. He had not been able to believe his good luck the night Rosalyn had appeared outside his jail cell. After eight years of imprisonment, she had somehow escaped the nunnery in Edinburgh and come for him. She had bribed her way into the asylum, with what, he dared not ask, and had released him from the confinement her sister had sentenced him to.

Finley loved Rosalyn for setting him free, but she had said they were going to London. She hadn't said anything of returning to Dunblane, where he had once been the beloved steward.

"Well?" she demanded, jerking hard on the pony's mane so that it halted. "Do ye want to go back?"

He shook his head adamantly. "Nay, nay, of course not."

He did not want to go back, but he didn't want to stay here, either. He did not like the dark castle ruin where they were sleeping, and he did not like doing the things she made him do. To kill an animal for meat was one thing, but just to kill, to mutilate, was another. Rosalyn said she made him do it to test him, but he was beginning to think she liked it.

"Then shut up and do what I say." She kicked the pony and it leaped forward. "Do ye love me?" she asked.

"I love ye," he muttered.

"And ye would do anything for me?"

"Anything."

"Ye'd better."

"Good morning."

Tor turned from the mare he was stroking to see his father enter the barn. " 'Morning," he grunted back.

"Nice eye." Munro walked up to him and stopped to gaze up at Tor's face.

Tor rubbed his sore jaw. "Got into a little . . . disagreement last night."

Munro grinned. "So I hear." He walked past Tor to the next stall and reached for a bridle that hung on the wall. "My brother and I used to fight when we got drunk, too."

"We weren't drunk," Tor mumbled. "Just had . . . a disagreement." He thought about Anne. About what Finn had said. He said she watched him. Finn thought she liked him. If Finn got within an arm's length of Anne, he would kill him.

"I nae know about that. I hear there's enough ale on the floor of my hall this morning to float a boat."

The look of amusement on Munro's face annoyed Tor—implying that he understood Tor, that there was some kinship between them. How could he possibly understand him? Munro had been raised the eldest son of a wealthy landlord. The blessed child of a union sealed by a priest's lips. Munro Forrest could have no way of understanding how Tor felt or what he thought about anything. The suggestion was insulting.

"I hear my grandda' took a beating as well."

Tor reached out to stroke the shaggy mare's mane again, breaking eye contact. It was nice here in the barn: warm and quiet. It smelled of hay and horses and men. Familiar smells. "I apologize for the mess we made. I told the boy we would clean it up ourselves."

Munro shrugged and eased the bridle over the mount's head. " 'Tis nae the first time Rancoff's hall has seen a good brawl between men. Probably nae the last, either."

Tor made no comment. He was at odds this morning, and his head ached. He didn't know if the pounding head was from the beating he had taken from Finn last night or from the ale. He was getting too old for both, he supposed. Finn and Olave were still sleeping it off on the floor of the great hall, but Tor had awakened at dawn and couldn't get back to sleep.

He didn't know what to do. A part of him wanted to gather his brothers, get back on his horse, and ride north again. Leave Munro Forrest and his pleasant life in the Highlands behind. Tor wanted to return to the only place he had ever known as home. But something—someone—was keeping him here, and it wasn't his father.

"I've a mind to take a ride this morning. Looks to be a good day. The sun is shining." Munro looked at Tor over the stall's wall. "Will ye join me? I could show ye the lay of the Forrest land."

Tor did not answer immediately. He rubbed his temples with his thumb and forefinger. A ride might clear his head. It would be hours before his brothers woke, and what would they do then? He glanced over the stall. Munro's back was turned to him as he saddled the pony. "Aye, I will ride with ye."

Munro turned around, that silly grin on his face again.

"What?" Tor demanded. "Why do you look at me that way?"

"Careful, there. Ye've only been here a few days and you're already sounding like a Scotsman."

Tor stalked off through the barn to saddle his horse.

Once out on the open fields and meadows, Tor's disposition improved against his will. He didn't want to enjoy the ride with his father, but he couldn't help himself. The Highlands on this side of the Grampian Mountains were breathtakingly beautiful, with hills and valleys, moors and meadows, and vast forests. Despite the snowfall only a few days ago, there were signs of spring everywhere. Green shoots of grass poked up from the brown peat, tempting the horses. Buds bulged on oak tree limbs and starlings called from branches.

The terrain was wet and muddy in some places, but the footing was sure. Tor and Munro made their way west and then north. At the edge of a forest, they stopped to watch a herd of roe deer. Though fresh meat might have been nice for the dinner table after so many months of pickled and salted meats and fish, neither man drew a weapon.

Munro and Tor said little as they rode on. Munro pointed out various landmarks and told clever stories about the land and the Clan Forrest men who had walked it before him. The only blemish on the morning was when they came upon a red deer that appeared to have been slain. Though the kill was less than twenty-four hours old, much of the meat had already been picked clean by the animals that lived off carrion. What was left puzzled them both.

"What do ye—you," Tor corrected himself quickly, "think killed it?" He hadn't even realized he had been adapting his speech to match those around him.

The skull appeared to have been shattered, and there were ragged tears on what was left of the hide on the neck.

"Wolf, maybe." Munro stared down at the carcass.

Both men had remained mounted. Tor took one last look at the deer and urged his horse up the path. "I have known many a wolf in my lifetime; I wear his pelts. No wolf kills like that."

Munro shrugged and fell in behind his son. "Who knows. Hard to tell from what was left. Maybe wild dogs."

"Maybe."

At noonday, Tor and Munro stopped to let the horses drink from a brook that trickled from a mountainside and eat some dried beef and slices of bread Munro had thought to pack.

"It is a beautiful land," Tor said grudgingly. He leaned against a tree with one boot up for support while he chewed on his beef jerky. Farther north, it is so barren. There will still be no green at home."

Munro sat on a rock, relaxed, his booted feet thrust out. "But your land has its own beauty," he said watching a sparrow flit from one dry branch to another. "I remember the cold, the rocky terrain, but also the beauty of it. There is a vastness farther north that I nae feel here."

Tor did not want to think of Munro in his mother's village. He did not want to think of the two of them together. "You traveled much when you were younger?" he asked. It was the first time he had initiated such personal conversation with his father.

"Aye. My father and brother and I traveled with the Bruce at times. I was at Bannockburn when Sterling Castle fell." Finished with his meal, Tor wiped his hands on his leather pants. "And now he is king."

"King in our eyes. Still nae recognized by the English bastards, though."

"And he is also Anne's father?" Tor didn't know what made him ask. He hadn't even been thinking of her.

Munro glanced Tor's way. "He is. I nae think he knew until her mother's illness that he sired her. He came here himself to ask Elen and me to take her in."

"She hates him, but I suppose you know that." Tor ground the heel of his boot into the mossy ground.

Munro chuckled. "She makes nae bones about that

issue, does she? 'Struth, I understand her point of view more than she realizes. But in all fairness, I must say I also see his."

"He does not have time for a bastard daughter, him being king," Tor quipped.

"We have never really discussed the matter. 'Tis nae my place, but I think he wishes to protect her," Munro said firmly. "Have ye any idea how many of the Bruce's family members have been killed? Do ye know the English dogs put his wife and daughter in cages?"

Tor wished he had not started this conversation, but he would not back down. "She thinks he does not care." Tor didn't know if he was referring to Anne's father, or his own now.

"Anne is stubborn. She willnae listen to me on this matter." Munro rose from his seat on the ground, brushing off his hands. "And how is it ye come to know so much of my charge? Hm?"

Tor started for his ground-tethered horse, uncertain how to answer.

"Ye know it would be unfair to her to pursue her."

"I am not pursuing her."

"Her father intends to marry her off. Soon, I suspect. The bridegroom will be a Scot."

Tor swung into his saddle. "And did ye not say only the day before yesterday that I was a Scot? That this land was in my blood?"

He sank his heels into the black mount's flanks and did not hear Munro's reply.

CHAPTER TEN

Tor heard the hoofbeats of his father's pony behind him and he slowed, allowing him to catch up.

Munro fell in beside Tor. His Highland pony was short-legged, but Tor was amazed by the animal's stamina.

"Tor, I'm sorry. That didnae come out as I intended."

Tor stared straight ahead. His father's words had stung. The idea that being bastard born made him unworthy of Anne cut him deeper than he would have guessed. He was more surprised yet that his father realized he was hurt and not just angry. He was surprised that the man cared. No one had ever cared how Tor felt before, except maybe his mother.

"I have no ill intentions toward Anne," Tor said carefully. "I did not come here for a woman."

"I nae know ye well, Tor, but I think I know ye well enough to see ye are an honorable man. I didnae mean to suggest that ye would take advantage of her.'' He gave a little laugh. '' 'Twould be more likely the other way around. Our Anne, she is a hard nut. I was only concerned for your heart.''

Tor shifted uncomfortably in his saddle. In all the years he had lived with his mother's husband, he had not once heard him mention anyone's heart. Tor had not even known for certain if the man had one.

''I would be a fool not to see she has an eye for ye. She thinks ye are comrades, somehow. That ye have a unity in being born bastards or something like that.''

Tor hated the word *bastard,* but it did not hurt as much coming out of his father's mouth.

''She had a hard life before she came to Dunblane,'' Munro explained. She was a lonely lass, still is in some ways. I just—''

''You want me to stay away from her.''

''Nay.'' Munro shook his head. But then he hesitated.

They had entered an open meadow, and a speckled hawk spiraled over their heads. Both men watched as it dove for some hapless creature in the knee-high grass.

''Aye,'' Munro conceded. ''I would worry less if ye would keep your distance.''

''It is not this Henneson brother that you need to worry about,'' Tor said, shifting the subject to ground he was more comfortable on. ''It is Finn whom the ladies like, both married and unmarried.''

Munro smiled. ''I appreciate the warning, but I do not fear your young brother will take my Elen from me. And if he did, he would soon toss her back.'' He laughed, amused with his own jest.

Tor could not resist smiling, too. ''She is not like any woman I have known before; I will say that,'' he admitted. "Anne said something about you having once resided in her dungeon."

" 'Tis a long story, best told when I am half sotted." He gestured. "But mind, I will tell it to ye one day."

The men fell into silence again as they rode back toward Rancoff. The ride was pleasurable for Tor, with the warm sun on his face and his ears filled with the sounds of the coming spring. As they neared Rancoff, they cut east toward the coast.

"Let's see if anyone has caught anything," Munro said. "A day like this and someone is bound to be fishing. There are some small eddies in the rocks on the beach between Rancoff and Dunblane. Good places to fish outside the rough surf. We'll swing around to Dunblane. Ye can ride home to Rancoff or stay to sup, whichever ye prefer."

"No doubt my brothers are already waiting in your lady's hall," Tor grumbled good-naturedly. "They keep saying they have never seen so much food in their lives. Never eaten so much."

On the beach, Tor and Munro did find someone fishing, though it was not men, as Tor had expected.

"Good afternoon to ye," Anne called from a perch on a rock. Her hand line dangled in the water below, where an eddy in the gray rocks formed a small pool that swirled with each wave lapping onto the shore. Beside her on the rock perch sat the elder of Munro's daughters.

Tor studied the little girl, trying to keep his gaze from straying to the bit of bare ankle and calf Anne flashed as she leaped up and waved.

The little girl, called Leah, looked like a miniature of her mother with her tumbling red hair, sturdy body, and bright, oval face. She looked to be a happy child. She also shared enough coloring and features with Anne that they could have been sisters . . . or even mother and daughter.

"Papa!" Leah jumped up at the sight of them approaching slowly across the sand on horseback. She jerked her fishing line out of the water, the live minnow bait squirming.

Anne ducked to keep the hook from striking her. "Easy there," she warned, throwing up her hands to catch the little girl's. "I told ye, if ye hook me again, you'll stay home next time."

"Caught anything?" Munro swung out of his saddle and left his pony ground-tied.

Tor didn't really want to dismount. Didn't want to talk to Anne. But he felt silly perched up on his big horse, looming over the others on the ground. Reluctantly, he dismounted.

Munro took the fishing line from his daughter's hand and gingerly passed it to Anne. He opened his arms wide as Leah hurled herself off the rock, through the air toward him. Tor was amazed by the absolute trust he saw in the little girl's face as she flew into her father's arms.

And he was just a little envious.

"Have a good ride?"

Munro was swinging Leah around in a circle by her arms, and the girl was squealing with laughter. Anne could be speaking to no one but him.

"Aye—yes. A good ride. His—the land is beautiful. Very serviceable, I can see. Good for grazing." Tor had no idea what he was babbling about.

"Nice eye."

"What?"

"Your eye." Anne pointed. "I like the color. A little green, a little yellow. Very nice."

Tor had forgotten the black eye Finn had given him. He lifted his hand self-consciously.

"Run into a door?" she asked with amusement as she rolled the fishing line up on a small piece of wood.

"Something like that."

She smiled again, and he knew that she knew how the black eye had come to be. Word obviously traveled fast around here.

"Didn't catch any fish?" he asked, wishing he had something to do with his hands besides let them dangle like dying fish at his sides.

"Of course we caught fish." She stuck out one hand, obviously wishing him to help her off the rock.

He caught her small hand, which was warm and firm in his.

She leaped off the rock into the wet sand. "Look." From the eddy, she pulled a small basket he hadn't noticed before. Inside were several squirming saithe of reasonable size. "Nae enough for the whole hall, but enough for my breakfast and Miss Leah's as well." She handed him the dripping basket.

Not knowing what else to do, Tor accepted it, holding it out so that the cold salt water didn't drip on his leather-and-woolen clothing.

"Play your die right and ye might get a little of my fish to break your own fast tomorrow."

She was teasing him. Flirting.

He liked it.

"How did you get here?" Tor watched thankfully as she unknotted her skirt and let it fall over her calves to her ankles.

"Walked."

Tor suddenly felt a tightening in his chest as he watched Munro climb onto his pony and reach down to lift Leah and place her in front of him. Surely, Munro would not expect him to ride Anne back to the castle in front of him.

"Nae worry," Anne said, seeming to know what he was thinking. "I've two feet to walk. Besides, the basket is messy if I dinnae carry it like this." She took back the fish basket and extended her arm a little. "Go on with ye." She pointed with her chin. "I've two legs that have carried me well so far. I'll walk back to the keep."

Tor glanced in his father's direction. He wanted to call out to him, but he wasn't sure what to say. He could not bring himself to call Munro "father," but "Lord Rancoff" didn't seem appropriate, either. "Munro!" he finally decided upon.

Munro looked over his shoulder.

"She wishes to walk." Tor hooked his thumb in Anne's direction. "I will walk with her."

Tor didn't know if it was his imagination, but Munro seemed to hesitate for a moment. He nodded. "Well enough. We will see ye back at Dunblane." His gaze lingered a moment on Tor and then he turned away, urging his pony up the beach to harder sand.

Tor knew Munro was thinking of the conversation they had had earlier today about Anne. But all he was doing was escorting her home. Surely, she was safe in his hands for a half-mile walk back to Dunblane's gates.

"So tell me what ye saw of our Highlands today," Anne said, seeming completely comfortable to be alone with him.

Tor was amazed at how easy she was to talk to. He told her about the trees budding. About the herd of roe deer they had seen and about the tiny shoots of green grass.

Anne was a good listener. She made comments, asked questions. She pushed him, making him sometimes reveal things about himself, yet she did not

push too far. He'd intended to say only enough to
satisfy her, to get through the awkwardness of the walk
up to Dunblane. Instead, he found himself describing
the smell of the wet spring oak trees and the sound
of the chattering birds in the branches. The only
thing he did not tell her about was the deer carcass
they had found.

By the time Anne and Tor approached the gatehouse of Dunblane, he was wishing the walk had been
farther. She was telling him about her ride through
the mountains in the snow with Munro to come to
Dunblane, and he wanted to hear more.

He liked the sound of her voice. He liked the way
she gestured enthusiastically, swinging the fish basket
as she tried to describe her and Munro's rough beginning.

"What is that?" Tor asked, pointing to a structure
in a nestle of trees to the west of the castle.

"That's the kirk. Elen says they think it's been here
longer than the castle. Want to see it?"

Before he could answer, she veered off their path.
Tor followed.

Anne set down her fish basket outside the front
door of the stone church.

"I—I do not need to go inside," Tor said.

But she was already skipping up the flagstone steps.
"Come on. 'Tis beautiful inside this time of day.
We've no priest; he passed away years ago. So there
are no regular services."

Anne grabbed his hand and he had no choice but
to follow. In truth, to hold her hand like this, he
would have followed her through the burning gates
of hell.

The tiny kirk was dim inside; its glass windows were
shuttered. It smelled of damp stone, old wood, and
the lingering scent of incense.

Anne dipped her hand into a small cup built into the stone wall and crossed herself. Awkwardly Tor followed her.

Tor's mother had been a Christian woman, and she had tried to share her belief with her sons, but his stepfather had had no tolerance for a woman's religion, so Tor had learned little of Christian beliefs.

Anne walked up the narrow center aisle and sat on a bench in the front before the altar. " 'Tis so peaceful here," she said quietly.

Tor stood in the aisle, knowing he should not be here alone with her. He knew Munro would be angry. But the serene look on her face, the memory of her hand in his—he couldn't take his eyes off her.

She patted the bench.

He felt as if he were under some strange spell. He sat.

"Listen," she whispered.

He could hear nothing but the pounding of his heart and the sound of her light breathing beside him.

"Hear that? Judith and Leah and I heard it yesterday. We think there must be a nest of baby birds in the eaves." She glanced upward, carefully surveying the ceiling. She turned her head in his direction, her gaze meeting his. He heard her breath catch in her throat as he slid one hand over the smooth wormwood of the bench and slipped it around her.

This was dangerous.

Tor knew it was dangerous. But he could no more have stopped himself from kissing her than he could have kept from falling after leaping off a mountain cliff.

She made no attempt to move away, as he half expected, half hoped. She did not close her eyes either as he leaned over her, lost in her blue-eyed gaze. Her mouth was soft, her lips slightly parted. He barely touched his mouth to hers, yet his head swam with the scent of her bright hair, the feel of her lips against his, the quiver of her hand as she slid it onto his knee.

When he pulled back, her eyes were half shut. She just sat there, exhaling softly.

She was so beautiful. Her cheeks were flushed from the sun and the wind on the beach. She smelled of the salt sea and dreams he never knew he had.

He could not resist a chuckle as she sat beside him, utterly still. "What are you doing?" he finally breathed, lifting his finger to her chin so that she would open those lovely eyes and gaze at him.

Slowly her lashes lifted and he was again lost to her.

"I want to savor it."

"Savor it?"

She smiled. It was a shy smile, but not one of shame. "My first kiss."

Her words startled him, and he looked away. He had certainly known she was a virgin, but to think that no man had ever even kissed her! He felt honored; this was truly holy ground. But he was also ashamed. Only hours before, he had told his father he had no intentions toward her. Now, all he wanted to do was kiss her. Touch her. He wanted to lower her onto her back right here on the front pew of the church and make love to her.

Tor stood so suddenly that Anne started.

"What's the matter?"

He turned away, took a step back down the aisle. "I am sorry. I should not have—I have no right to—"

She ran after him, her footsteps echoing in the vaulted eaves overhead. She grabbed his hand and made him turn to her, gazing up at him with those blue eyes he knew he would see in his dreams. "Ye and I are both full-grown. I am well past the age of marriage, and a woman who can make her own decisions, Tor. I let ye kiss me because I wanted ye to do it."

"You do not understand." He could not bear to look her in the eye, so he glanced away.

She laid her hand on his cheek, urging him to look at her. "I let ye kiss me because 'tis what I have wanted since I first set eyes on ye in Rancoff's hall."

"Anne, Munro . . . he has asked me to stay away from you."

She dismissed his words with a wave of her hand, her other hand holding him fast so he could not back away. "He forgets that I am nae Leah. I am nae his daughter and nae a child."

"I have to go. He will be looking for me—for us." Tor pulled away, his emotions in such turmoil that he barely knew the way out.

Anne stood where she was in the center of the aisle and watched him retreat. "See ye at supper," she called after him.

CHAPTER ELEVEN

Anne closed her paneled bedchamber door and leaned against it. She closed her eyes and held her breath, casting to memory the feel of Tor's mouth on hers, the pressure of his arm around her waist.

She opened her eyes and brushed her fingertips against her lips, giddy and unable to stop smiling. Her first kiss. Inside a kirk, no less. Surely, that was a sin.

She giggled, and the sound of her voice echoing in the dark chamber tickled her.

She knew she was well past the age of giddiness, but she couldn't help herself. She knew men and women kissed. She had rationalized that they must like it, otherwise why else would they do it? But what she had not realized was how much *she* would like it. And here she had thought men nearly worthless.

Anne walked to the fireplace, where coals glowed on the hearth, and used a straw to light the oil lamp on the mantel. She wanted to change her clothing before supper. She knew she must smell of the sand and wind of the beach, and probably a little of fish.

As she opened the chest at the foot of her bed to grab a different gown, there was a tap on her door.

"Anne."

It was Elen.

"Come in," Anne called. "I checked on the girls before I came up." She rattled on as Elen entered and closed the door behind her. "I sent Leah to change her skirt—the wool was wet and sandy at the hem. 'Twill have to be brushed out after it's dry. Judith is in the kitchen *helping.*" She removed a dress of green plaid from the clothespress and shook it.

Elen stood near the door, her arms crossed over her chest. She was wearing one of Munro's saffron yellow shirts, bound at the waist with a thick leather belt. From the belt, keys usually jingled, but they were silent right now.

Anne didn't like the look on Elen's face. She had something to say.

"Did ye see the fish Leah and I caught? I promised her we would fry them in the morning to break our fast. We had a wonderful afternoon," Anne continued, filled with nervous energy. "But she near talked my ears off."

"Anne."

Anne presented her back to Elen so that she might unlace her damp dress. "Aye?"

"Munro has asked me to speak with ye."

The coolness of the air brushed her back as she stepped away from Elen to undress. She lifted her gaze to meet Elen's, not knowing for sure what it was Munro wanted Elen to talk to her about, but having a good idea.

Anne bristled. "And he couldnae come to me himself?"

"That was what I said."

Elen gave a hint of a smile, and Anne breathed a little easier. Whatever the subject, it couldn't be too severe, else Elen would have her ire up.

"Coward," Anne accused.

"I said that as well. And a few other choice things that ladies such as yourself shouldnae hear."

The two women exchanged a look that only two women who loved the same man could share. True, they loved Munro Forrest in very different ways, but neither could deny the fact that he held their hearts and either would die for him without question.

"So, has my father—another coward, I might say— sent word of my impending marriage?" Anne didn't really think that was it, but she was putting off having a conversation about Tor. She didn't know if she was ready to speak of him. Of her feelings for him. If she didn't understand them herself, how could she talk to Elen about them?

"Nae yet, but we expect word soon."

Anne stepped out of her gown and tossed it onto the bed. "So what is it? Have I scared poor Alexi again? Spoken too harshly to a maidservant?"

Elen laughed as she came toward Anne to help her into her gown. "Nay, that would be me."

Anne stepped into the gown, and Elen helped her to lift it over her shoulders. "It's about Tor."

Anne grabbed both ends of the ribbon that would lace the gown at the bodice, over her chemise, and began to work them, keeping her gaze downward. "What about him?"

"Munro is concerned that . . ." Elen exhaled. "God's teeth, Anne, he's afraid ye are going to fall in love with his son, run off, and marry him, and then the king will lift his head from his shoulders."

Anne laughed nervously. "And this he divined from my walk back from the beach with Tor?"

Elen shrugged. "He is a man of the Clan Forrest. I cannae defend him. He's addle-witted, as they all are."

Anne concentrated on the ribbons of her gown. "Munro knew we were walking back to the keep. Tor saw the kirk, and I took him in to see it. 'Struth, I thought the heathen could use it."

Elen's eyes narrowed. "So ye are saying that Munro's fear that ye are attracted to Tor is unfounded?"

Anne turned away from Elen to fetch her boar's-bristle hairbrush. As she gathered her thoughts and considered her words, she tried hard not to think of Tor's mouth on hers. Of course, the harder she tried not to think about it, the more she could taste him on her lips. "Tor hasnae any interest in me."

"My dear husband doesnae agree. He thinks he holds great interest in ye."

Anne turned to Elen. "What makes him say that? Has Tor said something about me?"

Again Elen sighed. "As the wife of your guardian, Anne, I must warn ye to stay away from Tor. Your father intends to marry ye to a good Scott, a High-lander probably."

"Ye said that ye must warn me as the wife of my guardian." Anne unfastened the plaits of her hair, tossed the ribbon ties on the bed, and began to pull the brush through her hair. "But what do ye, Elen of Dunblane, say?"

Elen stared at the floor for a moment. "He is a rogue, Anne."

"Perhaps."

"He has nay intentions of remaining here. He comes for what he can take from Rancoff and then will ride home. It is true by his own admission. There can be no future in—"

"In what?" Anne asked pointedly.

Elen lifted her gaze to meet Anne's. "In falling in love with him," she said softly. "There is naught for ye to gain but a broken heart."

"So, 'tis better to have never loved than to have loved and then had one's heart broken, is that what ye say?" Anne rested the hairbrush on her hip and waited.

Elen threw up her hands. "This is why I told Munro that he should speak to ye and nae me. He could say what he had to say and get out of here without thinking." She brushed her hand across her breast. "Without feeling." She crossed the room to Anne and took the brush from her hand. "So, do ye fancy yourself in love with my husband's son?" She turned Anne around so that she could pull the brush through her thick red hair.

"I dinnae know. What do I ken of love?" Anne said wistfully. "I only know how he makes me feel."

"I understand your confusion. 'Twas the same way when first I met Munro. I couldnae decide if I wanted to kill him or make love with him."

Anne laughed. "Nae worry. I have done neither. 'Tis all quite innocent." She thought of Tor's kiss and then pushed it from her mind. " 'Tis just that we have found it easy to talk."

"And ye are lonely." Elen squeezed Anne's arm and then went back to brushing her hair.

Anne closed her eyes, enjoying the feel of the brush as Elen pulled it through her hair. "Nay, of course not." She didn't want Elen to think she was unhappy. Even without her mother, her years at Dunblane had been far happier than her childhood. "I have the girls. I have ye and Munro to talk to. I have—"

" 'Tis nae the same as having a man to talk to at your age, and I know it," Elen interrupted.

This time it was Anne who sighed. "I suppose."

"Anyway, Munro asked that I speak with ye, and now I have done my wifely duty." Elen tucked a bit of hair behind Anne's ear. "Leave it down tonight, it's so beautiful when the wind and salt air have curled it like this."

Anne returned the brush to its place on a small table. "I suppose *he* will be talking to Tor?"

Elen was at the door. "Already has. When they went riding today. He said they clearly understand each other and we've nothing to worry about."

Anne thought of the kiss in the kirk. Obviously, Tor had not taken his father's warning to heart as Munro had thought. Guilt must have driven Tor to hurry out of the kirk so quickly after he had kissed her.

Anne could not resist a smile. "Nae worry about my heart, Elen. I will protect it from the Norseman beast and save it for a mon my father chooses, who is probably elderly and bucktoothed and foul of breath."

Elen opened the door to go. "In honesty, I nae think 'tis your heart Munro is worried about." She winked. "But your maidenhead." She gave a wave. "See ye in the hall."

Anne half expected Tor to have returned to Rancoff, but when she entered Dunblane's hall with her charges, each holding one of her hands, she spotted him in front of the great hearth talking to two of Munro's clansmen. He stood a full head taller than both men, and it struck her how imposing he would be on the battlefield. What would her father give to see this man fight for Scotland? Dressed in a kilt with a halberd in his hand, the English would run screaming in terror.

"There he is," said Leah. "That mon. He was the one I told ye about who played the game with me."

Anne spotted Tor's brother, Olave, seated at a table. He sat alone with a horn cup in his hand.

"He was very nice to me," Leah said. "He made a bird out of Judith's lap cloth for her."

Judith, who spoke very little, nodded, her blue eyes round with excitement. "Nice mon." She giggled.

Anne wondered if Tor had noticed her enter the room, but she didn't want to look his way again. Servants were already entering the hall with great trenchers of food, but instead of leading the girls to the dais, she walked them to the table where Olave sat.

"Good even' sir," Anne said, smiling.

Olave looked up and his cheeks instantly went red. "Good even-ing," he answered stiffly in heavily accented English.

The girls climbed onto the bench, one on each side of him.

"Good even', sir," Leah said, grinning. "We went fishing today and we caught fish."

Judith said nothing, but stared up at the large blond man, not in the least intimidated by his size or heavy accent.

"You did? Olave likes fishing." He patted his chest.

"Then we should take ye, shouldn't we, Anne?" Leah looked to her. "Can we take Olave next time we go? That's what he said we should call him. His brother is that really big one over there." She pointed toward Tor, who was still engaged in conversation with the Forrests.

Anne had to cover the smile on her face with her palm. "Is he?"

"He's Papa's son, but nae Mama's." Leah wrinkled her nose. "I dinnae really understand, but Da' said it was a long story best told before the hearth, and that I would understand when I was older." She frowned. "He always says that when he doesnae want to tell me something."

Anne watched as Olave thrust out two meaty fists. Judith stared at them. After great contemplation, she tapped one. Olave opened it and the hand was empty. He opened the other to show a hazelnut.

Judith squealed with delight. "Again! Again!"

Once again, Olave put the nut between both hands and then made two fists.

"He plays the game under cups for me," Leah explained. "This is for Judith because she's still a"— she whispered the last word—"baby."

"I am nae a baby," Judith protested. She looked into Olave's broad face. "Tell her I am nae a baby," she ordered him, thrusting out her lower lip.

Olave turned to Leah. "It makes Olave sad when people call him names," he said, thrusting out a fat lower lip the way Judith had.

Properly admonished, Leah nodded. "Do it again for her," she said. "Let Leah pick. I'll wager she gets it right this time."

"Ladies, we should leave Olave. Supper is almost ready."

"Olave likes to play," he said, looking up at Anne. "I will bring them to the table to eat."

Anne nodded. "All right, then." She looked to her charges. "But nae be pests."

Without her girls to protect her, Anne found herself alone in the center of the great hall, wanting to look Tor's way, yet afraid to. The whole room was filled with men and women she knew. She could have sat anywhere, conversed with anyone. Instead, she walked to the windows behind the dais and stared out into the darkness. She could see little but the silhouette of the curtain wall around the castle. She could feel the chill of the air through the glass panes.

Anne tried not to act surprised when Tor appeared at her shoulder and looked out the dark window with her.

"Will ye stay a while?" she asked quietly.

"After we sup, my brothers and I will return to Rancoff. I have no right to be here."

"Ye have a right to be anywhere ye are welcomed, and ye are welcome here, but that was nae what I meant." She did not dare look at him. "I meant will ye stay here. Here in the Highlands."

"I do not know if it is the smart thing to do," he said. She could tell that he, too, was choosing his words carefully. And though he did not say, she knew that the kiss they had shared in the kirk had affected him strongly, too. An energy crackled between them, seeming to become stronger with each passing moment.

She gave a little laugh. "Munro has already sent Elen to speak to me of staying away from ye."

He looked down at his shoes. "I—I am sorry. I should not have—"

"Dinnae begin that again." She looked at him and he had no choice but to meet her gaze. "I told ye. I wanted it." She looked back toward the dark window. "Perhaps more than ye wanted it."

"Anne."

She heard him move. His hand touched her sleeve, and she thought it might burn through the fabric. "Elen says Munro has already spoken to ye of staying clear of me." She smiled slyly. "I am guessing ye didnae heed your father's words."

"I could not—would not dishonor his name. Or yours."

She lifted her gaze to him, her body still turned toward the window. If anyone saw them, they could not possibly know what a personal conversation they were sharing. "I want ye to stay. In a fortnight, there will be a Beltane celebration on Rancoff's grounds. 'Twill be the first of May."

"I do not know if we will stay in the Highlands. I do not know if I am still comfortable with the reason I came."

"To take Munro's coin, ye mean?"

He paused. "Perhaps I should gather my brothers and just go. Return to my mother's village."

This time she turned to him. "Ye cannae do that to Munro. He is your father. Ye owe this to him. One fortnight at least."

"Do you argue for his sake, *min kjærlighet,* or yours?"

"Which would be more likely to keep ye here?" she dared him softly, knowing she trod on dangerous ground again.

He caught her hand, lifted it to his mouth, and kissed it. Before she could exhale the breath that had caught in her throat, he had released her. "Yours, I am afraid."

For a moment, her gaze was lost in his. He wanted to kiss her again; she could see it in his eyes. And she wanted the same. Was Elen right? Was she in danger of having Tor break her heart?

Anne knew full well that her father, the king, would send a man to marry her, and she knew that no matter how she protested, she would wed him, as was her duty. She would do it, not so much for her father, but for Munro. It was duty to Munro and Elen to be a good daughter, a good Highlander, a good Scot.

But just a few more kisses from this Norse stranger could do no harm, could it? It was ridiculous for a woman to go to her marriage bed having never even kissed a man. Wasn't it? And what of this nonsense that Tor would break her heart? He could not break her heart so long as she did not offer it, could he?

Anne watched as Tor crossed the great hall, his head held high. Munro was calling his name, waving to him as he entered with Elen on his arm.

Anne knew she had to marry whomever her father sent, but that did not mean she did not have a right to live a little before then, did it?

She took her chair at the dais, her mind made up. She would not do anything to shame Munro's or Elen's name, or to shame herself, but she would live a little. What harm could there be in that?

CHAPTER TWELVE

"I do not understand why you wanted me to ride all this way with you," Tor said, adjusting the hood of his mantle so the rain did not fall directly in his lap. At least it was not cold today. A ride all the way to Aberdeen alone with his father was bad enough, but in freezing rain, it would have been unbearable. "My brothers—"

"Your brothers are righter than this spring rain. Last I saw them, Elen had Finn and Olave dragging old tents from Dunblane's cellars to set up for our guests to the Beltane celebration. Elen said Finn was more help than me, and sent us on this errand."

"Minstrels. Your wife sent you to hire minstrels?" Tor wiped the rain from his face. "I do not understand why this is a man's job. Servants could be sent to do this. Rob is very competent. Why did ye nae send him?"

Munro eyed his son. "I agree well enough that Rob is a competent young man. He's all his father, my steward is, maybe more. But ye must learn, Tor, how it is when ye have women in your life." He leaned in his saddle toward Tor. "I go on the errand so that I can get *away* from my wife." He lifted his shoulder. "And ride with ye. Talk with ye."

Tor focused on the muddy road that led to Aberdeen. He still was not comfortable with the ease with which Munro expressed his feelings, but he was growing used to it. And so long as the illness did not affect him or his brothers, he would pay it no mind. "And why do ye want to get away from Elen? Ye were just telling me yesterday that the sun rose and set on her in your eyes."

"That they do." Munro nodded. "But the woman drives me to insanity. Just last night she was telling me that I never hear what she says." He gestured. "She doesnae do anything but order people about. How could I nae hear her? Everyone in the shire hears her."

Tor could not resist a smile. Elen did often take command of a room. She was a woman who took charge without hesitation, and her manners were often very masculine. She was headstrong, determined, and as stubborn as any man he had ever come upon. But the longer he remained at Rancoff, the more he liked and respected her. She was an amazing woman, able to balance a daughter on her knee and dole out harsh punishment to a thief in the same breath. She was a mixture of toughness and femininity Tor had never known, and she intrigued him. And Anne worshiped her, reinforcing his own respect for his father's wife. Elen seemed to be Anne's mother, protector, confidante, and friend all wrapped into one.

He tried to push thoughts of Anne aside. Here he was berating his father for having made this trip to escape a woman when, in truth, it was the reason he had agreed to go.

Since the kiss he and Anne had shared in the little church, and the conversation that had followed that night in the hall, he had avoided her. He did not seem to be able to resist his attraction to her despite his father's request. Yet he could not bring himself to go from here, either. He knew very well that nothing good could come of their attraction to each other, yet he felt powerless to turn away from her. He lived for glimpses of her fiery hair. He waited endlessly to catch snatches of conversation she shared with her young charges or with his brothers, who had taken to her without reserve.

Olave fancied himself in love with Anne; even the mention of her name brought redness to his face and stole his ability to speak. And Finn was pursuing her like a tomcat. Of course, Anne was not the only woman he was pursuing. A few days ago, Tor had caught Finn tumbling in the hay with one of Rancoff's scullery maids, and he was blatant with his compliments to Elen. That was so like Finn. He loved all the women and they loved him.

Tor and Munro crossed a small stream that trickled over the road. "My brother and I crossed this stream many a time," Munro said nostalgically.

Munro had mentioned his brother before, and Tor knew he was dead. He also knew that he had died at Rancoff and that there was some scandal involving Elen's sister, but no one had told him any more than that. Tor wanted to know what had happened to his uncle; he just hadn't asked. He told himself it was not his business, but he knew that he had not asked because that would be one more tie to his father. To Rancoff.

"Tell me what happened to him," Tor said. "He was called Cerdic, right?"

Munro hesitated. "Cerdic was my brother." He looked straight ahead as they rode. " 'Tis actually because of Cerdic that I have my Elen." He shrugged. " 'Tis really no big secret; everyone in Christendom knows the sorry tale."

Tor listened, realizing that to indulge his interest in his father's family was to take another step closer to becoming more a part of the family of which he wanted no part. He became more of Munro Forrest's son.

"Cerdic and Rosalyn, Elen's sister, came up with the scheme that he would kidnap her, they would play slap and tickle, and then she would be returned to her family. Only what my daft brother nae took into account was the strength of our neighbor, Elen of Dunblane. When Elen realized her sister had been captured by the Clan Forrest, she rode over with a band of men and captured me."

Munro flashed a look at Tor that warned him no comment would be appreciated. "I resided in the oubliette at Dunblane while Elen negotiated with my brother for her sister's safe return. Eventually, we discovered the whole thing was a ruse. I was set free, and Cerdic married Rosalyn."

Munro glanced at Tor and shook his head. " 'Tis a tale hard to believe."

"Go on," Tor said quietly.

"By then, Elen and I had fallen in love. With a little help from our king, I persuaded her to marry me."

"I was told by a gossip that she was dragged kicking and screaming to the altar." Tor grinned.

"She wanted to marry me," he defended. "I swear by all that's holy, she did. She just didnae realize she wanted to marry me. Anyway, the marriage settled the centuries-old fight between our families over the woods that lie between our properties. What it didnae settle was the fact that Finley, Elen's cousin and her steward, had been in love with her for years and fancied himself a candidate to be her husband and the Lord of Dunblane."

"Her steward?"

"I told ye, 'tis a tale hard to believe."

"Anyway, the petals soon fell from the bloom of my brother's marriage. The bride was apparently ambitious enough, and flexible enough beneath the sheets to somehow convince my brother that he deserved Rancoff, and they could have Dunblane in the parcel, if they rid themselves of me."

Tor felt a weight in his stomach. "The steward," he said, almost in disbelief.

"Aye. Finley was not of sound mind. Obviously, none of them were. There were attempts on my life and I thought Elen responsible."

"Because she was forced to wed you and give up her hold on Dunblane?"

"Something like that. 'Struth, I was an imbecile. I doubted her love for me. Anyway, I went across the mountains to fetch Anne from the king's men. Her mother had recently died, and Robert feared for her safety under her grandfather's roof. Finley followed me to kill me. Elen started to come after me when she realized what was happening, but Cerdic captured her."

Munro wiped the rain from his face and continued. "After Elen was captured by Cerdic and Rosalyn, she was held in Rancoff's dungeon. When I returned home and found her missing, I came for my brother's help, only to find that it was he who had betrayed

me for the love of"—his voice caught in his throat—
"for the love of that woman."

Another long sigh came from Munro. Tor waited
patiently.

"In a fight in Rancoff's barn, my brother died,"
Munro said.

"The sister?"

"Sent to a nunnery. Locked away until kingdom
come—or hell, in her case. And I foiled Finley's
attempt on my life and sent him packing to the mad-
house with the king's soldiers."

Tor was silent for a long moment. Munro was right;
it was almost a tale too strange to believe. "I am
sorry," he said simply, feeling a pull toward his father
that he had not expected. It was all he could do not
to reach out and touch him in some way.

Munro nodded. "So am I." Then he pointed
ahead, immediately cheering, obviously relieved to
find something else to inspire conversation. "Look.
There she be. Aberdeen. I know a fine place to dine
where we can then bed down without fear of thieves
or lice." He glanced upward at the setting sun. "No
doubt we can find ourselves a game or two come
dark."

"I thought ye said we came to hire minstrels for
your . . . whatever it is you are having."

"Beltane celebration," Munro offered, once again
himself. " 'Tis a tradition."

"Whatever. Anyway, ye told Elen you would hire the
minstrels, we would stay the night, and head home in
the morning. If ye are playing at dice and drinking
yourself into a stupor, how will ye hire minstrels?"

"That is the beauty of the plan, my Viking son."
He raised a finger. "We find the minstrels there and
kill two doves with one stone." He grinned. "A bril-
liant plan, if I do not say so myself."

Three hours later, Tor's and Munro's clothing was dry, their bellies were filled with meat and bread, and they had sat down to game with two men Munro knew from his days of fighting. They had accomplished what they had come to do: Munro had hired a band of three minstrels to come to Rancoff for Beltane. Heady ale and sharp Scottish whiskey flowed. A musician made his way among the tables with a fiddle, a pleasant voice, and a bawdy tune.

Despite Tor's best efforts, he could not help but enjoy himself. Besides, he was winning. True, he had reluctantly started off on coin borrowed from his father, but Tor had already won enough to pay Munro back and be ahead of the others.

"What can I get for ye?" A young woman with dark, greasy hair and overflowing bosom leaned over Tor's shoulder. "More ale, luv?" She batted her lashes. "Or something else for ye, ye big mon."

Munro glanced at Tor with amusement and snatched up the dice to take his turn.

"Just the ale," Tor said awkwardly, trying to hold his breath until she moved away from him. She smelled of onions and stale sweat, and he wanted no part of her save the fresh round of ale. Ordinarily, he was not so squeamish with women. A little pungent odor had never bothered him before. Hell's bells, most of the Norse women he had known smelled of herring. But ever since he had tasted Anne's mouth on his, he could not even turn his eye to another woman.

Munro glanced up from the dice. "I am nae ready to bed down if ye wish to"—he lifted his hand in the direction of the rooms overhead—"to excuse yourself for a wee bit."

Munro shook his head. "Just the ale," he repeated.

"Ye want to stay in this sorry-arsed game?" the

man called John asked. "And pass up that snatch of sweetmeats?"

The other man called Robby B laughed, slapping his hand on the table.

"I am winning," Tor said affably. "It does not happen often. I can have a woman any time." He met his father's gaze and winked.

All four men laughed, Munro included.

"Ye've a fine son, there," John said, clapping Munro on the back. "Fine he is."

"Fine he is," Munro repeated, his words slightly slurred. He lifted his own horn cup that he carried. "To my fine son, Tor."

"To Tor," the others echoed.

Tor snatched up the ivory dice. "Enough of your foolish toasts. Can we play, ye drunken louts?"

"Listen to my son." Munro pushed his cup against Robby B's shoulder, sloshing ale onto the man's sleeve. "Been in the Highlands little more than a fortnight and already he sounds like one of us."

"A true Forrest," Robby B chimed in. "I saw it the minute I laid eyes on his hulking mass."

Munro met Tor's gaze across the narrow table and grinned. Tor grinned back.

The musician who had been playing fiddle approached the table and began to croon some Scottish tale of love lost. Munro rocked in his chair to the tune. "Ye've a way with words, sir," he said when the song was done. He tossed the player a coin. "Do ye play elsewhere or only here at the Bull's Ring?"

"I play anywhere a mon pays me to play, m'lord." The man tucked the coin into a bag on his waist. "I've two fine sons who sing, too, sweetest voices ye've ever heard."

Munro took a long pull of his ale. "That right? Well, would ye be willing to come to Rancoff Castle for Beltane?'' He rocked back in his chair. "Do ye know it?''

"Everyone knows Rancoff, m'lord.''

"Well, that's me.'' Munro slapped his chest. "And him, too.''

He pointed to Tor.

"M'lord,'' the musician greeted Tor, his nut brown eyes widening with surprise. He was obviously having a difficult time seeing the connection between the blond Norseman and the Scottish lord.

"But that is a story best told at the hearth with plenty of ale to wash it down,'' Munro told the minstrel.

"I think you have had enough ale already, Munro,'' Tor quipped.

The other men laughed as they placed their bets.

Undaunted, Munro continued. "I want ye to play at my Beltane revelry. Will ye come? I'll give ye coin for yer travel and trust ye to show. Ye come, ye play well, and there will be more.''

Tor leaned over the table. "Ye already hired minstrels,'' he said quietly.

Munro knitted his brows so comically that Tor had to laugh.

Munro leaned on the table and whispered loudly. "I did?''

Tor nodded and swept another pile of coins off the table. At the rate the others were drinking, he could make enough money to buy his own castle by the night's end.

Munro thought for a moment, belched, and then sat up again. "Come anyway. What harm can there be?'' Again that foolish grin of his. "The more the merrier, eh?''

Tor cut his gaze to Munro. "*She* will not like it. She said to hire one band of minstrels, not two.''

"I am the mon of my keep and of hers as well," Munro boasted, hitting his chest with his fist for good measure. "She wouldnae dare speak against my decision."

"The minstrels from Aberdeen are here," Anne said, approaching the table where Elen had strewn sheets of paper. Elen glanced up, looking harried. She pushed a stray strand of hair back behind her ear. "They're here?"

Anne grimaced, hating to be the bearer of bad news. In fits of anger, Elen had been known to toss cups and plates and the occasional dagger. "*Both* bands of minstrels," she said.

Elen slapped her hand on the table and bolted off her stool.

Anne took a step back to get out of the line of fire should Elen snatch up any missiles to hurl.

"What?" Elen shouted. "We have two bands of minstrels? How can there be two? I sent that mon to hire one band of minstrels." She threw up her hands. "How could he nae get this one thing right?"

Anne tried not to smile, knowing Elen would not appreciate her amusement right now.

"Where is he?" Elen demanded. "Do ye know where my husband who cannae count to one is?"

Just then, Tor walked into the hall carrying a load of firewood.

"And what of ye?" Elen demanded of Tor as he passed her. "Can ye nae count, either?" She cuffed him on the arm. "And I sent ye to watch over him."

Tor halted and frowned as he watched Elen disappear from the hall. He looked to Anne for explanation.

"The minstrels have arrived," she explained.

"Aha." He crossed the hall to the great hearth and dumped the logs into a wood box off to the side of the stone fireplace.

Anne followed him, unable to avoid noticing the size of his forearms, bared by his pushed-up sleeves. "And what makes me think ye knew there were two bands of minstrels coming and nae one?" She crossed her arms over her chest. She was glad to see him. She knew he had been avoiding her for the past fortnight and she knew why. She also knew that he could have returned to his homeland at any time and had chosen not to.

Tor tried to hide his smile. "I went because Munro asked me to." He lifted his palms. "I am completely innocent of any wrongdoing."

She laughed. "So ye nae deny knowing Munro hired too many minstrels."

"He is my father. I do not think I should be forced to bear witness against him."

Again she laughed, and he took a step closer.

It was a beautiful morning. The sun was shining, and its rays poured through the unshuttered window of the great hall, casting magical patterns of light and dark on the plank floor. Someone had left a handful of the first flowers of spring on the table Elen had been working at; the scent of their fresh greenery was intoxicating.

Standing so near to Tor was intoxicating.

"How have you been?" he asked.

"Ask Finn. He sat with me last night to sup whilst your seat remained empty."

"I . . . I was helping repair a grain shed. I—"

"Ye have been avoiding me." She didn't give him time to answer. "But 'tis all right. I understand. I am the king's daughter; few men would dare."

"Anne—"

"I am glad ye haven't gone, though. Ye fit together well, ye and Rancoff. Even Munro says so."

"He does?"

Tor took another step closer to her. There was no one in the hall, though anyone could enter at any moment. If Elen did not find Munro, she would be returning to finish her ledgers. Anne did not want to anger Munro or Elen. Tor was all she had thought about these past two weeks: his voice, how he scowled, what his mouth had tasted like against hers.

She took a bold step toward him. "Methinks m'lord Rancoff would nae wish me to repeat his words. Suffice to say, he is pleased with his son. Despite how ye grumble and drag your feet—"

"I nae grumble."

"He thinks ye are a good man with a good heart as well as a hard worker."

Tor raised his hands to rest them on her shoulders. His gaze lowered to hers. "Why must ye be so beautiful, Anne of Bruce?"

"And he likes the way ye have picked up the speech of our Highlands."

"I have . . . not—"

Anne pressed her finger to his lips. "If ye are going to kiss me, ye'd best do it quickly. I suspect Elen will be back in a moment, dragging Munro by some body part."

"I am not going to kiss you," he breathed.

"Nae?" She lifted on her toes, pressing her hands to his chest. He was wearing a simple green wool tunic this morning and looked as much like a Highlander as any man in the castle. "Then I will kiss ye."

Before Tor could work up a word of protest, she slid her hand around his thick, strong neck and pulled him down toward her. She felt his muscles tighten, as if he would not yield, but then they relaxed as his mouth met hers.

She pressed her body closer to his, not quite understanding her need to feel him against her, but unable to resist that need. When she felt the warm wetness of his tongue against her mouth, she parted her lips slightly. She knew nothing of kissing, very little at all of what went between a man and a woman. But what she did know was how good this felt, how perfectly they fit together.

Anne heard a little sound come from her throat as he deepened his kiss, thrusting his tongue into her mouth. She clung to him, knowing what she was doing was dangerous, but not caring. At this moment, she felt more alive than she had ever felt in her life.

When at last they parted, Anne was breathless. She could hear him, too, breathing heavily. Both took one great breath of air and their mouths met again. There was no need for verbal communication. He seemed to know what she wanted, what she needed.

As Tor wrapped her in his arms, she felt overwhelmed by his size, but not intimidated. She felt safe in his arms. Protected.

Hesitantly she slid her hand across his face. He had shaved his face this morning, and she reveled in the feel of his skin so different from her own. With her palm, she explored the line of his jaw, the bridge of his cheekbone.

"Have ye lost whatever sense ye ever possessed, Munro Robert Forrest?" came Elen's voice suddenly from the entrance hall.

CHAPTER THIRTEEN

Panic gripped Anne's chest as she tore herself from Tor's arms. He must have heard Elen at the same instant, because he turned away from her and leaned over as if he were doing something with the logs he had just brought in.

"What is the harm in two bands of minstrels?" Munro asked, his usual amiable self. "I nae understand why ye are so concerned."

"What is the harm? What is the harm?" Elen ranted. Spotting Anne, she motioned to her.

Anne casually stepped toward the table, farther away from Tor.

"What is the harm, he asks me? What is my concern? My concern," she said, turning back toward him, "is that I have a husband who is unable to count beyond one; that is my concern."

"Tor, help me, son." Munro extended his arms. "I'm drowning here."

Tor straightened to his full height. "One band of minstrels, two; it makes no difference to me."

"Coward," Munro accused, still retaining his sense of humor.

Elen dropped onto her stool in exasperation. "Now I've two bands of minstrels, and no players because the lead ran off with another man's wife. Half the tents I intended to use are moth-ridden." She threw up her hands. "And I cannae find my keys."

Munro walked up behind her and tried to put his arms around her shoulders.

"Leave me be," she muttered, pushing aside his hands. "I'm still angry with ye." She waggled her finger. "I know exactly what happened in Aberdeen. Ye got yourself so drunk at the tavern ye like that ye hired one group and then the other, nae remembering the first. Whilst I was here trying to organize this mess, ye were out throwing the dice and drinking yourself silly."

Munro made a face that would have made Anne laugh in any other circumstance.

"Dear wife, I am hurt that ye would suggest such a thing." He cast a quick glance in Tor's direction.

From the look on both men's faces, Anne knew that Elen had come closer to the truth than either father or son cared to admit.

"This isnae going to work," Elen cried. "There will be no Beltane celebration."

"Nonsense." Munro gestured. "Tor will see to the holey tents. Anne will find the keys. I will find players."

"Ye cannae find players two days before the first of May."

Anne started for the door, relieved to have something to do. "I'll look in your chamber. Ye probably just left your keys beside your bed. If they're not there, I'll check Judith's skirts. Ye know what a wee thief she is."

"Olave is good with a needle. I will see to the tents," Tor said as he followed Anne out of the hall.

Anne didn't turn back until she reached the grate of the oubliette in the entrance hall. "They didnae see us, did they?" she whispered desperately.

Tor caught both of their trembling hands. "They did not see us."

She lifted her gaze. "Elen and Munro have been so good to me."

"I understand."

She pulled her hands from his. Did he understand that she was such a wicked lass that she didn't really care what Elen and Munro thought? Did he understand that she was such a wanton that even now, with the taste of his mouth burning on hers, she wanted another kiss?

"I'd best find the keys," Anne said, turning away sharply.

"Tents," Tor muttered.

Anne went in one direction, Tor in the other. She was almost to the door that led outside before she turned on her heels and ran back to him, startling him.

"I cannae help myself," she breathed. "I may as well resign myself now to the fact that I will burn in hell." She rose up on her toes, pressed her mouth to his once more, and then turned and ran.

Tor just stood there as she made her escape, his fingers to his lips.

The next two days were such a flurry of activities that Anne did not have to try to avoid Tor. Elen had her running from sunup until well after sunset. She had invited neighboring families as well as members of the Clan Forrest and Clan Burnard to attend the celebration. Not only did she have to worry about the merchants and entertainers that would come, but both Rancoff and Dunblane castles had to be cleaned from cellar to dovecote.

While Elen organized the booths that were being set up at the foot of Rancoff castle, Anne saw that both keeps were cleaned. She had the chamber and scullery maids from both castles sweep the floors and add extra bedding to every nook and cranny they could find.

From what she could observe, Munro was keeping Tor equally busy. Animals were moved from barns to make room for guests' horses. There was hunting to be done to supply fresh meat. Calves were being born that had to be tended to, and there was such a general confusion around Rancoff castle that Tor seemed to be the man settling disputes.

Several times each day, Anne ran into Tor, but they were busy and there always seemed to be others around. Anne thought it just as well. After the kisses they had shared in Dunblane's hall the other morning, she was not certain she could trust herself with the Viking. Everything she knew to be true told her to stay away from him, and yet her heart tugged at her. When she saw him through the windows of Rancoff or across the great hall, all she could think about were his kisses. His touch. The sound of his voice, husky in her ear.

Shocked by her wantonness, Anne was beginning to think that maybe her father was right. Maybe it was time she wed.

By the evening of the last day of April, both keeps were full to bursting with Elen's and Munro's friends and relatives. Merchants were preparing to display their wares in the meadows beyond the castles, and many common folk from miles around had come to camp in the fields and glens to enjoy the celebration to which all were welcome.

"Wake up! Wake up!" Leah cried the morning of the first of May.

"Wake up, wake up," Judith echoed.

Anne awoke to find both of the girls, who slept with her on a trundle on the floor, bouncing into her bed. " 'Tis the first of May. Beltane," Leah said, yanking the counterpane off Anne. "Wake up."

Laughing, Anne grabbed the girls and pulled them against her in a hug. Hand in hand, the three walked to the window in their sleeping gowns and pushed open the shutters. The air was still morning cool, though the sun shone so brightly that it made Anne squint.

"It's going to be a wonderful day, nay?" Leah asked, beaming.

Anne hugged the little girls close to her and kissed the tops of their heads, one and then the other. She was as excited as the girls were. "Aye, 'tis. Now get dressed both of ye. No doubt your mother has need of all of us in the hall."

Downstairs in the great hall, Anne helped served the first meal of the day. By midmorning, though, Elen chased her and the girls outside. "Go," she encouraged, flapping her woolen skirts. "Out in the sunshine, all of ye."

"Are ye nae coming?" Anne was almost as anxious as the girls to go down to the village, but she didn't want to abandon Elen.

"I'll be down directly. I promised Judith she could see the puppets." She rolled her eyes. "Puppets and players, I nae know how that man did it."

"Ye certain ye nae want me to stay here and help?"

Elen shook her head. "I'm going to check with the kitchen one last time and then go to the barn. I thought I would hunt with the ladies this afternoon. Ye wish to go?"

Anne shook her heard. "I'll see to the girls; ye enjoy the afternoon. Ye deserve it."

Elen kissed her young daughters. "Be good for Anne and keep your mantles on. 'Tis nae as warm as ye think."

"Aye, Mama," the girls chimed.

Taking one girl in each hand, Anne led them out of the hall, over the drawbridge, and down the hill toward the village.

For the next few hours, they strolled from booth to booth. They watched the cloth puppets tell jokes and dance. They heard not one, but two bands of strolling minstrels, and sampled sweetmeats and pastries until Anne thought she would pop. Anne bought crowns of flowers for all of them and they danced with the girls on a grassy hill until they collapsed from fatigue and laughter.

All day Anne kept her eye out for Tor. She knew he was here somewhere, but many men were off hunting. There were horse races to enter and watch. There were even gaming tables set up at Rancoff for the men's pleasure. Anne didn't really expect to see him today, but she couldn't help looking for him. Hoping. Near dusk, Anne settled under a tree with the girls. They were both tired, their hair tangled, and their hands and mouths sticky.

As Anne leaned against the trunk of the tree, drawing both girls in next to her, Olave lumbered over. "Did you see the puppets?" he asked excitedly.

Leah bolted upright, instantly full of energy again. "I liked the dog puppet."

"Me, too," Olave said. "Olave liked the dog puppet."

"So you're enjoying yourself, are ye, Olave?" Anne asked, gazing up him.

His face reddened and he turned first one way and then the other. "Olave had a good day. Finn won a race. Nobody beat Tor arm wrestling." He beamed. "They're my brothers."

She smiled. She liked Olave. He seemed to be a hard worker. He had a good heart, and he was immensely devoted to his brothers. As an only child and a woman with no true relatives, Anne admired that trait in him. "I know they're your brothers. I . . . I was wondering where they were. I havenae seen them all day."

Olave continued to squirm with the pleasure of her attention. "Finn, he went for a walk with a lady-woman. I have not seen Tor."

"There ye are, my sweets!" Elen came over, dressed in a man's tunic and breeches. Her hair was wild with tangles, her face flushed from exercise. "Have ye had a good day, my poppets?" She put out her arms to her daughters.

Leah and Judith bounced up off the new grass and ran for their mother.

"Mama! Mama!"

"Did ye see the puppets?" Leah asked.

"Puppets," little Judith echoed.

"I havenae." Elen adjusted the crown of flowers that had slid back on Judith's head. "Shall we go see them now and give Anne some time to herself?"

"Can Olave come, too?" Leah asked.

"Why, certainly." Elen looked to Olave. "Would ye care to join us, fine sir?"

Olave beamed.

"Come with us! Come with us!" Leah and Judith both bounced up and down with excitement.

Olave stared at the ground, scuffing one foot. "Olave . . . Olave could see puppets."

Judith left her mother's side to grab Olave's large hand and lead him along.

Anne waved. "Have a good time, girls."

"I'll put them to bed tonight," Elen called over her shoulder. "Go dance. Eat, drink if ye like. I'll see ye later."

Anne had enjoyed a wonderful day with Leah and Judith, but as they walked off with their mother, she gave a sigh of relief. She leaned against the tree with pleasure and watched the men and women celebrating around her.

Everyone was in a jolly mood. Ale flowed. Pipers and fiddlers played. Merchants called out their wares. Women shopped and laughed. They flirted and danced. The men stood around sharing ale, betting on horse races, and flirting with the women who passed. The whole meadow surrounding Rancoff Castle and leading down to the village was alive with noise and activity.

Watching the others, Anne laughed and smiled and waved, not feeling the need to join them. For now, she was just satisfied to sit beneath her tree, sip the cool, fruited wine someone had brought her, and watch. At last, just as the sun was setting, she spotted who had been on her mind all day.

Tor saw her from across the dirt road. One of Munro's clansmen had stopped him. Anne could tell Tor didn't really want to talk. She knew he had seen her, but to be polite to his father's kinsman, he launched into conversation with the older gentleman.

The wine was making Anne feel warm and cozy

inside as she sat under the tree, watching—admiring—Tor. Today he wore the burgundy and green of Rancoff, with his mantle pinned to one broad shoulder with his father's brooch. His wild blond hair had been tamed with soap and water and a leather tie at the nape of his neck. Watching him talk, she wondered what that hair would feel like between her fingers. Would it be thick and coarse like her own, or smooth and silky like Leah's and Judith's. She had never touched a man's hair before and her curiosity was great.

Tor glanced over the clansman's shoulder and caught her eye. She couldn't tear her gaze from his. He had been watching for her all day, too. She could tell by the look he gave her that he was near to smoldering.

Anne casually rose to her feet. She knew the smartest thing to do would be to remain here. To talk with Tor when he came over, here in the midst of the crowd where she would be safe. But she didn't want to be safe. She wanted . . . she wanted . . . Anne didn't know what she wanted, except that she wanted Tor. Wanted to see him. Talk to him.

Kiss him.

Knowing he watched her, Anne casually crossed the road, then veered east toward the beach that was less than half a mile from the castle. She did not dare look back until she reached a small copse of trees. Darkness was settling in, and here in the open, away from the pitch torches, the natural light was now dim. But she could not miss Tor's hulking form in the semidarkness. She waited at the tree.

"Did ye have a good day?" she asked, leaning against the tree trunk. She felt strange inside. Her heart was hammering in her chest by the time he reached the tree.

He rested one hand on the trunk beside her head. "I had a good day. Ye?"

He leaned so close to her that she could smell the malted barley whiskey on his breath. He was not intoxicated, but she guessed he'd had his fair share today. His tone of voice sent a trill of excitement down her spine.

"The girls truly enjoyed the music and the booths. We bought flowers for our hair."

"I see." With his free hand, he brushed the crown of her head, where the ring of flowers still rested. He caught one of the ribbons that fell from the hairpiece and twisted it around his finger.

"Olave said ye won at wrestling."

"I saw him with Elen and the girls," Tor said. "He looked happy."

"Leah and Judith love him. He's so gentle with them."

They spoke casually, but the energy that sparked between them was anything but casual. Anne could feel a tightening in her stomach that seemed to be radiating outward to an ache she could not describe. Her breath was coming shorter, yet he had done nothing but lean close to her.

Anne pressed her back against the tree, feeling the roughness of the bark through her woolen gown and mantle. With the settling of darkness came the night sounds of spring. Crickets. Frogs. The sway of the beach grasses and the call of the seagulls.

Anne moistened her lips. If he did not kiss her soon, she knew she would perish.

"Would ye like me to walk you home?"

She smiled and reached out to brush his cheek with her hand. Was this what love felt like? This tightness, this excitement? She had told Elen there was no need to fear for her heart. Was it already too late?

Had it been too late the day he had barreled into the Highlands?

"Do ye hear yourself? Ye keep telling me ye willnae stay and yet ye sound more like us every day."

His grin was lopsided. "No hard questions tonight. It has been too fine a day." He reached over to guide her by her shoulder. "We could walk by the beach."

Anne thought about the lonely beach. About what Elen had said about being alone with Tor. But right now nothing could have stopped her from walking that strand of beach between Rancoff and Dunblane save her own death. "Let's go by the beach," she said.

"You are sure?"

Again, their gazes met. She knew he was asking if she wanted to walk with him, but there was an underlying meaning. She could pretend to deny it, but it was there, hovering between them. She lifted up on her toes and kissed him gently on the mouth, feeling as if she knew as well as her own. He tasted of whiskey and the forbidden. "Let us go to the beach," she repeated in a whisper.

He hesitated and she wondered if he was struggling inside himself.

She kissed him again. This time he needed no further encouragement.

CHAPTER FOURTEEN

Hand in hand, Tor and Anne walked over the dunes toward the sound of the crashing waves. The beach was deserted.

"Cold?" he asked. He wrapped his arm around her shoulder and drew her beneath his mantle.

The smell of his maleness was so intoxicating that her voice caught in her throat for a moment. "Nay. 'Twas so warm today that the cold air feels good." Her voice sounded calm, but inside, her body was quaking. What was she doing out here in the dark with this man?

"I looked for you all day," he said. "I could not . . ." He exhaled. "I wanted . . ."

She lay her head against his chest as they walked out over the packed sand. "I looked for ye, too."

"Do ye want to sit?"

" 'Tis a beautiful night. Stars will be out soon."

"We can just walk," he said, his voice sounding strained.

Anne knew the smart answer. She also knew she would not commit to it. "Over there near the rocks." She pointed. "We will be out of the wind."

Arm in arm they walked to the secluded place among the rocks. Tor pulled his mantle, a long rectangle of Rancoff plaid, from his shoulders and spread one end of it in the sand. "Sit," he told her.

She sat on the plaid, and he sat beside her and pulled the plaid up over both their shoulders. The wool was so long that it covered them both.

Anne closed her eyes and breathed deeply. The wool smelled of Tor, but there was something more to the plaid that she found comforting. It was the way it enveloped them both, protecting them both as only a family as powerful as Munro Forrest's could.

Tor held her close but made no move to kiss her or even touch her. She could never have imagined sitting on the beach in the darkness with a man, enjoying the silence, his nearness seeming so right that no words were necessary.

Anne snuggled against him as Tor pulled her closer, his arm around her shoulders. With his thumb he caressed the nape of her neck, sending trills of sensation down her spine.

She turned her head toward him, looking up. As if waiting for her signal, he brought his mouth down hard on hers without hesitation. Anne felt as if she were dreaming as he thrust his tongue into her mouth and lowered her onto her back on the woolen plaid. Surrounded by his arms and the weight of the blanket, she eased backward without fear. All conscious thought seemed to drift carelessly away. The crash of the waves on the beach faded. Anne could hear nothing but her own heavy breath and the pounding of her heart.

She strained against him as he pressed her deeper

into the sand. She could feel the coldness through the blanket, yet she was far from cold. Heat seemed to radiate from her abdomen outward, a heat Tor was creating.

They kissed and kissed again. Anne could not get enough of the taste of his mouth, the feel of his tongue. He slid his hand along her side and over to her breast, the caress seeming a natural extension of his kiss.

She moaned as his hand brushed the layers of fabric that covered her breasts. Her nipple hardened, puckering against the linen of her shirt. Suddenly, the soft, worn fabric of her undergarment felt abrasive.

Tor tugged at the ribbon that laced up her bodice. She pushed aside his hand and loosened it for him. She gave no thought to what they were doing, only to what they must do. What she must have.

"Anne . . ." He whispered her name thickly in her ear as he slid his cool hand beneath the open bodice of her gown. Though her shift still stood between his hand and her breast, she sucked in a great gulp of air in reaction to his touch. She had never known this was what it would be like to feel a man's intimate touch. This burning, this aching, this sense of flying.

"Anne, Anne," he whispered. "Where have ye been all my days?"

Their mouths met again in a fierce, urgent kiss.

Anne pulled her shift aside, knowing that if she did not feel his bare hand on her breast, she would . . . she would . . . Another moan escaped her as his bare hand met with her breast and found her nipple with the pad of his thumb.

She sought his mouth again, slipping her fingers through his hair, which had somehow come loose. The smell of him, the weight of his body pressing hers into the sand, was overwhelming. Intoxicating.

Tor lowered his head to kiss the hollow of her throat. He dragged his mouth over the layers of clothing until at last he found what he sought, catching her nipple between his lips.

"Tor," she moaned.

As he suckled her nipple, he slid his hand over her rib cage, over her stomach. The heat that had been building inside her was now roaring. The place between her legs ached, and when his hand brushed there, she arched her back in encouragement.

He slipped his hand under the hem of her gown and upward. She was drowning in sensation. The feel of his mouth on her breast. The sound of his voice in her ear as he called her name. There was no turning back. She knew there was no turning back, not even if the gates of burning hell lay ahead, waiting for her to enter.

A part of Anne feared the touch of his hand beneath her skirts, but another part ached for that touch—had been aching since the night she had first laid eyes on him.

Anne was taken completely by surprise, overwhelmed by the wave of sensation that washed over her as his finger found the dampness between her thighs.

His breaths were short and deep, yet his kisses were gentle on her lips, her cheek, her nose, the lobe of her ear. He whispered in her ear, Norwegian words she couldn't understand, but it didn't matter. They were sweet words of endearment just the same.

He rolled to his side beside her to better maneuver his hand, and she rolled onto her side to face him.

"Tell me to stop and I will stop," he said.

"Nay, do not," she breathed.

Anne moved against his hand, sensations of pleasure coming like great waves. She pressed her mouth to his, stroking his back, his chest, struggling to find her way through his clothing, to touch his bare skin. Because he wore a plaid around his waist like other Highlanders, he could not hide his desire for her.

Boldly, she reached down to stroke him through the tangled fabric.

Tor groaned and murmured in Norwegian.

He rolled her onto her back and she did not protest. Could not. She was burning for him. Needing him as she had never needed water or nourishment.

Instinctively, she parted her thighs, her legs shaking as she accepted him without reservation.

It was not what she expected.

No pain, only a fullness she could not have imagined. And pleasure. A pleasure that was first small like a spark of light, growing each time he moved inside her.

Anne clung to him, her arms around his shoulders. She had no idea what she was doing, and yet she seemed to know instinctively. She felt as if she were hanging on the edge of a cliff, not knowing what lay beneath. She was jumping anyway.

Slowly his movement became more rhythmic. Faster. The waves were gone; the beach was gone. All of Christendom was gone. Nothing existed but Anne and her lover, Tor. She knew she loved him in that moment. She knew she had loved him since the beginning of time.

Without warning, a great wave of sensation welled up inside her. Feeling as if she were caught in the tide and thrown suddenly onto the beach, she cried out with surprise, with incredible pleasure.

Tor gave a moan and was still.

"Anne," he panted. "I did not. I . . ."

She felt as if she were floating. Cast on a sea that

had suddenly calmed. Though it was dark and the wind cool, she could feel the sun on her face.

He slid off her and onto his side and gathered her in his arms.

For the first time, she felt the bite of the night air and shivered. He pulled the plaid tighter around them, encasing her in the warmth of the plaid and his body.

"No," he groaned. "I cannae believe—"

"Shhh," she whispered, pressing her fingers to her lips. "Dinnae say it." She lifted her gaze, her lashes damp. She didn't know why she was crying. She had never been happier in her life. "It . . . it was wonderful. The best gift anyone has ever given me in my life."

He opened his mouth to speak, then closed it. Instead, he leaned over her and kissed her forehead. *"Jeg elsker De,"* he whispered.

"Jegelskerde?" she repeated. "What does that mean?"

"It means . . ." He kissed the top of her head, not meeting her gaze. "I love you."

She knew that he was probably just saying that because of what had just happened, and she knew better than to tell him that she loved him, too, but his words still made her smile.

Anne and Tor lay on the beach for a long time, wrapped in the plaid and the warmth of their love-making, until finally he broke the silence. "They will be looking for you if we do not go."

Anne knew he was feeling guilty. Feeling as if he had betrayed his father. She knew she should share his guilt and pray for her soul. But not tonight. She felt too good. Making love with him had felt too right. Tomorrow would be soon enough for the regrets she knew would come.

Tor helped her up, as gently as if she were spun of Venetian glass. He smoothed her clothing and insisted he retie her bodice by the light of the moon rising in the sky.

Her clothes straightened, the sand dusted from her skirts, Tor wrapped his plaid around both their shoulders, and slowly they continued along the beach toward Dunblane.

At the keep, they found the drawbridge still lowered. Campfires glowed around the walls. They heard laughter from somewhere, and elsewhere the sounds of a man and woman that made Anne's cheeks warm, despite what had just taken place at the beach.

At the door to the tower house, Anne turned to Tor. "I wish that ye could come up," she whispered, knowing that even to suggest such a thing was absurd. No matter what she had just done, she was still the king's daughter.

"I wish that I could come, too, not to make love but to hold ye in my arms," he whispered in her ear.

Anne was shocked that she could already feel the prickles of desire in her loins again. Just his voice made her pulse quicken.

"Good night," she whispered.

He hesitated.

She smoothed his wrinkled shirt. "I have to go. They probably haven't noticed I have not returned, with all of the confusion of the day, but . . ."

"Good night," he said and pulled her to him.

They shared one last kiss and then he released her. Without looking back, Anne ran inside and up the twisting stairs to her chamber. She did not stop until she slipped inside to find Elen waiting for her.

CHAPTER FIFTEEN

"Where have ye been?"

Anne halted in the doorway, her hand still resting on the polished knob. "I . . ."

"Ye said ye would meet us at home." Elen rose from the chair near the hearth where she had been sitting.

"I . . ." Anne felt like a thief caught with her hand in the larder. " 'Tis nae that late."

" 'Tis after midnight."

Anne lowered her gaze to the dimly lit room. She could hear the soft breathing of the girls. Guilt wheedled at the edges of her reasoning. No one could know. If no one ever knew, no harm had been done.

"I stayed at . . . at Rancoff a while." She ran her hand over her head, only realizing now that somewhere she had lost her crown of May flowers. "Then I walked home by way of the beach." Getting better control of herself, having a plan in her head, she walked to the bed, where her sleeping gown lay.

"Alone?"

Anne had to think fast. Had someone seen her and Tor leave Rancoff's grounds together? She did not think so. Did someone on the beach see them?

"Please tell me ye walked alone," Elen said firmly. "That no one else was with ye."

Anne was not a liar. She did not think she would be good at it, but she thought she had better be. "I walked alone."

Anne took off her shoes and sat on the edge of the bed to remove her stockings. She hoped Elen did not come too close, for she could smell Tor on her clothing. She could smell their lovemaking on her skin. She could almost still feel his body pressed to hers.

"I walked alone," Anne reiterated. "I must have lost track of time. The beach was nice tonight. Quiet after the noise of the day."

It all sounded reasonable. This would not be the first time Anne had taken a walk on the lonely beach.

Thankfully Elen moved toward the door. "I said nothing to Munro about ye nae coming in. But I was worried. 'Tis nae safe for a woman to be alone in the dark these days. Ye nae know what kind of men lurk in the shadows."

"Ye dinnae need to worry about me," Anne said, feeling bad for lying to Elen. They had always been so honest with each other. Until tonight, Anne had never had anything to hide. "I am a woman full-grown. Besides, no one would dare touch the king's daughter."

"Well, I am glad ye are safe. God keep ye."

"God keep ye."

Anne waited until Elen closed the door before falling back onto her bed with relief. . . .

And the beginnings of regret.

* * *

The next morning the girls had to drag Anne out of bed. She had done so much in the past few days that it all suddenly seemed to catch up with her. She'd had too much wine the night before and too many rich foods. She wanted just to lie in bed and cast to memory every touch of Tor's hands, every word he whispered—even when she didn't understand what he was saying. But the girls would not wait, nor would the household.

Anne dressed, washed her hands and face, and escorted the girls to the great hall, where they would feed their guests again. She guessed she would spend the day with Elen, attending to those who would stay another night and saying goodbye to those who would head home after breaking their fast.

Knowing she would be kept busy today was comforting. If she had something to do with her hands, she could not spend too much time castigating herself for what had happened last night. She knew, of course, that it must never happen again. Though there was little chance of pregnancy the first time, she could not take that chance again. As she walked up the steps to the great hall, she hoped Tor was not there. She didn't know what she was going to say to him yet. How she was going to act with him. They would have to be careful not to behave any differently with each other, lest someone begin to suspect. How she would do that, she didn't know.

The girls broke free from her and ran to find their mother, leaving her at the top of the staircase, gazing into the room. No one slept on pallets on the floor any longer, but the pallets had not been cleared away. Tables and benches were in disorder. Women gathered in small clutches, talking frantically. Men lumbered about, grabbing bread and meat wrapped together by servants, taking skins of water.

What had happened? Where were they going?

Anne reached out to a heavyset man with a broad face and short, graying beard. "What is going on?"

He brushed past her. "We ride."

"Ride? Ride where?"

The hall was so noisy that he must not have heard her. She called to his brother, who was right behind him. "Banoff! What is going on? Where do the men ride?" She caught the man's arm so he could not escape. He looked much like his brother, with the same broad face and heavy frame.

"Someone slipped into Rancoff's barns last night. Took chickens. Killed horses."

Anne released his arm, shocked by what she heard. "Killed the ponies?"

"Slit their throats." He gestured with one finger across his neck.

Anne's stomach lurched at the thought of the animals suffering. Of the blood.

"Who would do such a thing?" She turned to him as he hurried down the stairs after his brother.

He shrugged as he walked off. "We nae know. Reivers?"

Anne gazed around the frenzied room and, spotting Elen, ran to her. "What does Banoff speak of? Someone slaughtered our ponies?"

The look on Elen's face was immediate proof of the truth. "It happened early this morning, before dawn." She held pitchers in each hand. "Most of the mounts were nae ours because ours had been moved to the far western meadow. It was our guests' mounts that died."

"Why would someone kill horses?" Anne followed Elen as she walked past tables and refilled men's cups. The conversations around her were terse. People were frightened. Angry.

"I nae know, Anne."

"And if they were going to kill horses, why come into the keep? Why did they nae kill ours in the far meadow?"

"It makes no sense. That is what disturbs us." Elen halted, her gaze meeting Anne's.

"Elen!" Munro called, his tone sharp.

Anne looked up as Munro approached them, his booted feet hitting the floor hard. Tor was right on his heels, his stride equally as determined.

At the sight of Tor, Anne's stomach gave another lurch. She thought to look away, but it was too late. Their gazes met and she knew he was struggling with the same emotions that she was. They were all there: the guilt, the fear of being discovered, the pleasure of the memories.

After that first moment of panic, Anne was amazed at how calmly she behaved. How deceitful she had become so quickly. She forced herself to look at Munro, focusing on what he was saying.

"How many horses?" Elen asked.

"Seven were found dead. We had to . . ." Tor paused. "Put one out of his suffering."

Anne pressed her lips together. "And no one saw anything? Heard anything?"

Munro grabbed his plaid bonnet and ran his fingers through his full head of hair. "So far, we have found no one who heard anything. Nae after yesterday's festivities." He raised a hand. "Once everyone went to sleep, I suspect they slept hard."

"What of the stable boy who sleeps there?" Elen set both pitchers of ale on the closest table.

"He was . . . occupied elsewhere," Tor said.

"Occupied? Occupied?" Elen dropped her hands to her hips. "Occupied how?"

Tor glanced at Anne, then at Munro.

Munro leaned forward and whispered in Elen's ear. Elen rolled her eyes.

Anne didn't like being left out. The stable boy had been with a woman, obviously. The three just thought her too innocent to hear such references. She frowned. At her age, her mother had already given birth to a bastard by the man who would be king one day.

"Have ye any idea which way they went?" Elen demanded.

"We ride shortly," Munro said. "I will lead one group, Tor another. At least we've plenty of men to ride with us. I want no panic, but I will leave both keeps armed with men on the walls. Men who would sneak into my keep to kill horses, there is no telling what they might do. I want ye two to remain here today. Our guests at Rancoff will have to find their own meals or come here." Munro reached out to take Elen's arm and brush a kiss against her cheek. "Stay here, Elen, and keep my girls safe." His voice was tight.

Anne glanced over Munro's bent shoulder to see Tor. He was looking directly at her, saying nothing, though his message was clear. He did not want her out alone until these men were found.

"I simply nae understand," Elen said, giving Munro a quick hug. "To kill horses and then steal naught but chickens. It makes no sense. Who would have the stones to do such a thing? Why?"

"There are times when things dinnae make sense, 'tis all I can tell ye." Munro turned away with Tor at his side. "Should we find anything, I will send word."

* * *

The slaughter of the ponies and the havoc they produced kept Tor's mind off the previous night. He made himself keep Anne out of his head so that he could concentrate on the task at hand. Later, when he had time, he would allow himself to wallow in the guilt that was already eating at him.

Tor rode with his father's clansmen over Rancoff land in search of any sign of the vandals, but to no avail. No one in the village, no one among the Beltane merchants, none of the guests, had seen anything. They had not left a trail. Not a sign that they had passed through, except the carnage they had left in the garrison barn.

It was almost sunset when Tor and the men with him met Munro's group.

"Nothing," Tor told his father bitterly. "The cowards have gone into hiding, but how far could they have gotten?"

"We found nothing either." Munro eased his mount up beside his son's and looked out at the sea of weary faces of the Scots who had ridden with them today. "Time to turn in, men. I invite ye all to come to Dunblane and sup with us. Please, those who must go home in the morning, do so. My son and I will find these filthy bastards and see they swing from a pike upon my wall. Ye will all be reimbursed for the loss of your mounts, and I will loan or give ye what ye need to get home."

A murmur rose among the men as they discussed who would go home and who would stay.

Munro turned back to Tor. "Come to Dunblane. Eat. Ye have served me well today."

They were at a fork in the road, where Tor could choose to go back to Rancoff's keep or accompany the men to Dunblane. He wanted to return to Rancoff, to roll out his sleeping gear and fall asleep in his clothes. He did not want to go near Dunblane or Anne de Bruc, who had changed his life forever the night before.

He felt like a coward. Never once since he had been forced to kill his first man at fourteen years of age had he avoided a confrontation. He was known among his mother's people as a fierce fighter, a force to be reckoned with. Yet he was frightened to the very marrow of his bones of seeing Anne again. Of speaking to her.

He didn't know what had come over him last night. He had not intended to make love to her. Not even when he had suggested they walk on the beach. There was no denying he had wanted to get her alone to kiss her. Perhaps he had even fantasized about caressing her breasts, but he had honestly not meant to take her virginity.

And now what? He had promised his father he had no ill intentions toward her. This was exactly what Munro had feared when he had asked his son to stay away from the king's daughter. What if she told Munro? What if she became pregnant?

"Are ye coming?" Munro asked.

Tor glanced up. He had been so lost in his thoughts that he had not heard Munro speak. The other men had already started down the road toward Dunblane, leaving him and Munro behind.

"Do . . . do ye wish me to return to Rancoff and be certain that all is well there?"

"Ye left your brothers. Ye said all was safe with Finn, and my steward and his son are there." He reached out and squeezed Tor's forearm. "I would like my son at my table tonight with my family."

Tor looked down at the reins twisted in his gloved

hands. How could he refuse? To refuse would be to dishonor Munro in front of the others.

Startled by the thought, Tor frowned. When had he come to care about his father's honor? When had it become as important to him as his own? And when had seeing Anne become more important to him than being sensible?

Resigned to his weariness and the questions he had a lifetime to answer, Tor made a clicking sound between his teeth, and his horse started forward down the road to Dunblane.

CHAPTER
SIXTEEN

Anne stood on Dunblane's rampart, looking out over the darkening countryside. From here, she could see the line of the dark ocean. She could see the peat bog and the North Woods far in the distance.

She hugged her mantle tightly. It had been a warm, sunny day, though the wind had picked up at sunset and the scent of cold rain permeated the air.

Where were they? she wondered.

Munro and Tor had been gone all day and there had been no word. What if they had encountered the reivers who had killed the horses? What if one of them had been hurt or gravely injured?

Anne had kept herself busy all day, trying not to think about what she had done last night. She went to the kirk alone to make her confession because there was no priest to confess to. She gave herself a stiff penance.

But even now she still could hardly believe she had given her virginity to a man who was not her husband.

She had played with fire, when she'd thought all she wanted was to feel a bit of his warmth. All she had wanted were his kisses. How could she have known how easily it could turn to more? How could she have known her own desires could be so strong, so uninhibited? How could she have known they would afflict her with stronger needs, deeper passions?

How could she have been so stupid? So naive?

And what if someone found out? Would Munro send her away . . . back to her father? What would he do to Tor? Would he send him away also, or take away the inheritance Anne knew Munro was so close to offering his son? And what of *her* father? Would he have Tor killed? She doubted that. A man who did not have enough interest in his daughter to see her probably would not have a man killed for despoiling her, but still . . .

This was all her fault, Not Tor's. He was a man. What man would not take what she had so blatantly thrown in his lap?

Anne tucked her hair that had fallen from her hood behind her ear. She felt guilty not only for what she had done and for the position she had put them all in, but also because she had enjoyed it so much. What kind of good Christian woman was she to have behaved so wantonly? She had touched him *there*. Liked it. Liked the feel of him in her hand.

Anne groaned. Her grandparents had always said she and her mother were headed straight for the burning pits of hell. Maybe they'd been right.

Movement caught Anne's attention and she leaned over the stone wall, squinting in the fading light. Men on horseback. She spotted Tor; he could not be missed. He was nearly a head taller than any of the others, and his blond hair was flying free in the wind behind him.

Anne bit down hard on her lower lip. She had a mind to claim she felt faint and go to bed. She didn't know if she could face Tor in the hall with the others. It was not the shame she feared, but self-betrayal. What if she could not look at him without reflecting the hunger she felt even now? Now, when she knew what she had done was wrong, she still could not stop remembering what he had felt like. What if others saw it in her eyes? She could probably fool the men, but could she fool Elen?

Anne turned away as the riders closed the distance between them and the castle. She was being a coward. If she did not want anyone to know what had passed between them, she had to pretend nothing had happened. It was the only way to carry the ruse.

And what of her desire for Tor?

It would have to be smothered. Locked away. Hidden forever.

It was that thought that, at last, brought tears to her eyes.

A short time later in the great hall below, Anne moved among the men and women who had remained at Dunblane. She served food and drinks, talked with the guests, and pretended Tor was not in the room. He supped with a group of men near the hearth. Not trusting herself, Anne allowed one of the kitchen girls to serve that table.

Tomorrow she would talk with him, when she was calmer. Besides, with the slaughter of the horses, he surely had other things on his mind. More important things.

Anne managed to avoid him the entire meal until she thought she might be able to safely make her escape. She grabbed two empty bread chargers to return them to the kitchen. With Leah and Judith having completed their meal, Anne could plead responsibility for her charges and take them off to bed.

She hurried down the dim hallway that ran behind the great hall to the kitchen. She had just reached an alcove in front of the swinging kitchen door when she heard Tor's deep, resonant voice from behind her.

"Anne," he called quietly.

She considered pretending not to hear him. If she reached the sanctuary of the busy kitchen, he could talk to her there without touching upon any subject more serious than the freshness of the bread.

"Anne, wait," he beseeched. "Please."

She halted in the dark alcove, but could not turn around. Her nerve endings seemed to be alive and crackling. If just his voice could do this to her, she knew she could not afford another caress, another kiss—not if she wished to resist him and her own sinful desires.

He closed his big hand over her arm and turned her toward him.

She brought the tin chargers up between them as if they could serve as armor to protect her from him. In truth, she needed defense against herself.

"Anne . . ."

She lifted her gaze to meet his. She wanted to cry. She wanted to throw her arms around him and taste his mouth on hers. She wanted him to proclaim his love for her, and to confess her own for him. Of course, that was not going to happen.

"I am sorry," he said quietly. "I do not know what came over me. You must believe me when I tell you it was not my intention to—"

She shook her head, silencing him. "We cannae

retrieve the milk that is spilt, but we can mop it up," she whispered. "As long as no one knows."

"It will not happen again."

"As long as no one is the wiser, we will be safe."

They spoke almost simultaneously, then were silent again. His gaze enveloped her. He wanted her as much as she wanted him; she could feel it.

Anne felt her heart tighten in her chest. "It cannae happen again," she said, as much for herself as for him.

"I will take my brothers and I will go."

"Nay!" She grasped his arm, holding tightly. "Please dinnae say that. Ye will break Munro's heart. Do ye nae think we have done enough damage already?"

He grimaced. "I have betrayed my father."

She shook her head again. " 'Twas a mistake. No one has to know. Ye cannae let this ruin your chance with your father—your chance at having a life here."

"And who says I want a life here?"

She stared at him, not speaking, wondering how she had come to know this man so quickly and so well. Her mother would have called them mates of the soul.

"Ye are mad if ye think Finn and Olave will return north. They like it here. Ye like it here and, if ye play your cards right, if ye continue to be the mon I know ye are, your father will make ye one of his clan and give ye all that entails."

Tor looked away. He pressed his hands to his sides as if it was the only way he could keep from reaching out and pulling her into his arms. It was all Anne could do to keep from flinging herself into his embrace.

"No one will know," she whispered. "My father can send his mon to marry me and no one will ever be the wiser." She gave a little laugh. "Surely ye dinnae think it has not been done before?"

Again he met her gaze with those blue eyes that were icy and yet so full of warmth. "I . . ." He halted and started again. "All right. If that is what you wish. If it is what ye want."

It wasn't what she wanted, but what must be. She gave his hand a quick squeeze. It was all she dared allow herself. " 'Twill be all right," she insisted. "I swear 'twill. Just a wee bit of spilt milk." She made herself smile.

"And what if ye are with child?"

She frowned. " 'Twas my first time. Women nae take the first time."

"No? How do you know?"

She tapped him playfully on the arm with the chargers, feeling that she was the one who had to be strong here. "How do I know? I know because I am a woman. Women know these things."

He eyed her carefully. "Ye are certain? I do not know. In my mother's village, men were not privy to such information. We did not talk the way you talk to each other. Between men and women," he explained awkwardly.

She shrugged. "Your loss." She smiled, her eyes twinkling. "Nae worry."

"But if ye were . . . if ye did, ye would tell me?"

"Of course."

"I would do my duty to ye . . . if you were. Duty to my child. Ye know that."

"That would certainly go over well with the king of Scotland. His daughter marrying a Norseman."

"I would go to him. Petition for your hand. I would nae dishonor you." Tor tightened his hands into fists at his sides, speaking passionately. "I would nae bring a bastard child into this world. Not after what you have suffered. What I have suffered.''

She sighed, feeling her heart tighten again. Tears burned the backs of her eyes. He was such a good man. He—

She pushed away her thoughts. They would serve no purpose. What was, was. She would marry whom her father ordered her to marry and she would do her best not to shame Munro and Elen.

"I have to go," she whispered. "Someone will come looking for me. We cannae be seen together alone like this anymore."

He nodded and turned to go. "You will tell me."

"Nae worry!" She forced herself to turn away from him and walk into the kitchen. Inside, she put away the chargers, keeping her smile frozen on her lips. Later, when she was in bed and alone, there would be time to cry for what she had lost. For what she would never have.

"Is it done yet?" Rosalyn leaned over the hearth, breathing in deeply. She had been waiting all day for this damned meal. " 'Tis been so long since I tasted freshly baked chicken that I cannae remember it."

Finley rotated the makeshift spit to be certain their supper roasted evenly. "I couldnae start the fire until after dusk, so as not to risk anyone seeing the smoke. Ye know that. Now get back. I will tell ye when 'tis done. Ye nae want it to burn, do ye?"

She met his gaze. "Nae speak to me that way, ye swine. Ye forget who I am."

"Forget who ye were, ye mean," he sniped.

She glared at him. "Ye only say that because of what I look like. Give me a few months and ye will be at my feet begging for me." She ran her hand over her closely shorn head, wishing for the hundredth time that it would grow faster. Without her long, blond hair, she felt as if she were someone else. Of course, after all that had happened, she supposed that she was.

"Begging? Me?" He laughed. " 'Twas nae me I heard begging last night."

"Swine," she accused again, as she sat on a chair they had scavenged from one of the other rooms. "Ye are a swine, ye know that? No gentleman would remind a lady of what she says in passion."

The castle they had taken refuge in had long been abandoned. Much of it had been burned out years before. Fortunately for them, with a little investigating, they had discovered that the kitchen and its larders were still intact. Because the castle looked uninhabitable from the outside, it was the perfect hideout, perfectly located for Rosalyn's needs.

"Swine? A swine am I?" He left the roasting chicken to come to her and went down on one knee. He boldly slipped his hands around her stockinged ankles and slid them upward, meeting her gaze.

"How dare ye?" Rosalyn said, yet made no attempt to push him away.

"Ye are like a water skin too long on the shelf," he said, his smile greedy. "Ye cannae get enough of me and ye know it."

She leaned back in the chair, spreading her legs as he slid his hands upward to her thighs. Her pulse quickened. "Are ye going to kiss me or are ye just going to flap your mouth?"

He rose up on his knees, his hands remaining beneath her stolen skirts. She had killed a woman in the mountains for these skirts, and they were not even of particularly fine wool. She met his mouth, gently at first, then nipped his lower lip with her teeth.

He immediately jerked back. "Ouch!" He yanked his hand out from under her skirts and touched his bruised lip. "I told ye I nae like that." He reached up and slapped her face.

Not hard. Just a little slap. Just the way she liked it. "Swine. Swine," she repeated. "I nae know why I put up with ye."

He pushed her back in the chair with his free hand and, with the other, grabbed her roughly between the legs. She flinched and gave a little purr. This time she met his mouth hungrily. "How long until the chicken is done?" she asked him.

"Long enough." He grabbed her skirts and yanked them upward, laughing deep in his throat as he jerked down his canvas pants. "Long enough, my white rose."

She laughed with him, her heart already pounding with excitement, her thighs damp with want. The drought had been too long, and now she could not get enough of a man.

CHAPTER
SEVENTEEN

A month later, Anne stood on a stool in the window-sill of the great hall and counted on her fingers once more. "Nay," she breathed, and counted again as if somehow the number of days that had passed would change if she kept counting.

Judith and Leah were on a bench beside her, laughing and flicking water at each other as they busily washed the sill with two wet, soapy rags. The windows were open in the hall and the June air was blowing in, ruffling their locks of red hair.

Anne felt as if someone had punched her in the stomach. She had spent the past two fortnights trying so hard to avoid Tor that it seemed little else had occupied her mind.

How could she be with child? Women never became pregnant the first time. How many times had she heard whisperings of how long it took some women to get with child when they were first married.

A lump rose in Anne's throat, and with it came an

unexpected wave of nausea. Was this another sign of pregnancy she had denied, or was she just working herself into a fit?

Anne stepped off the stool, afraid she might fall. The girls went on chattering, talking of a wedding they were soon to attend in Aberdeen. Anne and the girls rarely left Dunblane, not even once a year, so a trip to Aberdeen for a wedding would be the highlight of the summer.

"Please put me down." Elen's voice echoed in the outside hallway.

Anne heard footsteps as someone entered the hall.

"Finn!" Elen insisted.

Finn walked into the hall, the mistress cradled in his arms. "Anne," he called. "Run and get something for Elen's leg."

"Heavens," Anne breathed, dropping her rag into the bucket of water. "What happened?" She hurried toward them as Finn gently set Elen onto a bench.

"I am fine," Elen insisted. "I fell off the roof of the buttery."

"What were ye doing on the roof?" Anne looked at Finn. "What was she doing on the roof?"

He shrugged his broad shoulders. "I do not know. I only saw her fall."

Anne went down on one knee in front of Elen and pushed up the wool pants she wore. "Your ankle is swollen."

More masculine footsteps echoed in the entrance hall. Munro rushed in. "Elen. What's happened? John saw Finn carry ye into the keep. Are ye ill? Hurt?"

"She fell from the buttery roof," Finn explained.

Munro glanced at him. "She has been hurt so badly that she couldnae walk herself?"

"I did not know. I only did not want her to injure herself further," the handsome Norseman explained.

"Finn, I am fine," Elen said lightly. "Really. I appreciate ye coming to my aid, but ye can go back to what ye were doing."

"You are certain?"

She smiled and nodded. "A little swelling. Nothing more."

"Call me if ye have need of me."

Munro waited to speak until Finn had taken his leave. "Ye should have called for me," he said tersely.

Elen leaned over and rubbed her swelling ankle. "I knew ye were with the cattle. 'Twas naught. Truly. I lost my balance trying to fetch a boy's ball from the roof and I fell."

"And the Viking lover just happened to be there to catch ye when ye tumbled from the skies?"

Anne took a step back, surprised by the tone of Munro's voice. They always argued, but in a way she had come to understand as some kind of love play. In all her years in this household, she had not heard this kind of exchange before.

"He was trying to help, Munro." Elen stood up, gingerly putting pressure on her injured ankle.

"I merely think it is convenient that Finn is always there to lift ye when ye fall. To help ye dismount. To carry your damned ledgers."

Elen drew back, staring at Munro.

Anne was trying to think of how she could tactfully excuse herself from this conversation that she obviously had no right to hear.

"Munro Forrest!" Elen's voice was incredulous. "Surely ye are not saying ye are jealous of that lad?"

"Lad, my rosy arse," Munro spat. "Now if ye are certain ye are unhurt, I'll get back to the castrating, and ye, ye stay off the blessed roofs." He exited in a huff.

Elen turned to Anne and laughed. "The mon has lost his mind." Her anger was gone now. She just thought the situation funny.

Anne thought Elen was right; Munro was jealous. But she was feeling slightly nauseated again, and contemplating the matter took too much energy.

Elen sat down, not seeming to notice that anything was amiss with Anne.

Leah and Judith had abandoned their rags and were under a table with a family of rag dolls. They had glanced in the direction of the adults when they heard their father's voice, but neither seemed to be concerned now. They, too, seemed to accept their parents' arguments as part of family life.

"I swear by all that is holy," Elen said, rubbing her ankle. "The mon barely speaks to me except to tell me where he is going, what he is doing. What I should be doing. He falls into bed at night too tired for anything more than a good night kiss upon my cheek, and then he has the nerve to ruffle his manly dander over a mere lad helping me."

Anne lowered her hand to her stomach, another wave of nausea passing over her. She was having a hard time focusing on what Elen was saying, and felt guilty. She wanted to be a good listener for Elen in the same way that Elen was always there to hear her complaints.

Pregnant. Pregnant. The word kept echoing inside Anne's head.

What was she going to do? How was she going to tell Tor? Elen? Munro?

She felt faint.

Who would send word to her father? Would Munro

do it? Would the king himself ride to Dunblane after receiving word of his daughter's adultery?

Anne sank onto the bench next to Elen.

Elen did not seem to notice any green tinge to Anne's face. She went on talking, seeming to assume that Anne had sat down to continue the conversation.

"Jealous? I cannae believe that man could be jealous." Elen laughed. "After all I have done for him. Two children. A loving bed. A kind ear." She shoved down her pant leg. "I swear, he has taken leave of his senses, along with the madmen that roam our lands slaughtering animals."

Anne straightened her spine, swallowing hard as she tried to latch onto what Elen was saying—anything to take her mind from what was growing inside her. "Still Munro found nothing?"

"Naught but a trail of dead animals. Stolen swine and chickens. A crofter on the road to Aberdeen swears someone came into his home, took a kitchen knife, some clothing and shoes." She frowned. "Who would steal shoes? Tor thinks it is the same men, but I dinnae know." She shook her head.

At the mention of Tor's name, another wave of nausea washed over Anne.

This time Elen's forehead creased with concern. "Are ye all right, sweet?" She reached out to grip Anne's hand.

"Fine. Fine," she murmured. But bile rose in her throat and she struggled against it.

"Ye dinnae look fine. Ye look peaked."

Anne bolted off the bench, afraid she would have to make a run for the slop bucket in the corridor off the hall. "Could ye watch the girls? I . . . I feel a little light-headed."

Elen rose from the bench and put her hand to

Anne's forehead. "Ye dinnae have a fever. I hope it's not the ague."

"Nay, nay, just my flux." Anne didn't know how that came out of her mouth. God's brittle bones, if only that were what ailed her. "I'll just go lie down," she said, already walking away. "I'll be back shortly."

"Rest. The girls and I will finish the windows. I'll come up later and bring you a hot herb caudle to—"

Anne didn't wait for Elen to finish as she raced for the slop bucket.

As Olave walked along the path in search of the stray calf, he hummed a song his mother had sung to him when he was a boy. He missed his dead mother, but he did not miss Ny Landsby. He did not miss the cold, drafty long house he had lived in with the other single men, or the daily fishing. He did not miss the way his father's friends and their sons had teased him. He did not miss the fact that his father never cared what they said. Never pounded them the way Tor would if he caught them.

Olave liked it here at the foot of the mountains that Munro called Grampies. He liked the purple heather that grew in the meadows, and he liked the food. Best of all, he liked the girl, Anne. She was so nice to him. Olave loved her.

"*Herku, herku,*" Olave called, making a sound with his lips. He knew the calf had come this way. He had seen it take off across the peat bog and dive into the bushes at the woods line. It must have known what Tor was going to do to its stones.

Olave dropped onto all fours, looking for tracks in the soft dirt. "*Herku!* Here, cow." He pushed through the bushes that scratched his face and pulled at his long hair.

Olave broke out of the undergrowth into the forest and stopped short. There was someone there. Someone watching him.

He scrambled to his feet. They were on horseback. Two of them. One was a man with a black beard. The other was . . . Olave wasn't sure. He was small, with one of those little Scot hats on his head. He was wearing a knee–length wool skirt.

Was he a she?

Couldn't be. He didn't have any hair.

"Who are you?" Olave asked suspiciously. He heard the lost calf bawl, but he knew this was more important. He was a little bit afraid, but he didn't know why. It was just two people on ponies. Still, he wished he had a weapon. He had nothing but a little knife for eating that Anne had given him. He called it *dirk* because that was what she called it. It was a funny word, almost the same as the church word, *kirk*, so it confused him sometimes.

"Said who are you?" Olave repeated more clearly, knowing that sometimes people didn't understand him, especially here. Anne said his English was good, a lot better than her Norse. That was a nice thing for her to say.

"I would ask ye the same question," said the man with the beard.

"Olave." He tapped his chest. Anne had given him a tunic that was made of a light fabric. Not heavy and scratchy like the leather and furs he had worn before. He liked his new tunic. She had washed it and hung it out to dry so that it smelled like sunshine. Like her. "Olave Henneson," he added.

"Ye are nae from these parts. What are ye doing here?" the other one demanded.

It sounded like a woman, but still Olave was not sure. He'd never seen a woman without hair before.

They drew closer but made no move to dismount. The blackbeard had a sword and a bow on the back of his horse, but he made no attempt to retrieve them.

"Olave . . . . I come from Ny Landsby, north," he explained, pointing. He did not know which way was north from here, because he could not see the sun through the trees overhead. He just guessed.

"Viking swine," Blackbeard muttered to the other.

Olave stood a little straighter. He did not like the man. Olave was bigger than he was. Olave could yank him off his horse. Stomp him with his boot, but Tor had told Olave long ago, "No stomping men."

"What do you do on Dunblane land?" the small one asked.

Olave studied him/her carefully. She did look like a woman in the face. Pretty when he pretended she had hair. "Cutting calf's balls," he explained. "One got away." He pointed in the direction of the calf's bawling.

"Ye are going to get nothing from him," Blackbeard scoffed. "He is a halfwit."

The small one gave Olave a push with the toe of his boot. "I nae mean what ye are doing this minute!" she shrieked.

It was definitely a woman.

"Why are ye here on Dunblane land? Ye know what they do to trespassers here, do ye not? They cut your balls the same way ye will cut that calf's."

She was angry with him and Olave didn't know why. He just wanted to catch the calf and take it back. His brothers would wonder what had happened to him. They would think he was being lazy. Sometimes Finn rested in the woods when they were working. Sometimes alone, sometimes with women.

"Olave lives at Rancoff," he said proudly. "My brother is son to Rancoff."

"What are ye talking about?" the woman with no hair snarled.

Both riders pressed closer.

"Rancoff has no son. Only female urchins."

"Tor *is* Rancoff's son," Olave defended. "He is my brother."

"How can that be?" Blackbeard demanded. "How old is this Tor?"

"Tor is my big brother," Olave said. "We came from the north. Our mother told us to come."

Blackbeard spat words that Tor said were not supposed to be used in front of women.

Maybe the little one wasn't a woman. He had once known a man in his mother's village who liked to wear women's skirts, but only when he drank too much.

"Tell me what ye are talking about, or I will slit your throat," the little one hissed.

Olave saw the flash of the blade. He tried to step back, but he was a second too late. Blackbeard pinned him against the other one's horse so that the blade touched his throat.

Olave stared up at the little one. She had to be a woman. He swallowed. "Olave does not know what you want to know."

"Ye say your brother is Rancoff's son." She did not speak loudly, but she was so angry that spit flew out of her mouth. "Are ye telling me he is a bastard son?"

Bastard. Skurk. Olave knew that word in both languages. It was a bad word. A mean word.

"He is my mother's son," Olave said. "And Munro's." He refused to say the *bastard* word even at knifepoint. He would not say that about Tor. He loved Tor.

"God's bloodsucking bones," the woman muttered. "So the blessed Saint Munro has a bastard son. I wager that made for interesting supper conversation."

"Why are ye here?" Blackbeard demanded. "Why did ye and your bastard brother come?"

She still held the blade to Olave's throat, but he was not as afraid now as he had been when she first pulled it. "My mother told him to come."

"To collect his inheritance, of course," she whispered. "To take more of what should have been mine."

The woman pulled her blade away and Olave took a quick step back.

She seemed upset. Angry. Olave didn't know what he had done. He didn't like it when people were angry with him. Especially his brothers.

"Olave must catch the calf," he said.

Blackbeard looked to the one without hair. "Ye want me to cut him?" He said it the way a dog growls. Olave didn't like him. He didn't care if Blackbeard was angry with him.

"Olave! Olave, are ye here?" one of the Scots from Dunblane hollered. "Where the hell did ye get to?"

Olave turned in the direction of the Scot approaching though the undergrowth. He heard the man and what he thought was a woman ride away.

"There ye are." The Scot pulled off his plaid bonnet and wiped his balding head. He didn't have any hair either, but his was different than the riders. His was shiny skin. The other one had very short, prickly hair, as if it had all been shaved off.

"What are ye doing?" the Scot asked.

Olave considered telling the man about the two

riders he had seen, but decided against it. Who would believe him if he said he saw a woman with no hair who cursed at him?

"L-Looking for the calf."

The Scot's eyes narrowed. "Not runnin' off in the woods to steal somethin' or kill somethin', are ye?"

Olave stared at the red-faced man in confusion. "Olave does not steal," he said.

"Nay. Well, there's some that say none of this mess started until after ye came. Some says it might be ye and your brothers. Everybody knows that's what Vikings does."

Olave still didn't quite understand what the man was saying, but he knew the man didn't like him. "Olave does not steal," he repeated.

"Nay?" The Scot stepped forward, grabbing Olave's shirt.

He was taller than Olave but not bigger. Olave thought he could beat the man, but he wasn't supposed to fight with the Scots. Tor had told him and Finn when they came, "no fighting."

"Olave must get the calf," Olave muttered, looking the man in the eyes.

"Olave! Olave!"

Olave heard Tor's voice as his brother came crashing into the woods.

The Scot let go of Olave, but not before Tor saw him.

"What the hell goes on here?" Tor demanded.

Olave could tell his brother was angry. He just hoped he wasn't angry with him.

"Olave does not steal," Olave said. "Tell him." He pointed at the Scot, who suddenly looked afraid.

Tor turned on the Scot. "Nae tell me ye are up to that again," he growled. "I told ye once, I will nae stand for your accusations. My father willnae stand for them.''

The Scot took a step back, raising his hands. ''Just a misunderstanding,'' he said, backing out of the woods. ''Naught more.''

When the Scot was gone, Tor turned to his brother. ''Ye all right?''

Olave nodded.

''What are ye doing in the woods? I told ye to stay near the castle without Finn or me.''

Olave pointed farther into the woods. ''Olave thinks the calf went this way.''

Tor stared at Olave for a minute and then he smiled. Olave liked it when Tor smiled at him. ''Well enough. Let's go get that calf together, then, eh?''

''Herku!'' Olave shouted, running into the woods.

''Herku,'' Tor echoed.

CHAPTER EIGHTEEN

Anne sat in the semidarkness of the sanctuary, her hands folded in her lap. But she did not pray. She was past praying. The day after she had lain with Tor she had come here, confessed her sin, and asked her Lord for forgiveness. Because she truly believed in her confession and her regret, at least on a spiritual plane, she knew she had received that holy forgiveness. Anne knew the baby growing inside her was not punishment for her sin. Her God was not that vengeful a God.

What she did not know was what she was supposed to do now.

She had barely spoken to Tor in three weeks. He was busy with the new calves. Busy riding the land with his father, getting to know Munro. Anne knew that in Tor's mind, he was simply doing what he must to get the money he thought he deserved. But what Munro was actually doing was training Tor. He wasn't just showing him the Highlands. He was making his Norse son a Highlander.

Tor hadn't realized yet that he was finding a satisfaction here he'd never expected.

She had to tell Tor about the baby, but how? And what of Munro and Elen? She had betrayed them by giving in to her earthly desires. They had cared for her, protected her, loved her all these years, and she repaid them by shaming them in this way.

Anne twisted her fingers in her lap. It would be months before anyone could tell she was with child, so she had a little time. But, she had to tell Tor, and then tell Elen soon. They had to have time to make plans. Perhaps her father already had a husband in mind, and the nuptials could be sooner than the king had intended.

It crossed her mind that Tor could marry her. She knew in her heart that she loved him. But she immediately dismissed that possibility. Women did not marry the men they fell in love with. They married the men their fathers, their families, chose for them. She knew this had not been the case with Munro and Elen, but they were so extraordinary in so many ways that she could not even take them into account. Besides, though both were titled and of good families, they were not the king's children. Not even from the wrong side of the bedsheets.

Besides, Tor was returning to the Northland. He had no intentions of staying here. He wanted no part of the Scots. He was still repeating that incantation, even now after being here for two months. And then there was the matter of forcing him to marry her just because she was with child. What chance of happiness would she have with Tor if he married her because Munro forced it? What would her father think of a Viking son-in-law? Would he send someone here to kill him and make her a widow? It would not be the first time the Highlands had seen such an event.

Tears clouded Anne's eyes. What to do? She felt paralyzed. And, she had been so happy only a few weeks ago. How could her life have turned so quickly?

The door to the kirk opened and Anne brushed the tears from her eyes. The sound of two pairs of little footsteps came up the aisle.

"There ye be!" Leah came to the edge of the bench, with Judith right behind her. "Mama has taken to bed," she said. "Can ye come?"

Anne rose from the seat, glad to have something else to think about. "When?" She took a charge in each hand and led the girls out into the sunshine.

"A little while ago."

As long as Anne had known Elen, she had been cursed with headaches. These headaches hit her with such force that each month she took to bed for a day or two. The headaches were somehow linked to her woman's cycle, for they always ended with the coming of her menses, or ceased altogether during pregnancy.

Anne did not dawdle, but she didn't race to Elen's side either. Elen had made it clear years ago that she did not want her daughters to be afraid of these headaches or to think that they were in any way an illness to be ashamed of. After all, what if they fell upon Leah and Judith someday as well?

"Why don't we get a pan of cool water and a wash-rag for Mama and sit with her a while, hmm?" she asked the girls. "The two of ye can stitch quietly and let her rest."

"Stitch," Leah moaned. "Mama says my stitching is a . . . a tro-sias. I hate stitching."

"If your stitching is *atrocious*, that is all the more reason why ye must practice each day." Anne led the girls across the grass to the drawbridge and then into the keep. "Someday ye lasses will be the ladies of your own keeps, and ye must know your stitching as part of your housewifely duties."

Little Judith halted at the door of the tower house and crossed her little arms over her chest. "I am nae going to be a lady who stitches, I'll warrant ye that."

Anne halted, thinking that was more words than she had ever heard the five-year-old string together at once. Her tone was identical to her mother's.

"Nay, you say?"

"Nay." She stamped a little booted foot. "I am going to wear tunics and ride horses like my mama."

Leah leaned over and whispered something in Judith's ear.

"And marry Tor . . . or Finn . . . or Olave," Judith finished.

It was all Anne could do not to laugh aloud. She knew Elen would like to have seen this little declaration of Judith's. She was as much her mother's child as Leah. Maybe more.

"Well, we nae need decide what we will wear or whom we will marry right now." She pressed a hand to the small of each girl's back and ushered them through the door. "What we must do now is find our stitching."

Tor stood around the corner of the garrison stable in Dunblane's bailey and watched Anne disappear into the tower house with Judith and Leah.

He wanted to go after her. To talk with her, just for a moment. Since they had spoken after the night on the beach, he had been true to his word. He had stayed away from her. He had not given anyone any indication that there was anything between them, but he wanted to be sure she understood why—that it was not because he did not want her, but because he knew he could not have her.

Tor groaned aloud. His emotions were in such turmoil that he could barely think. He could not sleep. He could not eat. He was torn between doing what he had set out to do—taking the coin and running—and remaining here, accepting whatever that meant. It was not just Anne that had him in such a quandary. It was Munro. It was Elen, and even his little half-sisters. No matter how he tried to deny it, there was something about this place—the grasses, the meadows, even this part of the sea—that he could not escape, even in his dreams.

There was something about the people here and the way they had become a part of him without his realizing it that held him fast when he thought of leaving.

"Go," he heard Anne's voice say. "And I will be up directly."

Tor pressed his back to the barn, listening. Just the sound of her voice put him on a strange edge. What was it with this land that put men under such women's spells?

"Just to the kitchen. I want no excuses, Judith. Find your stitching. If the dog has taken it, get another square of linen and we will start again."

Because the tiny kitchen in the cellars of the tower house had been abandoned for the more modern kitchens off the great hall, Anne had to enter the bailey to reach them.

Tor looked both ways, saw no one of any consequence, and crossed the bailey to follow her. He stayed back, moving quietly along the corridor and waiting outside the door for her to emerge.

She appeared suddenly, carrying a pan of water

and a linen towel thrown over one arm, then halted abruptly, her expression startled. She caught her breath. "T-Tor."

"Anne."

"I . . . Elen has taken to bed with a headache. The lasses and I—"

"Anne, listen to me. I did not mean to frighten you—"

"Ye didn't frighten me," she exhaled finally. "I— I just wasnae expecting ye . . . here." She shifted the pan of water from one hip to the other.

"I only wanted to tell ye—you." He sighed, looked away, then back at her again. "I wanted to tell ye that I have kept my distance because ye have asked me to. Not for any other reason."

Anne's face seemed paler than before. Perhaps he really had frightened her. But there was a look he did not understand.

"Anne, what is wrong?" He lifted a hand lamely, then let it fall before it reached her.

She shook her head, pressing her lips together.

"Anne—"

"Elen is ill. I have to tend to her. The girls . . ." She passed him in the corridor, her skirts brushing his bare calf above his boot as she went by.

"Anne, wait."

But she didn't wait. She hurried down the hall and ducked through a doorway into the great hall.

"Tor. There ye are!" Munro stood with several of his clansmen. He waved Tor over.

Anne hurried down the steps and out of the hall, the water pan clutched in her hands.

"We just received word that a crofter lost his home last night. Burned to the ground."

Tor wanted to go after Anne. But his father was calling to him, and what right did he have to go after her, anyway? She was the king's daughter; he was a bastard Viking son.

"Spark from the fireplace?" Tor asked, reluctantly veering toward Munro.

"Nay." Munro's face was grim. "It was torched. Slaughtered sheep. A severed head left on a gatepost. The family got out alive, though it was in the middle of the night." Munro met Tor's gaze. "Will ye ride with me?" Tor admired the concern he saw in Munro's face. His father truly cared about these people. "I nae care what others say. This isnae the work of reivers," Tor said.

Munro shook his head. "Ye are right. I nae know what we have here yet, but 'tis no ordinary reivers."

Tor swore a colorful Highland curse and followed his father out of the hall.

"Feeling better?" Anne sat on Elen's bedside, looking down at her friend.

Elen lifted her gaze and smiled sleepily. "How long?" When Elen's blinding headaches hit her, there was no way to tell how long she would be incapacitated. She lay in an almost unconscious state for one to three days and then came out of it, the headache lifting as quickly as it had come.

"Nae long. A day, a little more. 'Tis almost evening."

Elen sat up in bed, brushing her hair from her face. "My lasses?"

Anne smiled. "With Munro. Riding before they sup."

Elen smiled. He's a good man. A good father."

Anne had no idea why, but Elen's words brought tears to her eyes.

"Anne, what's wrong?" Elen grabbed her wrist.

Anne leapt off the bed, turning her back to Elen. She felt foolish. What was wrong with her? Why would such a simple statement make her cry?

"Anne . . ." Elen slid her bare feet over the side of the bed and sat up. "What happened? Are Judith and Leah all right? Nothing has—"

"They're fine," Anne sniffed. "I'm sorry. All is well. Some crofters lost their cottage to a fire." She gave a little laugh that did not sound like her own. "Unless ye count the fact that one of the dogs has taken yet another of Judith's stitchings."

Elen laughed, too, relief obvious in her voice. "Good, good, I'm glad all is well."

A sob rose in Anne's throat, and though she tried to suppress it, a little whimper came out. She didn't know what was wrong with her.

"Anne . . ." Elen padded barefoot across the floor, her sleeping gown brushing the wood planks. "Tell me."

Anne felt cornered.

Elen slid her hand over Anne's shoulder. Anne pushed her away.

"Anne, whatever it 'tis, I am sure 'tis nae so bad. Tell me what's wrong and together ye and I can make it right. I wouldnae want some—"

Anne turned to Elen, tears welling in her eyes. "A baby," she whispered. "I am going to have a baby."

Thankfully, Elen did not flinch. She did not shout. She did not even ask Anne if she was certain. She took Anne's hand and led her to the bed.

Anne couldn't believe she had just blurted it out like that. She couldn't believe she had told Elen when she'd not yet told Tor. Tor had a right to know. The right to know first.

"How far gone?" Elen sat beside her and pressed a linen handkerchief into her hands.

Her fingers trembling, Anne raised the cloth to her eyes, afraid the tears would start again. "Nae far. A month."

"Ye havenae bled in that time?"

Anne shook her head. "Longer. My breasts are tender. I am sick to my stomach at strange times of the day and I . . . I am prone to tears."

Elen laughed as she slipped her arm around Anne, but it was a sad laugh. "I am assuming ye havenae told the father."

Anne sniffed. " Nay."

"Ye should have told me sooner. 'Tis a heavy burden to bear alone." She studied Anne, but Anne couldn't meet her gaze.

"Why didn't ye tell me?"

Anne lifted a shoulder. "Afraid ye would yell? Loud?"

"Me? Yell? Anne, I'm hurt."

"I nae know," Anne said miserably. "Mayhap because this is such a mess. There is no way to right it."

"Of course we can right it, but we must do so quickly."

Anne twisted the damp handkerchief in her hand. "My father is going to kill me. He is going to kill him. Munro is going to kill him."

"Nonsense. Robert will kill no one. No one need ever know. We'll find ye a husband, make sure the dowry is hefty, and naught will be suspected. The fortunate bridegroom will fetch two for the price of one."

It sounded like a reasonable plan, but when Anne looked up to meet Elen's gaze, she knew it would not be settled that easily.

"Ye have to tell me who the father is," Elen said quietly. "I have my suspicions, but I must hear it from ye." Another lump of tears rose in Anne's throat. This was all wrong. Tor had a right know first. She should never have said anything to Elen. But Elen was being so kind. So calm and understanding.

"Who?"

Anne lifted her gaze. She refused to show any shame. She could not change what she had done. And in honesty, even knowing the sin she had committed, she could not say that if she had it to do over again, she would have resisted his charms of that night on the beach. No matter where she went, or how far the journey would take her in this lifetime, she would always have that one night of loving to remember.

" 'Tis Tor." Her gaze bore into Elen's. "Tor is the father of my baby. I have known no other man."

"Tor!" Elen shouted so loudly that the mirror on the wall beside the bed rattled. "I knew it!"

CHAPTER NINETEEN

Anne covered her ears with her hands. She should have kept her mouth shut. She knew she shouldn't have said anything.

"Tor!" Elen shouted again. "How could he? How dare he?"

"Shhhhh," Anne hissed, dropping her hands to her sides.

"After the way Munro has brought him into our lives? After all—"

"Someone will hear ye," Anne warned. "The girls will hear ye."

"I nae care if every mon, woman, and child in the Highlands hears me. I will string that Viking up by his stones. I will—"

"It wasnae him," Anne interrupted, knowing she must take a stand. She loved Elen dearly, but she would not be controlled by her.

"Wasnae him?" She threw up her hands. "But ye

just said 'twas. Did ye nae just tell me the father is Tor?''

Elen was a formidable sparring partner. Anne had been around long enough to know that, but she would not allow her to lay blame where it did not belong. "Listen to me." Anne grabbed her sleeve, forcing Elen to look her in the eye. "What I mean is . . ." She swallowed. " 'Twas my fault, nae his. 'Twas—'twas what I wanted.''

Elen took a breath. For a moment the women just stared at each other.

"Anne, ye dinnae know what ye say." Elen was a little calmer, but her green eyes still flashed with anger.

" 'Twas Beltane," Anne confessed. "I lied to ye that night."

"He took advantage of ye on Beltane? That was why ye came in so late?" She threw up her hands and swore. "God's bones. I knew I should have kept a better rein on ye that day. There are more babes born in February than any other month of the year."

"Are ye nae listening?" Anne was surprised that she had raised her voice. "Why do ye think I nae wanted to tell ye that night? I knew this was what ye would say." She tapped her chest lightly, feeling surprisingly strong. "I am responsible. Nae Tor. Nae ye. Nae anyone but myself."

Anne squared her shoulders. She would not give Elen a chance to speak until she had had her say. "I could have said nay at any moment. 'Twas my doing, I tell ye. He . . . he was more than a gentleman."

"Gentleman, my rosy arse! A gentleman doesnae take a lass's virginity. A gentleman doesnae take the king's daughter's virginity," Elen flared.

"I willnae have ye hold him responsible like this.

I am a woman full grown, Elen. I willnae say it again. I knew what I was doing. I knew what I wanted.''

"And now have ye gotten what ye wanted?''

Anne lowered her gaze, Elen's words cutting her to the quick.

For a moment, a silence fell over them that was as heavy as the darkness beyond the lamplight.

"I didnae think of this ... *possibility* that night. I only wanted—wanted ...'' She lifted her gaze, tears stinging the backs of her eyes. "To be loved by him, if only for one night.''

"Aye, sweet,'' Elen crooned and pulled her into her arms. "I am sorry. I nae meant to make matters worse. What's done is done.'' She smoothed Anne's hair and Anne hung to her for dear life.

"I have to tell him,'' Anne murmured.

"That ye must.'' Elen lowered her arms after a moment and wiped one of Anne's cheeks with her thumb. "And I must tell Munro.''

"Must ye?''

"He is my husband, Anne. I have never, will never, keep anything from him. Ye understand?''

Anne nodded pushing hair off her forehead. She was overly warm, but at least her stomach was not upset. "May I first send Tor warning and then pack myself off to the Sahara or somewhere equally distant?''

Elen laughed, and the sound of her laughter gave Anne hope.

"Munro willnae be pleased, but he loves ye,'' Elen said. "And we'll fix this, I swear we will. I dinnae say this to trivialize your predicament, but ye are nae the first lass to lose herself to the passion of the moment. What is spilt can be tidied up.''

"And Tor?''

Elen walked to a chair and reached for a pair of

men's breeches. " 'Tis up to Munro, of course. He is his son." She slid her nightgown over her head and took up one of Munro's saffron shirts. "This is going to hurt Munro. He has really taken to Tor. I think he has hopes the lad will stay."

Anne heard Elen's words, but her meaning didn't really sink in. " 'Twas so stupid," she moaned, lowering her forehead to the heel of her hand. "I suppose we did just get caught up in the moment. He had been so kind to me, and—"

"Ye nae have to explain to me." Elen slid the shirt over her head and grabbed for a pair of stockings. "I made some inappropriate choices early in my life, too."

Anne looked up. "I cannae believe ye—"

"My sister's wedding," Elen confessed with a wry smile. "Everyone else was dancing in Rancoff's hall. Me, an unwed maiden, I was dancing with the master of the house in a chamber above."

Anne had to smile. She was shocked, but not as shocked as she would have been six months ago. Now she knew what it was to desire a man—to risk more than she had a right to risk just to be in his arms.

"Are ye going to tell Munro now?" All Anne could think of was a scene in the great hall. She prayed Tor was not below stairs.

Elen pulled on a boot. "I will speak to him privately and I will ask him to stay composed."

"I want to tell Tor myself. Make certain Munro understands that Tor nae knows yet. I dinnae care how angry he is," Anne said. " 'Tis my right to tell Tor. I owe him that much if I am to ruin his life."

Elen patted Anne's arm as she went by her on her way out. "No one's life is ruined. Trust me. We will fix this. In a year's time, 'twill be nothing but a memory, stale as yesterday's bread.''

Anne watched Elen go, praying she was right.

"I must speak with ye."

"And I thought ye coaxed me out here to have your way with me." Munro caught Elen's hand and swung it between them. They were walking in a small, enclosed garden behind the kitchen's outside entrance. In the distance, against the far wall, stood the maze Elen was growing for the girls. Elen and Munro carried no torch, but there was enough light from the setting sun to illuminate the pathway.

Elen sighed. This man of hers never knew when she needed him to be serious. "Munro, please."

"What?" He caught both her hands. "With child again?"

His smile so warmed her heart that she hated to go on. "I told ye. I think my days of childbearing are nearly passed."

He continued to gaze into her eyes, and she again thought of how poor his timing was. When she wanted him to be romantic, he was busy talking of hunting or cattle. When she needed him to listen to her and be serious, he wanted to woo her.

" 'Tis all right, ye know," he said. "There are few who can say the children of their bodies all live and are happy and healthy. And now I have my son. I am more than content."

Elen knew he was leaning over to kiss her. She considered giving up the conversation until later, torn between wanting to get it over with and wanting to enjoy this rare moment alone with her husband. But she knew she couldn't put this off.

Elen pressed both hands to Munro's chest. "Listen to me. I have something to tell ye, and when I say it, ye have to swear to me ye willnae go mad. No shouting. No tossing people about. No weapons."

He blinked. "What are ye babbling about, wife?"

She squeezed her eyes shut for a moment and then opened them. "Anne is with child."

Munro stared at her as a light breeze caught the graying hair that escaped his plaid bonnet.

"She is what?" he ground out.

"Gets better." Elen folded her arms over her chest. "Tor is the father."

Munro stood so long in silence that she began to wonder if he had not heard what she said. It was possible. He often stood there as if listening, yet did not hear. Somehow, she knew this was not the case.

"Ye are sure she is with child?" he finally said, his voice strangely without emotion.

"As sure as a woman can be."

"And ye are sure it was him?"

"Please dinnae say ye would question Anne's honesty," she said. She knew she should not be angry with him—he had done nothing wrong—but she couldn't help herself. "Never in all these years living with us has she ever once given us reason to disbelieve her."

"I'm sorry. " He raised his hands, palms up. "Ye are right. She wouldnae lie. Certainly nae about something like this."

"Now, we must handle this quietly and carefully," Elen said. "There is no reason for anyone to get upset. 'Tis nae—"

Munro strode away.

"Where are ye going?"

"Where do ye think I am going?" he roared.

Elen stepped in front of him. "Nay. Not yet. She hasnae told him."

"Get out of my way."

"Munro!"

"Get out of my way." The sound came from his gritted teeth.

"Please, I told her we would let her talk to him first."

Munro went around her. "I will kill him. I will take my son between my own bare hands, and I will strangle the life out of him." He reached into the air. "And then I will feed his body to my hounds, one bit at a time."

"Munro!"

He met her gaze, his eyes dangerously narrow. "Ye get your way when it suits me, wife, but only when it suits me, and ye well know it." He raised a finger. "Now, out of my path so I can deal with my son."

Elen thought a moment, then stepped out of his way. She had promised that Anne could speak with Tor before Munro did, but she also knew she could not let this come between her and her husband. No matter what rocky road their marriage was on these days, she loved him with all her heart, and not even for her beloved Anne would she risk that.

At the garden gate, Elen and Munro parted without saying a word. Munro headed for the stable, where she knew he would leap onto a pony—bareback most likely—and ride to Rancoff. At the back door to the kitchen, she seriously considered telling Anne that Munro was headed for Rancoff, but in the end decided against it.

She would let Munro talk to Tor first. She knew he really wouldn't kill him. He would bellow, shout, toss a few stools, and then he would tell Tor he must marry Anne.

She smiled to herself. If she had suggested the two marry, he might not have liked the idea as well. But if Munro thought it his own idea, it would settle better in his gut. It was a perfect plan. Munro, with permission from her father, would make Tor marry Anne and save her honor, and Anne would get the man Elen suspected she loved. Better yet, Munro would get the son he so desperately wanted.

Munro swung the door to Rancoff's hall open so hard that it hit the wall and rebounded backward with a crash. "What have ye done?"

Tor rose up off the stool where he had been sitting to clean his weapons. Finn, who sat on the far side of the table, glanced up with amused interest. Olave sat on the floor near the hearth. He looked scared.

Munro pointed to Finn. "Get out!" He pointed to Olave, but gentled his voice. "Leave us."

Olave scrambled from the floor and took the rear entrance that led to the kitchen steps. Finn slipped behind Munro and closed the door behind him.

"What have ye done to me? To my family?" Munro demanded as he grabbed the nearest three-legged stool and threw it, coming dangerously close to his granddad's portrait, which had only recently been rehung.

Tor had no idea what was going on, but he guessed it was going to be unpleasant. His hackles stood on end. He and Munro had been getting along well lately, but that gave him no right to talk to him like this. A few pleasant conversations did not make up for a lifetime of abandonment.

Tor glanced at the Forrest portrait and adjusted it slightly before he met his father's gaze. "Are ye going to say what you're talking about, or would you like another stool to toss?" He swiped up the nearest stool and offered it.

Munro crossed the room to grab the stool and drop it to the floor. It hit the planks hard and slid, halting only when it hit the wall. "Ye will marry her at once."

Tor's brow furrowed. "I will marry whom?"

The moment the words were out of his mouth, he knew who Munro was talking about.

Tor felt as if he had taken a sudden, long fall. He was instantly light-headed. His stomach was in his throat. He felt the air rushing by.

Anne. His Anne.

Tor gritted his teeth, meeting his father's gaze head on. Somehow, he knew about Tor and Anne. Tor had to get to her. Talk to her. Find out what was happening here. What would have possessed her to tell?

"How dare ye put my family in danger," Munro shouted. "She is the king's daughter, for sweet Christ's sake! Do ye understand what power the king has over me? Over my lands? Ye could have had any unmarried wench in this country, and she is the woman ye must take!"

Tor was so shocked by what Munro was saying that he could not think clearly. He could not grasp what was happening here. Instead, it was his father's anger, the shouting, that he focused on. Anger, he understood. Anger, he could deal with.

"What right have ye to speak to me this way?" Tor bellowed back. "I willnae be spoken to like a child."

"Ye are a child. Ye are *my* child!"

Before Tor could process that in his head, Munro flew headlong into his rantings again.

"Robert trusted me," Munro said. "And I trusted ye. I trusted ye, son."

"I will settle this matter." Tor's gaze still locked

with his father's. "But nae because ye order me. Ye have no right to order me to do anything. Ye gave up that right the day ye left my mother."

"God's fluttering bones! This isnae about ye, Tor." Munro walked away, gesturing. " 'Tis time ye grow up. For once, put yourself aside. This is about Anne. This is about the safety of my family." He turned on him. "This is about *your* child."

With child. Anne was with child, of course; that was how Munro had found out Tor had lain with her.

Again Tor could feel himself hurtling through the air. Disoriented. He had always been so careful not to plant his seed. How could he have done this?

Tor eyed his father, again, grasping at his anger. It was the only thing that braced him right now. "Ye insult me and ye insult my honor," Tor accused. "You insult me when ye suggest I wouldnae do what is right."

In truth, he was hurt by his father's words. Hurt more than he realized was possible. His father knew how much he had suffered being a bastard. Surely he did not think Tor would wish that upon his own child.

Tor spun on the heels of his boots.

"Where are ye going? We've plans to make. This must be handled delicately and quickly. I am nae finished with ye yet."

"You are finished." Tor did not slam the door, but closed it with quiet resolution.

CHAPTER
TWENTY

"Anne."

She stood near Dunblane's hearth, her back to him as he entered the hall. But she knew it was Tor. And she knew why he had come.

Her gaze swept the vaulted room, searching for Elen. A pigeon fluttered overhead and settled on a beam. Elen was standing at the head table behind Judith, cutting a bit of meat for her. Elen had heard Tor, too.

The two women locked gazes, Elen's one of gentle apology. Anne's anger stepped forward anyway. Obviously, someone had spoken to Tor.

Yet, as Elen continued to hold her gaze, Anne felt her anger slipping away as quickly as it had come. Why did it matter who told him? Telling him herself first would not have made her any less pregnant.

"Anne de Bruc."

She turned from the hearth, wiping her damp hands on her skirt. She was surprisingly calm; her heart only gave a little flutter. And that, perhaps, was at the sight of Tor's handsome form. She should have been ashamed of herself.

"I want to speak to ye."

He seemed taller tonight, even more imposing. She could hear anger tight in his voice. She walked past him, down the stone steps.

He caught her arm as she crossed the oubliette grate.

"Ye should have told me. Not them. *Me.*"

When she did not answer right away, he tried to turn her to face him. She twisted her arm from his hold. She would not let him treat her roughly. She did not care how angry or how large he was.

"I meant to tell ye," she tried to explain carefully.

"It was not their business." Again he reached for her arm.

Again she jerked away. "Touch me," she hissed, "and I will call for one of Elen's kinsmen. Ye think they willnae come?" she dared. "If the *king's daughter* calls?"

Slowly he lowered his hand to his side.

She took a deep breath. "I am sorry that I didnae tell ye. I was still in shock. I didnae set out to tell Elen. Only, it spilled out."

"Ye should have told me first," he growled.

"What? So ye could shout at me?"

"So this could remain private between us."

She arched a brow. "And how long would it have been private 'afore my belly began to enter the room before me?"

He looked away, then back at her. "This talk is senseless. Ye will marry me."

His statement was so simple. It was such a reasonable solution to the problem. So honorable on Tor's part. Considering her circumstances, her father could probably be persuaded to give her permission to wed if Munro insisted it was the right thing to do.

Anne thought about the way she had felt that night on the beach in Tor's arms. She thought about how wonderful it would be to feel that way every night.

She looked at him, at the way he stood, his legs planted firmly, his hands behind his back. He was not asking her to marry him. There had been no declaration of love. He was telling her what she would do. Another man telling her what to do.

Something inside her snapped in two. She practically heard the pop in her head. All she could think of was unhappiness. Her mother's unhappiness because of a man. Her grandmother's unhappiness because of a man. It was not what Anne wanted. "Nay." She turned and started up the steps to the hall again.

"Nay?"

She tried to hurry up the steps, but he was too quick. He somehow managed to get in front of her. He was so broad that he nearly blocked the arched doorway.

"Nay?"

"What is it ye nae understand?" she snapped. "I said I wouldnae marry ye."

He stared at her as if she had just sprouted another head.

"Ye willnae marry me?"

She rolled her eyes. "Get out of my way!"

Behind her, the outside door opened. She glanced over her shoulder to see Munro walk in.

"She says she will not marry me." Tor gestured.

Munro ran his hands over his wet tunic, sending droplets of water flying to the flagstone floor. "Raining," was all he said.

His comment seemed surreal, considering the circumstances.

Anne turned back to Tor. "Get out of my way, ye big oaf."

Tor looked over her shoulder to his father, who still stood behind her.

"What are ye looking to him for?" she demanded. "He willnae save ye. 'Tis nae up to him. 'Tis up to my father, and if he wants me to marry ye, he can damned well come here and tell me himself," she spat. "Now get out of my way." She gave Tor a shove and brushed past him.

For a moment, he just stood there on the top step, trying to figure what had just happened. He was solving her problem. He was going to marry her. Everything was going to be all right. Why was she not happy? Wasn't this what women wanted?

He looked at Munro, who seemed to have calmed considerably since last he saw him.

"She says she will not marry me," Tor repeated, feeling as if he were floating. Didn't she realize how important this was to him? After all she had been through, didn't she know that she must marry him to protect their child?

"I thought ye nae wanted to marry her," Munro answered, as always taking his time before he spoke.

Tor stared at the floor, his fists clenched at his side. "I did not say that." He made himself look at his father. "I do not want ye to think ye can tell me what to do. Ye do not have that right."

"I lost my head," Munro said simply.

When his father talked like that, Tor didn't know how to deal with him. "I do not know what to do." He pointed lamely in the direction Anne had fled. "She says she will not have me."

"Nae worry. She will come around." Munro patted

Tor's shoulder as he went by him. "We will talk later and figure out the best way to send news of this turn of events to her father." He halted just before entering the great room. "Now mind ye, I am still angry with ye." He gave a half smile. "But ye are still my son."

Tor stood on the landing, staring into the darkness, wishing Munro had not said that. Wishing he had never left Ny Landsby. Wishing he had never been born.

"That him?" Finley lay on his stomach at the edge of the meadow and watched the Viking chop wood.

"God's foul breath! Of course 'tis him." Rosalyn elbowed him sharply. "He looks just like the addlepated one." She stared in disbelief, disgusted and fascinated at the same time. A bead of sweat formed above her upper lip as she watched the Viking remove his shirt and toss it onto the grass.

He was a handsome specimen of a man, this man. She wouldn't mind having a taste of him herself. Just looking at his broad chest and muscled arms made her hot below stairs. "A son. Can ye believe the prick Munro had a bastard son and never told anyone?"

"Why do ye think he came?"

"Why else?" She slapped him soundly. "To take what should have been mine."

She watched as the blond giant pushed up his sleeves and lifted the ax again. She wondered why Rancoff's son was doing such a menial task as splitting wood. Like father, like son, no doubt. Munro had never seemed to understand his place or that of his brothers. He was always asking Cerdic to do servile work. It had always been a bone of contention between her and the great Lord of Rancoff.

"Ye nae think he's just come for coin? What would a Viking want with land?"

"Idiots. I have been surrounded my entire life by idiots. Of course he wants the land. He wants the castle. Wants to be a lord. Doesn't every mon?" Rosalyn eyed him shrewdly. " 'Twas your dream once, nay?"

He squirmed. " 'Twas a long time ago."

"But ye still want her, don't ye?" She turned to Finley, the Viking cock forgotten for the moment. "Don't ye?"

"Nay. He shook his head, his voice rising higher in pitch. "Only ye, sweet."

"Liar!" She cracked him on the head with a stick she swept off the ground, and he cried out in pain.

"Admit it. Admit now that ye still want to get beneath my sister's skirts, and we'll be done with this."

Finley rolled away from her, dry grass sticking to his tunic. "Nay. I willnae say what is nae true. I love ye. I have always loved ye." He lifted his arms, prepared for the next blow.

"Nae her?" She crawled back from view to the woods line and rose to her feet, brushing off the motheaten clothes he had stolen for her. The dress was not fit for blood rags, but it was all she had. "Tell me ye love my sister and 'twill all be over right here." She raised the stick over his head, certain she could hit him hard enough to crack his skull open. "Say it."

"Only ye, my love." He got up on all fours and crawled to her feet, where he prostrated himself. "Ye are mistaken. Your memory of the past is clouded by the things they did to ye. I never loved anyone but ye, Rosalyn."

Slowly she lowered the stick, her anger subsiding.

Finley was a good man, as loyal as any hound her father had ever owned. And so easy to manipulate. He was just the kind of man she liked.

He made little sobbing sounds, his cheek pressed to her foot.

She slowly lowered her hand to his head of black hair. She needed to give him a trim. The hair was long and tangled. He looked like some wild man out of the mountains.

"Say it again," she whispered. Through the trees, she could just make out the blond Viking. She could hear the echo of the ax each time it met with a log.

"I love ye," he whimpered, sliding his hands under her skirt, over her tattered stockings.

She closed her eyes and pretended the caress was not Finley's but the Viking's.

The heat of the June sun beat down on Tor, and he felt as if he were going to burst into flames himself. He gave the long handle of the ax a great heave and sank the blade into an upright piece of firewood.

There were plenty of men to chop Dunblane's wood; he was just using the empty wood box as an excuse. Here, outside the back gate, he could watch for Anne without being too obvious.

Anne was making him into a madman. It had been almost a week since he learned she carried his child. He could not sleep. He could not eat. He was either listless and resigned, or exploding at any provocation.

The thought that she was carrying his child and did not want to marry him infuriated him. Hurt him. The idea that his child might be born out of wedlock blinded him with rage.

Rage was not the way to deal with a pregnant woman. He had discovered that in the first days after learning of her condition. Surprisingly enough, her anger could nearly match his. But what did she have to be angry about? He told her he would marry her. He told her he would get her out of this trouble. He was willing to deal with her father. But so far, she would not budge. Worst of all, she would not say why she wouldn't marry him. She would barely speak to him.

As if conjured by his thoughts, Tor heard Anne's voice. "Only a short walk and then back to our studies, ladies. Remember, we'll be gone to Aberdeen for the wedding. Ye cannae fall behind."

Anne, Leah, and Judith walked through the gate.

"Fall behind, fall behind . . ." Judith chattered as she bounced along.

Tor couldn't resist a smile. She was good with children, his Anne. She would make a good mother.

"Stop repeating yourself. Anne, tell her to stop repeating herself," Leah complained.

Judith hopped and spun at the same time. "Repeat yourself. Repeat yourself."

Leah shrieked and lunged for Judith, but Judith was quick as a rabbit. The two little girls took off across the meadow, leaving a laughing Anne behind.

"Too much work, not enough play," Tor said, taking a chance she would speak with him. Of course, he knew there was an equal chance she would take the ax and split his head in two.

Anne turned. Apparently, she had not seen him there in the shadow of the curtain wall.

"They are already brighter than most of the females I ever knew," he said, a strange feeling of pride coming over him. Somehow, at some point in the past weeks, his half-sisters had burrowed beneath his skin.

Anne rested one hand on her hip as she regarded

him. She had to be contemplating whether or not she would dignify him with an answer. "I threw the flowers ye sent up with Olave out the window."

"Did ye?" He took a daring step closer. Another step and she'd have to get by him to reach the ax.

His father had warned him that women in her condition got like this sometimes. Irrational. He'd told Tor not to worry, that she would come around. Tor was worried.

"First I crushed them beneath my foot, and then I threw them out the window."

She'd spoken two sentences to him. This was definite progress.

"I wanted ye to know I was . . . thinking about ye," he said awkwardly. He didn't know how he had picked up on the Scottish accent so quickly. At first, he had tried to fight it, but lately he'd given up. Anyone could look at him and know he wasn't a Scot.

"Ye think I can be bribed into marriage with a handful of flowers?" she demanded.

"Nay, I just—"

"I told ye. I will not marry ye. Which part of that was not clear?"

"Anne . . ." He took a breath. He had vowed that next time he spoke to her he would stay calm. He would not shout. "Anne, ye must be reasonable. Munro says he cannot wait long to send word to your father. He would like that word to be a request for us to wed."

"And then what?" she demanded. "Ye pack me off to some ice float in the north, never to see Elen or the lasses again?"

"I—"

"Ye said yourself," she came closer, "ye said ye still intended to return to your village. Ye said ye wanted his money and nothing more."

"Anne." Again, he lowered his voice. "Ye cannae continue to put this off. These matters can be settled later. That child must have a father." His last words came out harsher than he had intended.

Just then, Judith and Leah galloped across the grass.

"Tor!" Leah squealed. She threw herself into Tor's arms, and without thinking, he lifted her and spun her the way he had seen their father do.

"Me! My turn," Judith hollered, flapping her arms like wings.

Tor lowered Leah gently to the ground, suddenly feeling self-conscious about being naked from the waist up. But Judith seemed to take no notice. He swung her into the air.

"Are ye coming to Aberdeen for the Macrae wedding?" Leah asked Tor.

"Are ye coming? Are ye coming?" Judith repeated.

"Nay," Anne said.

He lowered Judith to the ground. "Aye. I am."

Anne glared at him. "Someone must stay home to defend our walls."

"Our father wishes me to go," Tor explained.

"Wishes to go, wishes to go," Judith babbled.

Leah reached out to grab her sister's braid, and the two girls took off again.

"Ye are nae going," Anne hissed.

He realized that even if the girls hadn't noticed his bare chest, Anne had. Her cheeks were pinker than normal. "My father has asked me and I will go. Finn has offered to stay behind with Olave. There are plenty of men here to defend the walls of both castles."

"I dinnae want ye to go. I dinnae want ye near me."

"Anne." He gave a little laugh but he was not

amused. "Tell me what is going on here, because I swear I do not know. Ye wanted to be near enough to make love with me on the beach that night; then, when I tell ye I will marry ye, ye act as if I am a leper." He spread his arms wide. "I am willing to defend your honor. Why are ye being so stubborn?"

"Ye are willing to save my honor?" She tossed her head. "Willing?" Without another word, she stalked off.

Tor considered going after her but, catching a glimpse of the ax, decided against it. He was definitely making progress, but he decided not to press his luck. With a few days in Aberdeen in her company and no duties to attend, he would have plenty of time to talk to her. Surely in a week's time he could convince her.

CHAPTER
TWENTY-ONE

A week later, Anne stood on the Macraes' balcony off their great hall, studying the midsummer bonfires that blazed below and as far as she could see over the hills that lay north of the city. The isolated bright blazes in the darkness seemed to her to be spots of hope.

Behind her, she could hear the fiddlers and pipers as they struck up another merry tune. Cousins Mary Macrae and Ian Macrae had married at midmorning. The celebrating had begun by midday and would not cease until Mary was kirked come Sunday.

Behind her, Anne heard laughter and the clapping of hands, but it seemed distant. The merriment seemed distant. She could hear the stomp of boots and slippers as men and women made their way around the center of the great hall, dancing until they were dizzy and breathless.

Ordinarily, Anne liked to dance, but tonight she was not in the mood. She leaned over the balcony wall, pressing her forearms to the rough stone. She heard a footstep behind her and knew who it was.

Tor leaned on the low wall and stared out at the bonfires burning on the dark horizon. "Why do they burn them?" he asked.

She could feel the heat of his body beside her, though he was careful not to brush his arm against hers. "Midsummer's eve. I nae know why, other than we have always burned them on this night."

"Elen said ye did not feel well this morning."

She kept staring into the darkness. "I am fine."

He turned his head so that the torchlight near the arched door cast a shadow across his face. "I am glad to hear that one of us is."

For once, his tone was not adversarial. She stared out into the darkness, breathing the faintly sweet scent of the burning woodpile below. Applewood, perhaps, from a fallen tree? She thought about the baby growing inside her. About Munro's insistence that he must soon send word to her father. That it was his responsibility.

"Anne, tell me what is it you want," Tor said.

"I nae know." She looked to him.

He wore his long blond hair pulled back by a leather tie tonight, but a lock that was only chin-length had slipped forward to brush his shaven cheek. She wanted to push it back. Wanted to touch him. She pressed her hands to her sides.

"That is not an answer."

"Of course 'tis an answer." She turned to face him. "Just nae one ye particularly like."

He was dressed like a Scotsman again tonight, garbed in a burgundy-and-green plaid with his mother's brooch pinned at the shoulder.

Staring at him in the darkness made her heart flutter. Would it be so bad to do what everyone wanted her to do, and marry him? she wondered. She knew he would never harm her. She knew he would be a great protector. Perhaps with some persuasion he could even be convinced to remain here in the Highlands. And even if he didn't, wouldn't marriage to him be better than marriage to a stranger her father chose for her?

Anne wanted more than the lesser of two evils. She deserved more.

"Ye know that your father can force ye to marry me. 'Tis what Elen and Munro want. From what I hear, I think your father respects Munro's decisions."

"I know that." She studied his Nordic blue eyes, wondering what he was really thinking. "He could also force me to marry another."

She thought she saw a possessive light spark in his eyes. "And you would rather marry a man ye do not know, than marry me? This is *my* child we speak of, too."

Anne felt the scratch of tears behind her eyelids and remained silent.

"Anne." He slid his hand around her waist.

She fully intended to pull away. She didn't want to marry another man; she wanted to marry Tor. She knew she was being stubborn, unrealistic, but she wanted him to *want* to marry her. She wanted him to love her.

"Anne, Anne, nae cry," he murmured.

She let him draw her into his arms, just for a moment.

He smelled of clean wool, tobacco, and soap. When he pulled her against his chest and enfolded her in her arms, she felt as if she was without the ability to resist.

"This is my fault," he whispered. "I should not have—"

" 'Twas the most alive I have ever felt," she said, feeling as if she were dreaming, floating in his arms. She was intoxicated by the male smell of him, by his size. "Please dinnae tell me now that ye wish ye had not taken me. If ye tell me that"—her voice cracked—"I nae know what I will do."

Tor glanced over his shoulder into the light of the great room. The pipes were still singing merrily. There was still clapping, dancing, shouts of well-wishers. Anyone who cared to look out onto the balcony could see them.

Tor drew her to the dark corner of the balcony, backing her against the wall so that the doorway lay to his left. He pushed her hair back off the crown of her head, lifting her chin in his palm. "Anne, ye must listen to me. Tell me what it is that keeps ye from agreeing to take my hand. I swear by my mother's grave that I will be loyal to you. That I will not stray. I will protect you and our child. . ."

He continued to talk in a flood of sentences, but she barely heard. They were all gallant words, but still she did not hear the three words she needed to hear. Words he had uttered once before, yet she had been afraid to trust. More talk would resolve nothing. How could she tell him what she wanted? If she told him, he would say it. He would say anything to keep her from giving birth to a bastard child. There were worse things than being born a bastard. Being born unwanted. Unloved.

Tor continued, making promises to speak directly to her father.

Anne slid her hand over his chest, upward to his shoulder, skimming her fingertips around his thick, muscular neck as she closed her eyes. He kissed her midsentence.

If possible, his kiss was even better than the others

they had shared. There was something in the bitter-sweetness of the kiss. Each wanted what the other feared could not be given.

"Marry me," he begged.

She was nearly breathless. Logically, she knew what she was doing was right. But her heart was pounding, her blood rushing in her ears. She could feel that aching heat inside her that she had only recently come to know as desire.

She shook her head, unable to say yes, unable to stop kissing him.

"At least promise me ye will think on the matter."

"I . . ."

"Anne . . ."

She fluttered her lashes, taking a half step back. She was still in his arms, but at least at this distance, her heart did not beat with his. "I—I will think on the matter; I can promise naught more."

He brought her hand to his mouth. " 'Tis all I ask tonight."

She pulled away. "The lasses. I should check on them."

"Let me walk with ye."

He still held her hand. She let him, and together they walked into the light of the great hall.

"Look at them. She looks kissed." Elen pushed her elbow into Munro's side. He was talking to a gentleman on his left who was so intoxicated that the old badger was confused as to who the bride and bridegroom were.

"Munro," she said in his ear. "Are ye listening to me?"

The gentleman tottered off for another draught of Scotch, and Munro turned to her. "What?"

"Look at them," she said wistfully. "I think he is making progress." She pointed to Tor and Anne walking along the perimeter of the hall. Even amid the folds of Anne's gown, Elen could see they were holding hands. "They've been kissing."

Munro's forehead furrowed. "How does one look kissed?"

She sighed, sipping her mulled wine. "Do ye nae see the stars in her eyes?"

He looked into her goblet. "Have ye imbibed a great deal, wife?"

She pushed him away. "Listen to me. I am being serious. Ye and I once looked that way. Hiding in the dark corners. Stolen kisses. Do ye remember the wolf pelt ye once sent me? 'Twas the most romantic gift. A pelt for my bed."

"Methinks I was merely hoping to join ye on that pelt."

She groaned. "Munro! I am being serious. Do ye nae miss those days when we searched for each other in a crowded room? When we went all day hoping to catch a glimpse of the other?"

He sighed and leaned against a stone pillar, seeming to realize he was not going to be able to get away from her. "I do not recall starry-eyed exchanges, wife. Ye and I were different. Our love was different."

"Was it?" she mused.

He frowned. "What has gotten into ye tonight, Elen? Are ye feeling ill?"

She studied the rim of her glass, knowing this conversation would go nowhere. Munro just didn't understand. "What are we going to do if she does not agree to marry him?"

"I nae know. Ye were the one who said there would be no more forced marriages in Dunblane's kirk."

"Do ye think Robert will come? Will the king think

this a matter needing his attention, or will he want ye to deal with it?''

He shook his head. "Honestly, I nae know. He has a bit of a temper, our Robert, but he is a sensible man." He watched in the direction his son and Anne had disappeared between vaulted arches. "I cannae for the life of me figure out why she doesnae want to marry him."

"Ah, I think she does," Elen said. "Let him woo her. Every woman wants to be wooed."

"Whatever ye say, dear."

Munro leaned to kiss her cheek, and she let him, wishing it were more. Wishing she had been on that balcony with Munro. But she didn't know how to tell him that without appearing foolish. Maybe she was being foolish. She was a woman married eight years. She had two beautiful children and a husband who did not have a straying eye. What more could a woman her age expect?

"Now I see Albert waving to me. I've been looking all evening for that grouse." He offered her a smile that still charmed her after all these years. "Nae turn in without me."

Elen forced a smile as he walked way, looking as handsome as ever. Despite the fact that he was nearly five decades old, he still made her heart patter.

Munro was probably right. It was just too much wine that was making her so melancholy. Resolved to owe it to the wine, she took another drink.

"I cannae believe ye would risk this," Finley hissed, pressing his back to the wall as they passed down Rancoff's unlit corridor.

She walked down its center as if she owned the keep. She *should* have owned the keep. If only Cerdic had not been so soft, so weak. "Ye heard the milk-maid. The master of the house has gone to Aberdeen with his family for a wedding. Everyone else in the keep—those guarding it—are down making merry in the fields. Singing around their bonfires. Drinking, dancing," she said, getting angrier with each word. "Whilst I scrape for my next meal."

"Ye never said we would come here," Finley whined. "When we came ye said we would stay away. Ye said we would hide out whilst we made a plan—whilst we gathered supplies, and then we would go. Ye said we would go to London and there we would marry."

She glanced over her shoulder at the dark-haired man who was fast going gray. She would no more marry him than she would that rat back in the old kitchen where they were hiding out. She had captured the rodent under a cooking pot and beat it to death with a piece of firewood.

"Ye said naught of revenge."

"Shh," she warned, scowling. "Who said anything of revenge? I told ye, I look for candles. All that darkness is yellowing my skin."

"Someone will come. We will be caught." He shuddered as the rat had shuddered after she had hit it the first time with the stick. "I cannae go back to that place. I told ye, I wouldnae go back."

He sounded like a frightened child to her. A stupid, frightened child. She reached out to caress his cheek. She needed Finley. She did not know exactly what her plan was yet, but she knew she needed Finley.

She watched as he picked at a self-inflicted burn on his arm.

She brushed his hand aside, annoyed that he would not let the wound be. "Just some candles," she hissed. "And we will be on our way, my love."

He covered her hand with his.

So easy to manipulate. So like a man.

"Well enough?" she whispered.

He nodded, though he still looked frightened.

She slipped her hand over his and drew him down the hall. "Come, now. Let us find those candles and be gone from here."

"Ye promised," he muttered to himself, allowing her to take him by the hand and lead him deeper into private rooms of the keep. "But ye promised."

CHAPTER
TWENTY-TWO

"Ah, brother, you have it bad," Finn teased, shaking his head as if in mourning. The three brothers sat on the ground in one of Rancoff's hayfields and ate bread and cheese. They leaned against a new haystack, the early August sun beating down on their faces.

Tor grabbed the water skin from the grass and tipped it to his mouth, catching a stream of cold water. "Shut up."

"Got it bad. Church on Sunday. A clean shirt every morning. You bathe so much you stink."

Tor turned the water skin on Finn, squeezed it, and water shot out, hitting him in the face.

Olave laughed from his belly.

"The rumors are divided. Some say you court the Lady Anne to win more than just a handful of coin from your father." Finn wiped his face with his bare forearm. "Others say she's got a loaf baking and you fear you cannot run far enough from the king of Scotland."

Tor leaped up, pushing Finn into the sweet-smelling grass, and drew back his fist. "Ye will not say that of her. Ye will not allow others to say it."

Finn raised a hand in defense. "I only tease you, brother." He gave him a playful shove. "I told them you were pursuing her because you were mad in love with her."

Tor backed up. "What I do is not your concern."

Olave chuckled.

Tor turned to Olave. "Or yours."

Olave stuffed a handful of bread into his mouth. "Olave will marry Anne if you do not."

Tor eyed him but said nothing. He turned his attention back to Finn again. "Are ye saying ye are not content here? You want to go home? Is that why ye dinnae want me to marry her?"

"I never said I did not want you to marry Anne. Where did you get that?" Finn leaned against the haystack again. "As for me wanting to stay in the Highlands, the first fortnight we were here, I told you I would stay."

"Olave will stay."

"I told you there was nothing left in Ny Landsby for me," Finn continued. "Not since my father died. Not since our older half-brother died. Mor was right. Our way of life is dead. It was dying before you and I were born." He slipped a thin reed of grass between his teeth and leaned back against the haystack. "Besides, I like the women here." He opened his arms to the world. "They like me."

"Women like Olave."

Tor eyed his youngest brother. Olave sat contented, his legs spread wide, cheese and bread on a linen cloth in front of him. Each day since they had begun cutting hay, Anne had wrapped the food for Olave and sent it over with a house lad. She always sent it to Olave, but always sent enough for all three of them.

He thought she was warming to the idea of marrying him. As the days passed, he was warming to the idea as well. Ordinarily, once Tor had a woman, his desire for her abated. He rarely made love to the same woman twice. But with Anne, it seemed that one taste of her was just the bread brought before a meal. He felt he had barely touched her sensuality. He could think of nothing but holding her in his arms again, feeling her arms around him. Tor could wield a sword or a halberd, a war ax or a spear, with utter confidence in himself, yet he had never felt safer than that night on the beach in Anne's arms.

"No, I think Olave and I will stay no matter what you do, my brother. Who knows?" Finn went on, philosophically crossing one leg over his knee. "Perhaps I will even marry a wealthy lass and find my own castle."

Tor struck his knee with one hand as he laughed. "Marry a—"

"Tor! Tor!"

Tor heard his father call his name from behind him. At the same moment, he heard hoofbeats.

Something was wrong.

Surely not Anne . . . not the baby. Tor took off across the field toward his father, who rode through the cut hay toward him.

"What is it?" Tor panted as he met Munro.

Munro pulled the pony up short and led it into a tight circle around his son. "There's been a murder," he said.

His father was calm as always, but Tor could hear the shock in his tone. "Who was murdered?" Tor grabbed the pony's bridle so Munro could not turn in a circle again.

"The tanner—Charlie."

"How? What happened?"

Munro gazed down at Tor. "That is what is so abominable. I want ye to come. Ye must see this for yourself. I've told them to leave the body where it lies until we have returned."

"I nae understand." Tor was so relieved that nothing was wrong with Anne or his half-sisters that he only half heard what Munro had said. "What must I see?"

"I want ye to see the body. You were right. These are no damned reivers! Wait until ye see what these curs did to him." Munro circled his mount around Tor again, to head for the keep. "I only hope your stomach is well settled."

That evening, Anne served Munro and Elen and the girls and then walked to the end of the table. "Tell me," she whispered as she leaned over Tor's shoulder to pour ale in a leather tankard for him. "Elen said the tanner was dead, murdered, but not how he was murdered."

Tor accepted the ale she offered. He still did not have the stomach to eat. "Anne, I am tired. Please do not gnaw at me."

She glanced at the others on the dais. Munro and Elen were talking quietly to themselves. Olave was entertaining the girls by pinching bits of bread into animal shapes. Finn had gotten up to sit at another table in the hall to flirt with the daughter of a vassal come to visit her father.

Anne sat beside Tor in Finn's place and pushed

Finn's trencher aside. "Everyone is trying to protect me. I have a right to know."

He lifted the horn cup to his lips and let the cool ale run down the back of his throat. Tor had seen his share of death. Men who had drowned fishing, farming accidents, battle wounds, but he had never seen anything so barbaric as this.

"Ye want me to be your wife?" She lowered her voice. "And yet ye are already keeping things from me. I couldnae live with a man who—"

"He . . . burned him."

Anne blinked. "What?"

Tor took another drink of the ale, trying to push the awful image from his mind. Distance himself. But he could still smell the scent of the charred flesh.

She slipped one hand over his bare forearm. "What did ye say, Tor?"

"Munro didnae want you to know that whoever did this burned the tanner. Burned his body whilst he still lived."

Anne's lower lip trembled, but she did not turn away in sickness as many women would have. "That is dreadful," she gasped, crossing herself.

He nodded, staring down into his cup again. He wondered how he could manage to distance himself from such a hideous scene and yet could not distance himself from this woman. She made him think of things he did not want to think of—made him feel what he did not want to feel.

"Who do ye think did such a thing?"

"Everyone has their own opinion. There are those who avoid me and my brothers, as if they think we did it. Not long ago some men tried to pick a fight with Olave. They made accusations against us."

"That is ridiculous. Ye have ridden these lands for days searching for who is doing this."

"Ye cannae blame them for being wary. Remember, the trouble didnae begin until our arrival."

" 'Twas spring. Reivers always come in the spring."

Tor toyed with a slice of dove pie. He knew he needed to eat, but he wasn't certain he could keep anything down yet. After carefully studying the scene, Tor had helped his father take down the tanner's body, and then they had carried it to the man's cottage. They had laid him out on his family's flour-dusted table.

"We kid ourselves to talk of these men as reivers. They are no reivers. They are men who hate Munro. Hate Elen. There can be no other motivation. Only hatred could make one man do these things to another."

Anne leaned close to him, and he found the warmth of her slender body somehow comforting.

"So who do ye think is doing this?" She looked at him with such a trust that he wanted to kiss her. "Who would hate us so much?"

"I nae know. A man collects enemies with the years. An Englishman Munro once met in battle. A neighbor with a land grudge. I cannae say." He finished the last of his ale. "What I do know is that people are afraid, and rightly so. Afraid of me, of my brothers, of any strangers to these parts."

"So what will ye do? This cannot go on. Our people cannae live in fear." She watched him intently.

Tor reached for the leather pitcher of ale. "We will stop them."

Approaching the north woods a few days later, Anne stared at the forest. Though the sun had not yet set, the light filtering through the lush August foliage was dim, the forest overcast in shadows.

Anne had not intended to ride from Rancoff to Dunblane alone. She had every intention of waiting for Alexi and Banoff to escort her, just as they had escorted her here at midday to inventory the kitchen larder. But she had sent them to buy some roots for the kitchen from the root woman down in the village, and they had not returned. It should not have taken this long.

For some unknown reason, Elen had decided she wanted Rancoff's kitchen better stocked and had sent Anne off with Banoff and Alexi first thing this morning. Because Anne had felt cooped up the past few days, going nowhere beyond the walls without escort, she had been anxious to ride anywhere, if only to count bins of flour and strings of onions.

Anne had completed her task by late in the afternoon and was looking forward to getting outside and riding home. Munro and Tor had been gone three days, riding Rancoff and Dunblane lands, talking to men and women who lived and worked on the land. There had been no word that they had found the murderers, but Anne hoped they might have discovered something.

"Where are they?" she muttered as she glanced about the woods.

She sighed in regret at her hasty action in leaving without her escorts, but refused to dwell on it. She wanted to get home to change out of these dusty clothes, to brush her hair before the men arrived.

Anne was still refusing to marry Tor under the basic principle that he had not asked her. He had not said he loved her, but she felt that they were growing closer, and she was beginning to hope things might change before she was forced to choose between marrying Tor and taking whatever her father offered. She knew she was just stalling, but she was

beginning to hope it had been the right choice—
hoping Tor might begin to see her in a different
light. She wanted him to see her as a person who
could be a companion, an equal, and not just the
mother of his child. She wanted him to want to marry
her.

With another sigh, she pressed her heels into the
sides of her pony, urging him on toward home.

The moment she entered the woods, a strange feeling came over her. Her first thought was that she
should turn back . . . but that was silly. She had passed
through this forest hundreds of times, often unes-
corted.

The deeper into the forest she moved, the more
uncomfortable she became. The pony beneath her
tensed. He danced sideways on the path, shying first
one way and then the other.

"Whoa, whoa," she soothed, slowing him to a walk.
She patted the shaggy pony's mane, trying to calm
him. She didn't want to lose her seat and fall; if
anyone at Dunblane found out she had taken a fall
from a horse, she wouldn't be permitted to ride again
for months.

"What's the matter, boy?" Anne murmured.

Even as the words left her mouth, the hair on the
back of her neck stood up as she peered upward.
The foliage was so thick overhead that light only
squeezed between the leaves and branches in narrow
slits.

Anne saw no one, and yet she knew someone was
there, watching her. Should she continue forward or
ride back? She prayed Alexi and Banoff were behind
her rather than ahead of her.

Her pony nickered, the sound high-pitched, nervous.

Anne wished she carried a weapon as Elen did.

"Who's there?" she demanded, pulling the horse up short.

The pony threw his head down and she struggled with the reins to get his head up. "Did ye hear me?" she shouted angrily.

She saw a shadow, heard movement.

Suddenly, a man appeared on the path. He was on foot, but she heard the nicker of a horse and knew he had a mount hidden in the brush. "Who are ye?" Anne asked as her pony nervously danced sideways.

He didn't look like a murderer, but then what did murderers look like? He was a small man with wiry black hair streaked with silver-gray. He had sad eyes.

"Who are ye?" he questioned back.

He was a Scot. And from near here; she could tell by his accent.

"I am Anne de Bruc of Dunblane, and this is our wood."

He glanced up into the trees, a strange look on his face. "Ah, the north wood," he said, seeming to speak as much to himself as to her.

The man made her skin crawl, and she had no idea why. He was clean, his hair washed and brushed, his beard neatly trimmed. He wore a common man's clothing, a simple dirk at his waist. He appeared no different than any other working man of the Highlands, save the fine leather of his boots.

Anne didn't know what to do, what to say as he stood blocking her way, staring at her.

Again, she wished she had something better to defend herself with than her dinner knife.

"Ye are very pretty, Anne de Bruc. Any relation to our king?"

Was he a kidnapper? Did he know who she was?

She chuckled. "There are many of the de Bruc

family. If I was of relation to the king, do ye think I would live in this back wood?''

His eyes narrowed and she detected a strange light in them. She knew her instincts were right: she should be afraid of this man. Abruptly, she spun her horse around. If he chased her, she was certain she could get back to the meadow before he caught up. She prayed Alexi and Banoff would be there looking for her.

CHAPTER
TWENTY-THREE

Anne sank her heels into her mount's side, leaned forward, and urged the pony to turn back the way they'd come.

Her mount needed no further prodding and wheeled around. Anne did not look over her shoulder until she cleared the forest edge.

She nearly collided with Alexi and Banoff on the path from the keep.

"M'lady? Are ye all right?" Banoff said.

At the sight of her escorts, she took in a great gulp of air, nodding. Her heart pounded and she was breathing hard, but she was all right. He had not followed her.

She reined the pony in and around in a circle. "Something scared me, 'tis all." She gave a little laugh, still trying to catch her breath. "I should have waited for ye." She wasn't sure why, but she didn't want to say anything to Alexi and Banoff about the man in woods. "Please dinnae speak of this to m'lady

or m'lord.'' She gave Alexi a shy look. "I wouldnae
want them to know what a simpleton I am. Scared
of shadows.''

"I am sorry it took me so long in the village," Alexi
said. "I thought ye said ye would meet us in the
village, but then I wasnae certain."

"Are ye ready to go now, or do ye need a minute
to catch your breath?'' the older man, Banoff, questioned. "If ye want to dismount—"

"Nay." She waved him away. "I want to get home.
I just saw something in the shadows that was not
there. I truly am fine." She reined the pony back
onto the path, headed toward the north wood. In
truth, she was fine. She was no longer afraid, because
as surely as she knew there was something suspicious
about the man, she knew he was gone.

Judith lifted her skirts and darted into the maze,
laughing as Olave chased her.

"May I go, too?" Leah asked.

It had grown dark long ago, but the garden was
well lit by the moon and numerous torches. Elen and
Munro sat on a bench while Anne sat on another
across from them. Tor sat on the grass, plucking at
stems.

"Go," Elen shooed. "Because 'twill soon be time
for little girls to go to bed. Just dinnae leave the
garden."

"I willnae," Leah answered, darting into the maze.
"Olave! Judith! Wait!"

Anne reached for the mulled wine on a makeshift
table between the two benches. It had been a perfect
evening. Munro and Tor had returned, and though

they had found absolutely nothing, they were safe and glad to be back. They had all shared a light evening meal of fresh fish, broad beans, and stewed apples. Elen had suggested they retire to the garden because it was such a beautiful night.

Tor had started to make excuses to return to Rancoff. Anne had asked him to stay.

She knew she was confusing him with her behavior. She had seen it in his eyes when she had laid her hand on his arm. But she was mixed up herself. Munro was beginning to push her. He wanted to send word to her father, requesting the marriage before anyone realized she was pregnant. Anne wanted to be able to agree to marry Tor, but he had to meet her halfway, and so far he had not.

"What a beautiful night," Elen remarked lifting her arms above her head to stretch.

Munro smiled, but Anne could tell that he was preoccupied. After the tanner's murder and the fear rippling across the countryside, how could he not be preoccupied?

Tor tugged at blades of grass between his feet.

Anne could hear the girls' laughter and Olave's rumbling voice as they frolicked in the small maze Elen had started when she was pregnant with Leah. She called it Leah's and Judith's maze, much to the children's delight.

Anne glanced behind her. In the darkness, she could see the top of Olave's head as he made his way through the maze. In a few years, the hedges would be too tall for even him to see out.

"Ye would think there would be some sign of these men somewhere," Tor said, thinking out loud. "It is as if they are invisible. Ghosts."

Anne brushed her hair off her face and breathed

deeply of the sea air blowing in gently from the coast. "Ghosts nae leave burned barns and dead bodies behind."

All evening she had been thinking about the man in the woods. She knew he should not have been there. Of course, she wasn't supposed to be in the woods alone, either. So should she say something or keep silent? Chances were he was just a traveler passing through. A traveler with strange eyes. But what if there was some connection?

"I just keep thinking that someone knows something," Tor continued thoughtfully. "I keep thinking we have missed something. Some clue to who this is or why they would do this."

"But the acts are so random." Elen gestured. "They have nothing in common except that they take place on our land, and even that is not particularly odd."

Anne toyed with the hem of her sleeve. Something told her the man she'd seen today was somehow involved with the murderers. She didn't understand how she knew, but she did and she had to speak up.

"I . . . I saw something odd today," she said slowly. She wanted to choose her words carefully. She didn't want any of them to think she had been in danger. "Someone."

"Who?" Tor was immediately attentive.

"I was waiting for Alexi and Banoff at the edge of the north wood." Not a complete lie. "I saw a man."

Tor rose to his feet. "A man? A stranger, ye mean."

"He was on foot, though he had a mount nearby." She kept her voice calm, her tone even. "I am certain he was just passing through, but . . ."

"But?" Tor pressed.

Anne glanced up. Elen and Munro were both listening. Tor was staring at her . . . waiting.

"I—I cannae explain it. There was just something odd about him."

Munro leaned forward. "Ye have never seen him before?"

She shook her head. "But he was from here. I heard it in his speech."

"A poor man? A rich man?" Elen asked.

"Neither. Worn clothes, but nice boots." Anne tried to remember each detail. "He had coarse black hair and a black beard, but there was a lot of gray— as if someone had painted it with silver paint. And his eyes . . ."

"Aye?" Elen listened.

"I cannae explain it. It was not that he had the eyes of a killer marauder or anything like that. He just seemed . . . sad. A little lost."

"Did he speak to ye?" Tor asked.

"Only a moment, and then I rode back for Alexi and Banoff." She met Tor's gaze. "Nae tell me I should nae have been there alone. I know that. It was foolish and I willnae do it again."

Tor opened his mouth to speak, closed it, then started again. "At least ye have given us a good description. We will ask around. If he is seen again, we can question him."

Anne heard a peal of laughter and turned to see a flash of Judith's skirts as Olave lifted her high in the air. They were deep in the maze now and barely visible in the darkness.

"I suppose ye know your way through." Tor pointed toward the maze.

Anne lifted a brow. She was pleased that he had not shouted at her about riding alone today. "Is that an invitation to walk with ye?"

She rose, knowing it was. "Ye want to walk?" she asked Munro and Elen. " 'Tis the perfect night for it." She gazed up at the glimmering half-moon that hung low in the sky.

"Go," Elen said. "The old folks will sit here and finish off the wine."

Tor offered his hand and Anne hesitantly took it. They walked out of the circle of torchlight and into the maze. She could hear the girls laughing. Olave had to be chasing them again.

The close walls of the hedge were high enough so that Anne could not see above them, but Tor could. For a few moments, they walked in the darkness, the moon lighting the path.

Anne swung his hand with hers.

"I know that ye said ye would think on the matter, but Munro says the letter must be sent to your father."

She liked his gentle tone tonight.

"If I knew why ye did not want to take my hand in marriage, perhaps I could . . ." He let his sentence trail into silence.

The more time that passed, the more likely she knew it would be that her father would force her to marry Tor. Munro seemed pretty certain he could convince his friend the king that Tor was as good a match as any. He had even suggested Tor would come into some sort of inheritance.

Tor seemed to be taking his time tonight. Giving her time. "It would be better for me if my father could say ye were in agreement."

She halted on the path at a turn in the hedges. "I do not think I have ever heard ye say that."

"Say what?" The moonlight that cast over them shone off his hair.

"Call him your father." She stood very close to him, enjoying the feel of him.

She could tell that he wanted to look away, as men always did when faced with some form of emotion.

She knew he wanted to change the direction of the conversation.

She was impressed that he did not.

"He is a good man," he said.

She smiled up at him. "That he is. And a good father, I think, even to a grown man."

Tor exhaled slowly. "Nothing here is what I expected." He looked to her. "Ye are not what I expected."

"Whatever do ye mean?"

He smoothed her hair and caught a lock, twisting it between his fingers. "I would have expected that ye would have gone to Munro and told him to force me to marry ye when you found out ye carried my child."

"Is that nae what happened anyway?"

He lifted one shoulder. "Munro was angry with me, and he had a right to be. What I did was not right. But believe me when I say I would not marry ye if I did not want to, Anne."

"Are ye saying ye would marry me if there was no child?"

His expression immediately changed. "Ye did not—"

"Nay." She slid his hand over her breasts to her belly. "Still safe, and I am not even getting fat yet."

She laughed, amazed that she could speak so calmly of the child who slept inside her. She was an unwed woman who was going to have a child. She would be blemished forever for committing this sin upon God.

"Marry me," Tor said, "and we will discuss remaining here."

Again she had to smile. "Ye are as stubborn as I am," she accused.

"Let me kiss you," he whispered, leaning close to her.

She gazed up into his eyes. "That is it? The end of the conversation? Ye are nae going to try and bully me again? Perhaps bribe me with gifts or sweet words?"

He slipped his hands around her waist. "Would it do me any good?"

She laughed deep in her throat and leaned against the pressure of his hands at the small of her back. "I think not."

"Then on to kissing."

He leaned toward her and she leaned back. "And if I dinnae wish to kiss ye?"

"Aye, ye wish it."

As his lips met hers, she whispered against them. "Ye sound more like a Scot every day, Tor Henneson. Send the letter."

"Does that mean ye will marry me?"

"It means I am thinking about it. What I decided willnae matter anyway if my father doesnae give his consent."

His only answer was the pressure of his mouth, and Anne surrendered to it. She did not know where she was going on this journey with this man, but something told her it would be long. And in the end, a good one.

"Why did ye not bring her here?" Rosalyn lifted her head from the pillow Finley had made her from a blanket he had stolen off a wash line.

He closed his eyes, wishing he had said nothing to Rosalyn of seeing Anne de Bruc. He should have known she would not be happy. Nothing he did made her happy. "Why would I?"

The kitchen in the cellars of the abandoned castle was dark save for the glow of one candle, but they did not dare burn more for their supply was low again.

Rosalyn dropped her head to the pillow. They had just made love and her voice was still husky. He liked her like this, softer, not so shrill. "I'd have killed her had it been me."

"Why?"

She turned to face him, her eyes glimmering in the light of the single candle. "I nae know." She lifted one thin shoulder. "Why not?"

Finley stared at the smoke-stained rafters overhead, barely able to make them out in the darkness. Rosalyn confused him. He did what she asked because he loved her, but he did not necessarily like it as she did.

"She was very pretty," he said timidly.

She turned to look at him again, her voice sharply edged. "Ye wanted her? Then why didn't ye? Why didn't ye take her right there?"

He lifted his head from the mattress. "She is the king's daughter. We were here when he went to fetch her. Remember?"

"King's daughter," Rosalyn scoffed. "All women are the same between their thighs, ye fool."

He lowered his head to the bed again. Roslyn was a very jealous woman. He knew that. It was stupid of him to remark about how another woman looked. He had not even intended for her to see him, but she had taken him by surprise. He had seen her at a distance, but even that close, she looked much like Elen had the year they had returned to Dunblane. She'd been so beautiful, her eyes so full of life.

"Ye could have had her," Rosalyn spat. " 'Twould nae have bothered me."

"I dinnae want anyone but ye, Roslyn." He slid his

hand beneath the blanket to her hand. "Ye know I love ye."

"Aye, ye love me, all right. Love me because I pulled ye from that madmen's place."

"Nay, I always loved ye. Secretly, I always loved ye." It wasn't true, of course. His first love had been Elen, but since Rosalyn had come to him and led him out of Inverness, he had come to love her. He loved her more than anything on earth now. More than life, perhaps because she was so full of life and he was so dead inside.

Finley scratched at a scabbed-over sore on the back of his arm.

"Stop scratching." She slapped his hand. "You rock the mattress. And I told ye to stop scratching or it will fester and ye will drop dead with pus running from your eyes." She sat up in the bed and blew out the candle, leaving them in complete darkness. "Is that what ye want, to die?" She lay back in bed again. "God's bloody bowels. I nae know why ye do that to yourself." She slapped him again, but gentler this time. "Burning yourself, cutting yourself. I vow, ye belong with those drooling idiots."

Finley closed his eyes, close to sleep now. He paid no attention to Rosalyn's ranting. She talked constantly.

"Scratch my head," she ordered, snuggling against his naked body. "It itches."

He lifted his hand from beneath the bedcovers and scratched the top of her head, through the bristly hair. In the nunnery, she had been forced to keep her head shaved bald so as not to be afflicted by lice. The hair was growing in nicely now, as beautiful and blond as it had always been. She didn't like the bristly locks, but he did. He liked the feel of her hair beneath his fingertips, short and unwomanly like this. No one would want her like this. She was all his.

"Ah," Rosalyn moaned. "At least ye are good for something."

CHAPTER TWENTY-FOUR

"He wants what?" Tor laid one end of the floor-board in position while Munro maneuvered the other. It was the Ides of August and already time to think of harvesting for the coming winter. They were putting the floor down in a loft above a new shed. Grain would be stored below, hay here above.

"He wants to speak with you."

Tor wiped at a bead of sweat from above his upper lip. He had not expected word so soon. "The king comes here?"

Munro frowned. "Nae. He has business south of here. He asks that we meet . . . and dinnae speak of the meeting to Anne."

Tor stood, but not to his full height for fear of striking the rafters overhead. "He wants to meet secretly? So he can kill me?"

"I think not. If he wanted to kill ye, he would have sent an assassin, nae a messenger." Munro stood and reached for a skin of water that hung from a rafter. He took a long pull and tossed it to Tor.

Tor caught the water bag in midair.

"Besides, he doesnae know whether he wants to kill ye. Nae yet. Ye read my letter. I gave few details— only said ye were requesting Anne's hand in marriage and that Elen and I approved."

"I am nae a Scot. What if he does not like Norsemen?"

"Ye are half Scot." Munro opened his hand for the waterskin. "And what is there nae to like of a Viking?"

Tor laughed. His father was so accepting of him, of his differences in belief, in the way he did things. Anne was right; he was a good man. Tor would be a fool not to accept his embrace into the family and whatever that might entail. But Tor was thirty years and then some. He had grown up on the milk of distrust, and change did not come easily to him.

"So I go to meet the king alone?"

"We go. We can be there and back in two days time."

Tor walked toward the pile of wood they had pulled into the loft with pulleys. He grabbed another floor-board. "Ye think it is safe to go? To leave the women here?"

"We will double the guards on both walls, and the women will remain inside the keep until we return."

"That will certainly please all four of them." Tor swung the board around so that Munro could catch his end.

"I do not care. In matters such as this I will be obeyed, and they all know it."

What he said was true. When Tor had first come, he had thought his father weak, and Elen controlling. He had thought that his father was entirely too easily persuaded by her womanly wiles. But he had discovered that Munro let Elen have her way in matters he did not care about. When something was important to him, it was done his way and Elen agreed without complaint. She seemed to know where Munro's line was drawn in the turf.

"What will we tell them?" Tor carefully lowered his end of the board into place. "Anne will be hurt if she knows her father is so near and doesnae come. If she knows that we speak face too face." Hurt? She would be insanely furious, but he saw no reason to bring that up now.

"I dinnae understand Robert's reasoning, but I have to respect it." Munro dropped his end of the board into place. "I'll tell Anne that we received word of suspicious characters to the south of here. Elen must, of course, know the truth."

Tor nodded. He was fascinated by the honesty between Munro and his wife. In the home he had grown up in, his mother and stepfather had never been more honest with each other than they were forced to be. He thought about what Munro had said in the first days he had come. He had said he never received word from Henne that he had a son.

Yet, when Tor was a boy, Henne had silenced his requests to go to his father, telling him that Munro Forrest never replied. Henne had lied to Tor's stepfather. Could she have lied to him?"

Tor walked to the lumber pile again. Sweat ran down his back and soaked the waistband of his baggy Norse-style trousers. He did not like the idea that his mother had lied to him. He did not want to alter the image he held in his mind of her. But he did not want to be an idiot, either. This man was about to go before the King of Scotland to speak for him, to ask that Tor be granted his daughter's hand in marriage. When had Henne ever done anything so brave?

Tor brought another board. "Ye never knew about me, did ye?" he asked his father across the wide expanse of the loft. "Ye never got a message about me."

Munro caught the end of the board with surprise. "Nay. I told ye I never heard from her. What makes ye ask me that now?"

He shook his head, noncommittal.

Munro seemed to know not to push him. "I think we should go day after next. Robert willnae be there long, and then he returns to the borders."

Tor nodded and went for another floorboard. He could not meet his father's eyes because his own were watering.

It had to be the sawdust in the air.

"Do ye think the murderers have moved south?" Anne asked. She was pinning one side of Judith's new dress while Elen pinned the other. They did not catch the girls often to fit them for clothes, so when they did, the task had to be completed quickly.

Elen was making both girls new gowns, though for what, she had not said. Anne guessed it was for her impending wedding, though they had not yet heard from the king, and Anne had not actually agreed to marry Tor. Elen was clever. She had not brought the subject up in days; she was simply making preparations as if there might be a wedding.

"I couldnae wish such a monster upon others, but," Elen said, her mouth full of pins, "I cannae say I would nae be happy to hear they were gone."

"Well, maybe the journey was successful. I imagine they will be home soon, do ye nae think?" Judith squirmed and Anne caught her hand, stilling her. "Just a few more minutes, bobbin, and then ye can go."

"Perhaps they will be here soon, but I willnae worry if they are not. Ye never know what could be keeping them, weather, a run-in with old friends from the fight days . . ."

"A keg of ale," Anne offered.

The two women laughed.

"Tor and Munro are getting on well," Anne ventured. "Do ye nae think?"

"Are we done yet?" Judith moaned. "I have to piss."

Elen glanced up at her daughter. "Judith Mary! Such word from a young lady."

"Papa says it." The little girl thrust out her lower lip. "And I do have to piss."

Elen sighed, reaching for her daughter's hand to help her off the wooden crate she stood on. "Run to the garderobe and right back." She gave her a swat on her bottom as the little girl took off. "And dinnae tear the dress; 'tis not even finished yet."

With Judith gone, Elen sank onto the stool her daughter had been standing on. "I'm sorry, what were we saying?"

Anne laughed as she perched on the edge of the bed Elen and Munro shared. Anne liked this room; she liked the coziness and the sense of history here. Elen had been born in the room, as had her daughters. Anne wondered if she would ever have her own history. If she did, would it be with Tor?

"Munro and Tor. I think they are getting on well, nay?"

Elen smiled, pushing up her sleeves. It was a warm day and a breeze blew through the open windows, carrying the sounds of the keep below and the scent of the tide.

"I think Munro has loved him since the day he set foot on Rancoff land. Tor is coming around."

"Do ye think he would honestly return to his homeland now?" Anne questioned.

"Ye mean marry ye and then take ye from us?" Anne nodded.

"Well, who is to say what a mon will do, but I think he is beginning to consider this his home. His brothers are certainly content here. I heard Finn went to Aberdeen earlier in the week to woo some lass he met at the Beltane celebration."

Anne met Elen's gaze.

"Ye know," Elen said, "I nae think your father or Munro will force ye to wed Tor. But ye must marry someone, sweet. Why nae take the evil ye know, rather than the one ye do not?"

Anne shifted her gaze to the open window. She could hear sheep bleating. "I—I cannae explain these feelings. 'Tis as if I would rather nae have him at all than nae have him the way I want."

"I nae understand."

Anne rubbed her temple. "He told me he would marry. Ordered me to marry him, but he didnae ask. There has been no declaration of love save one murmur that I fear was merely . . ." She felt her cheeks grow warm. "In the passion of the moment."

Elen chuckled.

"What?" Anna questioned. "Is that too much to ask?"

"Nay, nay, of course not." Elen got up to take both of Anne's hands in hers. " 'Tis just that men are different in so many ways. I'll wager if I asked him, he would tell me he has asked ye repeatedly to marry him. And as for love . . ." She shrugged. "I cannae say what is in the mon's heart, but I can say that those words are easier spoken by some than others. I think he loves ye, Anne. And I think ye love him."

Anne frowned. "So I should just give in."

Elen squeezed Anne's hand. "Of course nae. But ye may have to compromise. Ye may have to tell him what ye want. What ye need. Then see what he can offer. Ye cannae expect him to read your mind." She released her hands and rose.

"Tor came here a bitter, angry young mon, and I think he has matured greatly." Elen walked to the window and glanced over her shoulder at Anne. "But I also think he has much to learn. Sometimes men and women have to learn how to love, be loved, and how to tell those they love how they feel."

Anne walked to the sill and leaned on it beside Elen. "I nae know," she sighed. "I just nae know. I dinnae want to settle for less than I want. Less than I think I deserve."

Elen hugged her. "I understand your concerns, but we must also keep in mind the morals we must live by and the world we live in. The fact is that ye are carrying a child and ye must wed. So where do ye think your better chances lie, with a mon ye nae know, or with the mon who made love to ye and gave ye that babe?"

Judith bounded into the room with Leah behind her. Leah spoke for the two of them. "Olave is here. He says he must help look for one of the yearling ponies that broke free, but then he will be back and he will play with us. Can we play with Olave?"

Anne rested her cheek on Elen's shoulder and gave her a quick hug. "Thank ye," she whispered.

Elen hugged her back and then released her. "Perhaps some playtime might be found." She grasped Judith's hand and helped her up onto the stool. "It depends entirely on how much wiggling we have and how long it takes us to finish these alterations.''

"No wiggling,'' Leah said.

"No wiggling,'' Judith answered, beaming.

Anne laughed and wondered for the very first time if the babe she carried was a boy or a girl.

"He never came back?'' Elen asked her bailiff, Donald. Donald was getting on in years. Her father would be his age if he were still alive. But Donald was loyal to the bone, and Elen had treasured his companionship these years.

Donald stood almost at attention before Elen. Ponies nickered, and a confused rooster crowed. The sun was setting. Olave had left hours ago.

"Basil said he went out when that yearling broke free,'' Donald explained. "Northwest he went.''

Elen nodded "I know. The girls spoke with him early this afternoon. They were expecting him.''

Donald's wrinkled brow creased like an old hound's. "He should have been back long ago, m'lady. I got a bad feeling on this one.''

Anne crossed the yard and threw a small rectangle of Burnard plaid over Elen's shoulders. "No sign of him?''

Elen shook her head. "Basil and John are still out looking. Banoff went to find Finn at Rancoff.''

The sound of shouting broke the still, evening air.

"What is it?'' Elen called up to her clansmen on the wall.

"Riders,'' someone barked. "Coming fast.''

"Lift the bridge,'' she cried upward.

"Nay. Looks to be the Norseman Finn and Banoff. Finn carries something in front of him wrapped in a plaid." The man leaned over the wall, and Elen squinted in the darkness.

"What is it?" Elen called up.

The man crossed himself. "God save us. Looks to be another body."

Elen and Anne ran across the drawbridge to meet Finn and Banoff in the meadow.

Finn reined in his horse, a body wrapped in plaid balanced across the front of his mount. There was something dark and wet on the plaid. Tears streamed down Finn's face. "Help me," he called to the women. "Please help us. They . . . they've skinned him."

Elen reached the horse first. "Stand back, Anne."

Anne halted, staring at the boots that dangled at the far side of Finn's mount. She had seen those this morning. Different from Highland boots. Boots that came nearly to the knee and were made of thick leather with hair still left on them.

Olave's boots.

CHAPTER
TWENTY-FIVE

Anne watched, stricken, as Elen gently lifted the blanket, reached beneath it, and then withdrew her hand. She looked up at Finn.

Finn shook his head, his face contorted in emotion. *"Ingen,"* he whispered.

Anne met Elen's gaze. She did not have to ask. Olave was dead.

Anne walked to the other side of the mount and offered her hand to Finn. Tears ran down the man's face. He did not seem to understand what she wanted.

"Come down and walk with me over the draw-bridge," Anne murmured, still holding her hand out to him.

He shook his head and laid a hand on his brother's still body. "I have to take care of Olave," he said. "Have to—"

" 'Tis all right." Elen rested a hand on Finn's knee. "Ye can leave him to me. I'll take good care of him. I swear that I will."

Finn's gaze shifted from the older woman to the younger. "I have to take care of Olave," he repeated.

Anne took his hand in hers, fighting back her tears. "Come with me," she said firmly. "Let Elen take care of him."

Other men had joined them from the keep. They stood back, waiting for their mistress to give them orders.

"Help Finn down," she said. "Be careful." She laid one arm protectively over Olave's body so it would not shift as Finn dismounted.

Woodenly, he eased out of the saddle. As his feet hit the ground, he swayed, and Anne grabbed his arm. " 'Tis all right," she whispered as if he were one of the girls.

Slowly she led him up the crest of the hill to the drawbridge and over it into the bailey. From there, she took him to the great hall because she did not know what else to do.

As Anne led Finn inside, she glanced back over her shoulder at Elen, who had aided her men in leading Finn's mount into the bailey. She was holding one arm over Olave's body, like a mother hen protecting a chick.

Elen nodded to Anne. Slipping one arm around Finn's waist, she took him into the hall and called for strong drink. A half hour passed before other men joined them and Anne felt that she could go to Elen.

As Elen's and Munro's clansmen gathered around the Norse brother, murmuring words of comfort and sorrow, Anne slipped away. She crossed the bailey to the tower house and went inside. On the first floor there was a small chamber no longer used regularly. Elen had already seen to it that candlelight was brought in. This room had been the castle's great hall a long time ago, before its many additions and improvements.

Olave's naked body lay on the table in the center of the room. When Anne entered the shadowed chamber, Elen was alone with him. She had a wash rag in her hand.

Elen turned to her. "Ye didnae have to come in."

"I want to help."

" 'Tis a terrible sight," Elen said. "In your condition—"

"I want to help," Anne repeated, pushing up the sleeves of her linen shirt. "I have to, for Tor."

Without saying a word, Elen handed her a clean cloth. Both women dipped the rags into the water, which was already beginning to turn brown. Anne stood on one side of the old table, Elen on the other.

Anne slowly drew the rag over Olave's leg. His skin was a gray color, the blond hair of his legs standing out in contrast. As she worked her way upward, his skin became darker with bloodstains.

The two women worked in silence. Even when Anne came to his chest and saw what the murderer had done to him, she made no sound.

Tears trickled down her face as she thought of Olave running in the maze with Leah and Judith. Blowing seed flowers in the meadow with them. Carrying one girl on each shoulder into the great hall. She thought of the way he'd always blushed when she had spoken to him.

Elen cried as quietly as Anne.

When they'd finished cleaning his defiled body, they drew first a clean linen cloth over him and then one of Rancoff plaid. Elen was just raising the light sheet over Olave's face when someone entered the room.

It was Elen's clansman John. "M'lord has returned."

"He and Tor are here?"

John nodded.

"No one has told him?"

John shook his head.

Anne knew he was thinking that whoever was the bearer of the bad news risked life and limb. Tor was well known for the ease with which he lost his temper, even these past few weeks when he seemed to be much more easygoing.

Elen turned to Anne. "Go up to your chamber. Meggy took the girls to the kitchen for their supper, so ye need not worry over them. See if ye can lie down a while."

"I can—"

Elen cut Anne off before she could speak, grasping her arm. "Go above stairs. I will tell him."

Anne did as she was told. As she climbed the steps, she heard Elen go to the door. She heard Elen's voice and the rumble of male voices, though she could not make out what was said from the distance of the second story.

Then she heard a cry that ripped her heart.

Anne sank to her knees on the stair landing, grasping her head and lowering her forehead to her knees. She heard a door crash open and she knew Tor had entered the old hall. It slammed shut.

Elen's and Munro's voices floated upward as they talked in privacy in the front hall down below.

For a long time, Anne sat there, tears soaking her skirt. She thought of Olave. Of Tor and how much he had loved his brother. How well he had cared for him. How he had never held Olave responsible for any of his shortcomings. Tor was a good man.

A long time passed. The stairwell grew dark. Few sounds drifted upward.

Anne wiped her eyes and went down the steps again. Elen and Munro were on the bottom step. They were sitting quietly beside each other; Munro had his arm around his wife's shoulders.

"How is he?" Anne asked, descending the last flight of steps.

Elen and Munro rose. "He has not come out," Elen said.

Anne glanced at the closed door. "Go get Munro something to eat. I will see to Tor."

The husband and wife exchanged glances and then Elen nodded. "Ye know where to find us if ye need us."

Anne waited until they were gone and went to the closed door leading into the old hall. She took a deep breath and then pushed it open.

Tor sat on a small bench beside the table, his back to her. He held Olave's hand in his. "Leave me," he grunted.

She closed the door behind her.

"Did ye hear—" Tor turned on her and then halted in midsentence when he realized who it was. He turned back toward Olave's body.

Anne didn't know what to say, how to comfort him. She only knew that she wanted to.

She grasped a stool and dragged it over beside him and sat down. She thought of a dozen things to say, and almost started to speak more than once, but in the end, she knew that all she needed to do was sit beside Tor, letting him know that he was not alone.

Olave was buried the following day in Dunblane's kirkyard. Munro had offered to bury him at Rancoff.

Though the church was long gone, there was still a burial ground. But Tor insisted Dunblane was where Olave would want to rest. Near the little girls he had loved so much. So in the end, he was buried among Elen's family members.

Tor had been so quiet since coming home the evening before and finding his brother dead, that Anne had become concerned. She was sitting down to pick at her meal when Tor came up behind her. "I want to talk to ye," he said. "I ride to Rancoff now, but this evening, will ye meet me in the garden?"

His face was so serious, so sad, that Anne wanted to take it between her palms and kiss away his pain—take some of it upon herself just to lighten his burden.

She nodded.

Tor spoke briefly to his father, and then he and Finn took their leave of the hall.

Anne was waiting for Tor in the garden at sunset. She did not light a torch, but preferred to sit in the darkness and listen to the night sounds. She heard insect song and the occasional flutter of bird wings. She heard the neighing of horses in the distant stable and caught bits of various conversations on the wind. It was warm tonight, and she had pushed up her sleeves and loosened the ties of her bodice to give herself some air.

When Tor entered the garden by way of the kitchen, she knew by his slick, damp appearance that he had bathed and washed his hair. He had shaved and changed into a Scottish plaid. "Thank ye for meeting me," he said, sounding more formal than she had ever heard him. His voice sounded strange in her ears: his Nordic accent, the hint of a Scottish brogue he had picked up. He was an enigma, this man. This father of her baby.

Tor sat on the bench beside her. "I want to thank ye for caring for Olave. Finn told me what ye did."

She wanted to protest, but she knew he needed to speak, so she let him.

"It means a great deal to me that ye and Elen—" He halted when emotion filled his voice, waited, and then started again. "He cared for ye both."

She smiled, slipping her hand over his that gripped his knee. "I loved him."

"And that brings me to why I have come." He gazed into her eyes, and she felt as if she were drowning in the depths of their sadness. "This is hard for me to say," he murmured.

She listened.

"Losing Olave made me realize . . ." He halted, took a breath, and started again. "I have spent so much of my life thinking about what I did not have, that I did not realize what I did have. Anne, I would like to ask ye if ye will marry me. Not because ye are with child, not because it is the right thing to do, but because . . . I need ye and . . . I think ye need me. Let me take ye for my wife. Let me care for ye." He tightened his hands into fists. "I need to take care of ye."

He was asking her at last. Not telling her, asking her. Anne knew she was going to say yes, but she let him go on.

"If ye will marry me, I vow to ye we will remain near to this place so that ye do not have to leave your girls and Elen. I do not yet know how I will care for ye and the baby, but I will figure it out." He took her hand in his. "Please tell me that ye will marry me. That ye will carry my child, and the babe will be born in a wedding bed."

Anne's lower lip trembled, and for a moment she feared she would begin to cry. This was what she wanted. Just for him to *ask*.

He had made no speech of love, but that was all right. Anne had taken to heart all Elen had said. Love could grow between a man and a wife. And even if it didn't, she knew that she and Tor liked each other, respected each other. This was the right thing to do. "We will still have to wait for permission from my father."

"I have it." He placed a hand on a small bag tied on his belt.

Her eyes widened in surprise. "He wrote to ye? To Munro?"

Tor gazed down at his lap, then up at her. "Munro and I went to see him. That was where we had gone when Olave . . ." He did not need to finish his sentence.

Anne tightened her grip on Tor's hand. "I dinnae understand. Ye saw my father? I thought he was on the borders. Munro said there has been fighting all summer."

"He came north; we rode south to meet him. He . . . he wanted to see me in the flesh before he gave his permission."

Anne pressed her lips together, trying not to be hurt. Being angry with her father was so much easier, less painful. The Scots were fighting the English on the borders. Her father was the king, for heaven's sake. Of course he did not have time to ride all the way to Dunblane to see his daughter and give his permission in person. Of course he could not summon her to meet him; it would take too long for her to prepare and then travel to meet him. It made perfect sense that Robert would meet with Tor and Munro.

If it made perfect sense, then why did it hurt so much?

Anne lifted her lashes. "What was he like?" she asked softly.

He offered a sad smile. He seemed to sense she was hurt. He understood. "Very kingly."

She chuckled.

"And I liked him."

That did not make her laugh. She wanted Tor to hate him the way she hated him. "But he gave his approval?"

Tor nodded. "I think he was surprised to see that I was not a Scot. Apparently, my father left out that minor detail." He took her hand in his and turned it to smooth her palm. "We talked briefly. They were already breaking camp by the time we arrived, so he didnae have long."

"So he just said aye and off he walked?"

Tor smoothed the pads of her fingertips. "He said he wanted ye to be happy. He said he would send a wedding gift of coin when he could."

She gave a snort of derision.

"Perhaps ye should nae be so hard on him." Tor looked down at his hands and then up at her again. "He asked me if I could make ye happy."

"And what did ye tell him?"

"That I hoped I could." Tor raised her hand to his mouth and kissed her knuckles one at a time.

"So I suppose that is it." She looked into his eyes, feeling a strange mixture of fear and anticipation. Her fate was sealed. She would be this man's wife. Go where he bade her to go. Do what he bade her to do. She only prayed her judgment had been good.

"That is it," Tor repeated. "So may I tell Munro and Elen ye have given your consent? I would like to marry immediately."

"No one will talk of such a hasty marriage?" she wondered aloud.

"I am on the path of a madman. I want to take you as my wife before I face the danger that could be ahead. 'Tis no different than a hasty marriage before a man goes off to war."

"I suppose 'tis true."

"I go back to Rancoff now. Finn waits for me in the bailey. We make plans to find our brother's killer." He rose from the bench. "A kiss, and I will be on my way."

Anne stood and rose up on her toes to kiss his cheek, relieved the decision had finally been made. Before she could press a chaste kiss to his cheek, Tor caught her chin with his fingertips and lowered his mouth to hers.

Nothing more needed to be said.

"What do ye think? Who could have done such a thing as that?" Elen murmured in the darkness. "Why Olave? He was so harmless. So . . ." Without the right words to express herself, she did not finish her sentence.

Munro lay still beside her, but she knew he was not yet asleep. " 'Tis as Tor said weeks ago. Obviously someone has something against me."

"Or me."

Munro slid his hand beneath the bedsheets until he found hers.

She turned to look at him in the darkness. "The question is, what kind of hatred would a man have to carry to do that to another human being?"

"I nae know. I have gone over each incident in my mind and there seems to be no connection. They all seem random, except that in each case 'tis our

property, our lives that are affected in some way."
He sighed. "At least one good thing has come of
this. No one suspects Tor now."

Elen stared at the ceiling. "True. I nae know how
anyone could have suspected him to begin with. If
he had come to wreak havoc on your life, he would
never have shown his face that day at your wall."

"I dinnae blame them. When things like this happen, people who are scared do not think logically."

Elen continued to stare up into the darkness. "I
have never seen such hatred in my life," she mused.
"Never witnessed—" She halted.

"What?"

She gave a little laugh, knowing that what had just
popped into her head was too ridiculous even to
voice. " 'Tis naught. I am tired and I am beginning
to lose what little sense I ever possessed."

"Tell me what ye were thinking."

"Rosalyn," she whispered.

"Rosalyn? But Rosalyn is safe in Edinburgh. We
send a stipend each year. The sisters guaranteed she
would be kept safely locked up the rest of her days."

"I know. I said 'twas foolish." Elen pulled her hand
from Munro's and rolled onto her side away from
him. "It is just that she is the only person I have ever
known who hated to the very core of her being. Hated
us."

"Dinnae worry, Elen. Someone would write to us
if she had somehow escaped," he assured her.

"Ye are right, of course. Ye know," she said. "Ye
know, I had nae thought of her in a very long time."

Munro slid over in the bed and laid his head on
her pillow as he slipped his arm around her waist.
"So wipe her from your mind now, else ye will be up
with nightmares."

Elen smiled sadly in the darkness as she snuggled against him. " 'Night, Munro.''

"God bless ye and keep ye,'' he answered sleepily. "Now go to sleep. Tomorrow will be a long day.''

CHAPTER
TWENTY-SIX

Anne leaned against the door of the largest bed-chamber in Rancoff's keep and took a deep breath. She didn't know how Elen had managed it, but in less than a fortnight from the time she had given her consent to marry Tor, she had put together a wedding. In two weeks, she had found a priest, min-strels, wedding guests, and enough food to feed her father's army. It had been a beautiful wedding, as beautiful as if Anne had been planning it for years.

"So, now we are married," she said aloud, still unable to believe it.

Tor stood at the window gazing out into the dark-ness. "Married," he repeated. "I have a wife."

The way he said it made her nervous. Was he already regretting his decision? "Are ye sorry?" she asked, still at the door. If he had changed his mind, she would just go. She didn't know where, but she would not stay with a man who did not want her on their wedding night.

He turned from the window, and to her relief, he was smiling.

"I am nae a mon who does what he doesnae wish to do, and ye know it." He walked toward her, still dressed in his wedding finery. He was wearing the Clan Forrest plaid and the old brooch he had held fast to all these years. Were it not for the yellow hair and Nordic blue eyes, he could have been a Highlander.

He took her breath away.

"I am only honored that ye were willing to take me for your husband. I know my faults are many, and I know that I will be difficult to live with at times. And until we catch who murdered my brother, I fear I will not make much of a husband."

She closed her eyes. "For tonight, Tor, just tonight could we pretend that Olave is asleep in his bed?" she whispered. "Asleep with his belly full, thinking of how many times he danced with Judith and Leah."

"I think I could pretend for just one night," he answered softly.

And I will pretend ye tell me ye love me a hundred times a day, she thought.

He clasped both of her hands in his and took his time in closing the distance between them.

"What are ye doing?" She watched him watch her.

"Drinking in your beauty."

Her nervous laughter bubbled up. This was a side of Tor she had not seen before. Her forever-practical Norseman a romantic? The thought intrigued her.

"I am sure there has never been a more beautiful bride than the woman who took my hand in church this day."

She could not stop smiling.

"A woman whose beauty is only surpassed by her wit and by her intelligence."

"A shameless woman, already three months gone with child."

Still holding her hands, he encircled her waist, pinning her arms behind her. "Three months gone with *my* child," he murmured.

Anne closed her eyes in anticipation of his lips, and was not disappointed. Though they had certainly kissed intimately before, this was somehow different. Tonight was the first night of a new life for them both, a life begun with more than a little uncertainty.

Still, there was something exciting about the thought of entering this new life with Tor.

He took his time kissing her, releasing her hands to stroke her. Standing against the door, he kissed her, teased her with his tongue until he took away her breath and every last sensible thought that she possessed. With every kiss, the reality of the world faded further until there was nothing left but the two of them and the shadows of the chamber.

Anne held fast to Tor's broad shoulders, feeling herself melt against him.

He tightened his arms around her. "Are ye all right?"

She gave a little laugh, feeling foolish. If he let her go right now, she would slump to the floor.

"My knees are weak."

"Do ye feel badly?" He lifted his head from where he had just pressed a kiss to the hollow of her throat. "Should I call for Elen?" His face was immediately etched with concern.

She laughed again, her face growing warm with a mixture of embarrassment and passion. "I am fine, only weak-kneed from my husband ravishing me."

He swept her into his arms, still not seeming to understand. "We do not have to do this now. We have our whole lives together. Maybe it would be better if we wait until after the child is—''

As he lowered her onto the great four-poster bed, she pressed her finger to his lips. "I am fine. The baby is fine. Elen says the best time in a woman's life to make love is when she is carrying a child, because she does not have to worry about becoming pregnant.'' Relaxing on a heap of goose-down pillows, Anne reached out to her husband. Now that she was here and they were wed, she was anxious to claim her wifely rights. Apparently more anxious than he.

"Come here," she coaxed.

He leaned toward her, still seeming unsure.

Made bold by the ceremony in the kirk a few hours before, she slipped a hand around his neck and pulled him to her. He resisted for only a moment and then brought his mouth to hers.

Anne moaned as Tor slid onto the bed, pressing her deeper into the feather tick. When he began to pull at the ribbons of her bodice, she giggled. "Let me up, oaf," she teased, her voice husky. "And let me at least take my slippers off.''

He sat up. "Let me.''

Anne wanted to argue. She did not know if she felt comfortable having him remove her shoes and stockings. It seemed so . . . so unromantic, so ordinary. But as his gaze locked with hers, his eyes filled with desire for her, and the way she looked at matters seemed to shift.

He drank in her gaze as he sat up and pushed up her skirts. Taking his time, never shifting his gaze, he removed one shoe and then the other and dropped them to the floor. A shiver of anticipation ran up her spine as he clasped one ankle, pulled her foot to his chest, and reached up to untie the ribbons of her stocking at her calf.

His touch was gentle. It seemed innocent enough, yet her body's reaction shocked her. Every touch of his fingertips sent a tiny rivulet of pleasure through her. By the time he had peeled off the second green stocking, her pulse had quickened and she could feel a warmth in the pit of her stomach that was quickly radiating outward.

"Tor . . ." She could barely keep her eyelids open as he stretched out over her again.

Anne fumbled with the laces of her bodice. She did not know the proper etiquette of loving. She did not know what she was supposed to do and what she was supposed to let him do. She only knew that she had to free herself from the constraints of her clothing. She only knew that she had to feel her naked body against his. She needed that as dearly as she needed the air to breathe.

Tor covered her face, her neck, her chest with kisses.

She yanked at the ribbon of her bodice and threw it aside as he pulled open the gown and lowered his face between her breasts.

Even through the fine, thin linen of her shift, she could feel the heat of his mouth and the wetness of his tongue. She moaned as he licked one nipple through the fabric.

He tugged at the ribbon that gathered her shift at the neckline. When it knotted, he mumbled something in Norwegian and yanked it as she had the ribbon of her bodice.

Anne laughed as the delicate white ribbon snapped.

"I did not mean to—"

"There are more ribbons," she hushed. "Kiss me."

Her breasts free of the confines of linen, he cupped one breast with his hand and lowered his mouth to her nipple as Anne threaded her fingers through his long, thick blond hair, guiding him.

He suckled one nipple, and she closed her eyes, reveling in the tug of his mouth and the feel of his rough cheek on her tender breast. He had shaved this morning, but that had been so long ago that his skin was no longer smooth. Instead of causing discomfort, it increased sensation.

"Anne . . ." He was speaking in English and then Norwegian. Muttering sweet words that she could barely take in.

He slid a hand up her bare calf to her inner thigh. She moved instinctively toward him. She knew he must think her a wanton, a hussy, a woman without morals, but she could not help herself. She wanted to feel his touch. Wanted to feel it *there.*

At last, his warm fingertips met with the place between her thighs and she cried aloud with pleasure.

He was still kissing her, teasing her breasts with his tongue, nibbling with his teeth.

Anne panted and made sounds a lady certainly should not be making, but she couldn't help herself.

She tugged at the lengths of Forrest plaid wrapped around him, wanting to feel his bare skin against hers. He helped her push away the fabric, helped her pull his shirt over his head.

He had managed to get her arms out of her gown, so that all of the fabric bunched around her waist. He grabbed the dress and tugged. "Lift," he whispered.

She opened her eyes to take in his handsome face. Her husband—this magnificent man was her husband. She could not believe her luck in marrying a man not only pleasing to look at but pleasing to her heart as well.

At last, Tor threw off her gown and his clothes, and they were naked on the sheets.

"Please," Anne whispered and held out her arms to him. She knew what she wanted, what she must have.

Tor stretched over her again and brushed her damp hair out of her eyes as he stared down at her, half smiling, his blue eyes eloquent with desire for her. She could not wait another moment. Feeling the hardness of him against her bare leg, she arched up to meet him. He took her in one long thrust and she cried out, sighing in relief.

Anne had not meant to hurry. She wanted these moments to last as long as she could possibly make them, but when he slipped inside her, she could not control herself. The rhythm of his lovemaking overcame her and she moved beneath him, faster, closer to the edge of the precipice.

Tor also seemed to be trying to make the moment last, but when she raised her hips so that he could thrust deeper, he, too, lost control. Suddenly they were both breathing, moving as one, no longer able to hold back.

Anne thought they cried out simultaneously, she wasn't sure. Her world burst around her in heat and light and oceans of pleasure. She was surrounded, engulfed, overwhelmed by the smell and heat and feel of him. All she could do was hang onto him and call out his name.

Tor stilled, remaining where he was, buried inside her, cradling her in his arms.

Little tremors of pleasure rippled over her and she sighed, feeling as if she had sunk deeper into the bed.

Tor kissed her forehead, supporting himself on his arms so that he was not too heavy on her. "I think I will like this," he said, his voice still husky.

"This?" She laughed, feeling silly. Filled with joy.

"Aye, this." He kissed one of her eyelids and then the other. "But what I meant was being married to you," he whispered, his voice almost trembling. "No one has ever made me feel like this."

"How?"

"Safe."

"How I do love a wedding," Elen said wistfully. Anne and Tor had retired to Rancoff, and though there were still well-wishers drinking and dancing, pipers piping, the evening was almost at an end. Elen and Munro sat side by side on a bench and leaned against the wall of Dunblane's hall. "I think this is for the best."

Munro lifted one brow. "God bless me, I hope so. I felt as if I was laying my stones on the table when I went to Robert." He chuckled. "Ye should have seen the look on his face when the big brute walked in, tall as a garrison wall and mane of blond hair."

Elen slipped her arm through Munro's and pressed her cheek to his arm. " 'Twas the right thing to do. Did ye see them? They may nae realize it yet, but they are in love."

"Or at least in lust."

Elen drew back her fist and punched him playfully.

"Ouch, that hurt, wife!"

"Where is the romance in ye, Munro? Where is the man I married who sent me poetic notes and brought me gifts tied in rich cloth?"

He eyed her, tipping his horn cup. "Romance is for youngsters, and ye and I are long beyond those years."

Elen frowned. Realizing this conversation was headed for a stone wall, she changed the subject. "It was good to see Tor happy today. I know how deeply he cared for Olave. He was so good to him." She sighed, leaning against Munro again. "I just hope we catch them soon. I cannae bear the thought of losing someone else."

He kissed the top of her head. "We will catch him and string him up. I promise."

"And then?" she asked.

"Then," he continued, "Anne will have the baby, and ye and I will be grandparents."

She groaned at the thought of it. "I'm too young to be a grandmother." She paused. "And then what? I understand Tor and Anne will remain at Rancoff until the babe is born, but what then, husband?"

He did not answer, but went on watching the two couples dance. Finn had a young woman on each arm.

"Ye need to think of Tor's inheritance, Munro," she said gently. "If ye wanted him to prove himself worthy, ye know he has done it and then some. If ye want sacrifice, Olave's blood is more than enough." She tried not to become impatient. "I want them to stay here, Munro, but ye must give him reason to stay."

"I am thinking on the matter."

Elen groaned again. "God above. Ye know I am right. Ye know he deserves a healthy portion of what ye have, and ye know we have more than enough to give away. I swear by all that is holy, ye are as stubborn as Tor can be. Ye deserve each other," she said, rising from the bench. "Now come with me. 'Tis time for those of us who will be grandparents to be abed." She offered her hand and he took it. Arm in arm they left the hall.

* * *

"A damned wedding, that's what it was," Rosalyn grumbled as she threw herself onto the lumpy bed in the dingy kitchen. "I hate weddings."

Finley grabbed a bent iron and stoked the coals on the hearth. When they had seen all of the travelers headed for Dunblane, he had not wanted to go see what was about there. He had wanted to hide, but Rosalyn had made him go. He was glad to finally be back in the relative safety of their hiding place. "I cannae believe the king would allow his daughter to marry Munro's bastard," he said haltingly.

"Bastard for a bastard. They deserve each other," she spit.

He glanced over his shoulder. "Do ye think perhaps it's time we move on? Ye see the guards, the patrols. 'Tis only a matter of time before they find us, my love."

"They are too stupid to find us." She grabbed one muddy slipper, pulled it off her foot, and threw it. "How many times have they passed this razed castle and still they havenae found us?"

Finley set the iron aside and rose. "I have been careful with the fire. No smoke during the day. And the entrance is well blocked from view." He took a deep breath. "But Rose, I still dinnae understand why we came here at all. If we can start a new life elsewhere, we should—"

"Shut up," Rosalyn ground out. "Shut up before I shut ye up. I came here because I want what is rightfully mine. That is why they hauled me off to the nunnery." She grabbed the other slipper from her foot and threw it at him. "Because when my husband died, they didnae want me to get a single coin. Naught from my father, naught from my dead husband."

"I thought Cerdic had spent all of his inheritance. Lost his lands north of here gambling."

Rosalyn sat up in bed, her eyes narrowing. "Did I ask ye to speak? Did I?"

He shook his head.

Finley was a worm. But even worms could be useful at times. "Now listen to me; I have a plan. I may nae get a seat at the head table ever again, but at least there is coin to be had."

Finley dug at a wound on his forearm.

"Are ye listening to me?"

His head snapped up. "I . . . I am listening."

"I was thinking." She undressed as she spoke. "If we are to make our journey to England we will need coin and much of it." She glanced over her shoulder, pleased with herself. "And who has coin, if nae good King Robert?"

CHAPTER TWENTY-SEVEN

Anne woke the next morning in Rancoff's master bedchamber to find Tor already dressed. She yawned and stretched in the big bed and smiled at him. Last night seemed a hazy dream now, a delicious dream of lovemaking and whispered words. It had been a night she would always remember.

"Where are ye going?"

He glanced up as he shoved his foot into his boot, then walked to her and sat on the edge of the bed. He took her hand in his and kissed her knuckles. "We ride. This murderer who killed my brother must be found," he said bitterly.

So soon the world intruded again.

She rubbed the sleep from her eyes. The coverlet slipped, reminding her that she was completely naked. She grabbed the corner of the sheet to cover her bare breasts, but he gently tugged it from her hand.

"Let me look at ye."

"I wish ye didnae have to go today." She smiled sadly. "But I understand."

For her wedding night, she had been able to pretend Olave was not dead, but with the coming of dawn, the horror of it all came flooding back again.

"I wish I didnae have to go, either."

Tor pushed her hair back from her face, and she wished there was something she could do to ease his pain. Anything. But it seemed that the only thing she could do was be here for him.

"I know, I must be a mess," she said, smiling.

"To me," he whispered, "ye are beautiful. Now give me a kiss and I will be off."

Without reserve, she threw her arms around his shoulders and hugged him tightly. "Swear to me ye will be careful," she whispered.

"I will be careful."

He kissed her and then he was gone.

A fortnight later, Anne stood at Rancoff's gatehouse to see her new husband off yet again. Though it was still only September, it had become cold the past few nights; frost dimpled the dying grass beyond the drawbridge.

As the days since the wedding passed, Anne and Tor had slowly settled into a routine at Rancoff castle that suited them both. In the mornings, Anne saw Tor off either to fulfill duties given to him by his father, or to ride in search of the killer who had still not been found. Because of the coming winter and the duty Munro had for his people, he and Tor had decided that one of them would ride with a search party each day. The other would remain home to oversee the crops and all the hundreds of other tasks that had to be seen to before the snow began to fall.

Every day, Tor or his father and a group of men rode the perimeters of Munro and Elen's lands in search of the murderer. And with each passing day, they became angrier. More frustrated.

Today was a day Tor would ride.

Anne pulled a plaid tightly around her shoulders. The wind whipped at her hair and she pushed it out of her mouth. "Be careful today," she told Tor quietly so the other men would not hear her.

She worried every time he rode out of the keep, but she knew she had to keep those worries to herself. She did not want Tor to know just how concerned she was for his safety for fear he would worry about her. If he was distracted, he might not see danger coming until it was too late.

"I will be careful." Despite the import of today's task, he gave her a lazy smile that was nearly identical to Munro's. "And today I will find him," he finished resolutely.

Anne didn't know if it was her imagination, but Tor seemed to have mellowed since the wedding. Despite his lingering grief for the loss of his brother, despite his burning need for justice that seemed to increase with every passing day, he seemed calmer. Though he still lost his temper on occasion, he did not seem as quick to do so. He was more patient not only with her, but also with those around him. Now that the crofters did not think Tor responsible for the crimes that had been committed against them, they were beginning to respect him. Tor would make a good lord of a keep; Anne was sure of it.

Although Anne and Tor remained at Rancoff, Munro had said nothing of an inheritance for his son, and Tor had not asked. When Anne brought the subject up, Tor said it was not his place to initiate the matter with his father. Munro would have to make the first move. In truth, Tor seemed completely disinterested in receiving anything from Munro but his company, and Munro appeared to feel the same. While it warmed her heart to see father and son forming such a strong bond, she couldn't lose sight of the practicalities. She was with child and her child would need a future, a birthright.

The two men drove her to distraction with their stubbornness until Elen convinced Anne that the best thing to do was to leave the matter to them and see what happened. Anne had little experience with trusting her fate to others, but she agreed to give the men she loved a chance.

Tor swung up and into his saddle. "And ye take care, my wife."

Anne couldn't resist a smile. She knew it was silly, childish, but she loved it when he called her that.

"Ye be careful. Do not work too long. No scrubbing on your knees, no lifting heavy objects—"

"No leaving the keep, even if winged dragons attack the walls, and," she lowered her voice, "and keep your bed warm for ye."

He broke into a broad grin. "Ye are shameless," he teased in a whisper.

"The way ye like your wives," she said.

"Exactly." He grabbed his reins and waved to the men who would be traveling with him today. "I will see ye by sunset."

Anne stepped back and waved.

Tor lifted his reins, and his mount headed for the drawbridge. Halfway there, he turned around and came back.

"What's the matter?" Anne asked. "Ye forget something?"

He dismounted coming right for her. "I did. A kiss."

She laughed, delighted with him. "Did ye nae already have your share of kisses this morning?" she teased, referring to their early-morning lovemaking. Anne was shocked by the things she was willing to do with this man in bed.

"There are never enough kisses," Tor said as he grabbed her around the waist and pressed his mouth to hers.

Anne hung onto him for dear life.

One of the men walking the wall above gave a hoot of approval.

Breathless, Anne pushed Tor away. He had still not spoken of love to her, but wasn't this love? Wasn't this more than just lust? "God keep ye," she murmured and crossed herself.

"God keep ye," he repeated.

Anne watched as Tor mounted and rode off over the drawbridge. This time he did not look back.

Still grinning, Anne walked back to the keep. She had a full day ahead working in the kitchen, though her thoughts would not be on the fish.

Shortly after noonday as Anne took a break from the boring work of wrapping and packing fish, Rob entered the kitchen.

"M'lady?"

Anne was drinking cool, fresh water from the well. "Aye?"

"A message from Dunblane." Anne rose from the bench, immediately concerned. "From Elen?"

"Nay. Actually from m'lady Leah."

"What is it? What is wrong?"

"She asks that ye come to tend her mother. A headache. She says 'tis worse than usual, and m'lord has gone for cattle to the south properties." He slid his gaze to the floor, his face pinkening.

Everyone in both keeps knew of the Lady Rancoff's

ailment. Anne knew it was not life threatening, but she also knew that because it was related to Elen's womanly bleeding cycle, it made the men uncomfortable.

"Of course I will come." Anne turned to one of the kitchen girls. "Finish the last barrel and then go on with the baking."

"Will ye be back soon, m'lady?" one bold girl asked. "Ye said to have supper ready for the master at sunset."

"I will be back at sunset, I swear it. I'll tell the lasses I cannae stay, but I will help them make their mother more comfortable. Surely, Munro willnae be gone long today. Then I will return here."

The maid nodded.

Anne turned to Rob. "Saddle two horses. Ye will escort me to Dunblane and then home."

Rob hesitated.

Anne rolled her eyes. "I know. He said I was to remain in the keep, but I willnae remain here with Elen sick." She opened her arms. "How could he have known she would fall sick today? Obviously, Munro nae knew or he wouldn't have gone for the cattle."

Rob lifted his gaze, still obviously unsure of what to do.

Anne brushed passed Rob. "Ye've your choice. Ride with me, or stay and I will go alone." She pushed through the door. "Because I am going."

Despite the chill in the air, it felt good to get out and ride. Anne had first been concerned about riding astride when her belly began to round out, but Elen assured her that as long as there was no bleeding, and she was always on a quiet horse, she could ride until she gave birth. After all, the blessed virgin had ridden nine months gone, Elen had pointed out.

Rob escorted Anne to Dunblane armed with a bow, a long-bladed sword, and a scowl as manly as any she had seen. All the way across the meadow, he argued with her to turn back. At the edge of the woods, she had sweetly given him the choice of shutting up or turning back alone. Now he sulked like any scolded man.

Anne didn't care. If Elen needed her, she had to go. Tor would be angry when he found out, but he would simply have to get over his anger. She had already made it plain to him that though they were married, he would not control her. He would not keep her locked up in the keep, and he would not prevent her from being with those she loved.

As they entered the woods, Anne noticed a change in temperature. It had been cool in the meadow, but with the sun shining on her face, she had been warm enough. Now she wished she had worn a heavier mantle.

Anne lifted her hood, thankful she had worn gloves.

"If ye are cold, we can go back," Rob offered.

She chuckled, leading the way because they had to travel single file through this part of the forest. "Nice try."

The black-haired man Anne had seen before appeared out of nowhere, almost as if by magic. Anne saw a flash of a dingy mantle, and then the flash of an arrow. As the scream left her mouth, she heard Rob cry out and fall from his horse.

Anne's next shout was one of anger as she tried to wrench her pony around to see Robert.

Someone rushed out of the underbrush and grabbed her arm. Anne struggled, trying to look back to see who was reaching for her. Losing her balance, she fell off the pony's back and hit the ground hard, her head striking something solid protruding from the ground. Pain exploded in her head and her hip, and then there was nothing but blackness.

"If ye killed her, this is a waste of time," Finley grumbled, coming to stand over Anne, who lay unconscious in the fallen leaves.

"She isnae dead," Rosalyn snapped. "Now throw her over the pony and let us go."

Finley glanced at the young man on the path. The arrow protruded from his chest, now outlined in red. "Leave him?" he asked.

Rosalyn did not even look at the son of the steward who had once served her. "Is he dead?"

"Aye." Finely didn't know if he was or not, but if he wasn't, he would be soon.

"Drag him into the woods. Maybe the crows will find him before anyone else does."

Rosalyn walked through the brush in search of her horse and left Finley to clean up . . . as always.

Tor hurried to Rancoff's stable to see to his mount, then went to the well and washed the dust from his face and his hands. Anne would be waiting for him.

It had been another fruitless day of riding in circles, finding nothing. Seeing nothing out of place. Tor was so frustrated that he wanted to punch something. Break something. He could not help thinking that he and his father were missing something somewhere. The murderer had to hiding out less than a day's ride from Rancoff and Dunblane, but where?

Tor had gone over this a hundred times in his head today, and still he had no better answer than when he left this morning. He needed to let it rest. Perhaps after a good night's sleep he would be able to think more clearly. A good night's sleep with Anne.

He smiled tiredly to himself as he crossed the torch-lit bailey. Perhaps he and Anne would eat in their chamber tonight. He liked it when they locked themselves up in their bedchamber, where he didn't have to share her with anyone else.

Tor was surprised by how well he liked being married. He and Anne still had their differences of opinion, but all in all, he thought they were well suited for each other. In time, he was confident she would come to love him as he loved her. He felt like the luckiest man on earth.

Tor entered the keep and went up to the great hall. Anne wasn't there. He checked their chamber. She wasn't there, either. He walked back down the winding steps all the way to the cellar kitchen.

"Have ye seen my wife?" he asked, sticking his head through the door. The kitchen smelled of roast fish and baking bread, and his stomach grumbled.

A curly-locked lass glanced at another, then at him. They both looked as if they would jump out of their skins at any moment. Tor didn't understand why everyone was afraid of him. Anne said it was because he was big and loud. He wasn't *that* big and loud.

"Where is she?" he repeated, fighting an ominous feeling in the pit of his stomach.

"Gone . . . gone to Dunblane, m'lord. Rob escorted her," she added quickly.

Tor was immediately annoyed. "When?" He had told her to stay put. She knew he wanted her safely within these walls when he was gone. Hadn't they just discussed that this morning?

"Sometime after midday, m'lord," the curly-haired one answered timidly. "She said she'd be home by nightfall."

"It's already after dark."

"Just a wee bit," the maid answered, obviously trying to protect Anne. "I'm sure she will be here any minute, m'lord."

Tor scowled. Once upon a time, he might have yelled at the chit. Instead, he turned back into the hall, letting the door swing shut behind him.

"Disobey me, will ye?" he muttered under his breath. "I think it is time we came to an understanding, wife." He shoved though the keep door, into the bailey, and hollered to the closest man. "A mount!" he shouted. "I ride to Dunblane."

CHAPTER
TWENTY-EIGHT

"What do ye mean, she isnae here?"

"Shhh," Munro said, pressing a finger to his lips. They stood in the doorway of Elen and Munro's bedchamber. Elen slept in the bed. "I am telling ye what I know. I just got home, too. There were lost cattle."

Munro brushed his graying hair off his forehead. "Anne isnae here. I asked Leah." He pointed to the staircase, where the little girl had just gone. "No one has seen Anne. Leah said they sent word Elen was feeling poorly, but Elen and the girls assumed she didnae come because ye were gone today."

"And no one thought it odd that no word came back from Anne?" Tor demanded loudly.

"Calm down." Munro reached out, but Tor pulled away. "Elen was sick and Leah is only seven years old. Ye cannae hold her responsible."

"She isnae there. Do ye understand?" he demanded frantically. "Something has happened to her. Something has happened to Anne!"

"Son . . ."

Tears filled Tor's eyes and he was mortified. "Anne, Anne," he mumbled, gripping the doorframe for support.

"Tor, ye must calm down." Munro took his son's hand and led him into his bedchamber.

Tor could barely see where he walked for his tears. He didn't know what was wrong with him. He didn't cry. He had never cried in his life.

Munro pushed Tor down into a chair.

"We will find her," Munro said. "I swear we will."

Tor lowered his face to his hands. "I told her to stay," he muttered. "Told her to stay safe. I should have known she would—"

"Tor, listen to me." Munro took Tor by both shoulders.

Tor lifted his gaze and wiped his eyes with his sleeve. "Ye must get yourself together, and we must go looking for her. Ye have to be strong for her. Do ye understand?"

Finally, his father's words penetrated Tor's thoughts. Munro was right, of course. He had to be strong for Anne. It was the only way he could save her from whatever terrible thing had kept her from making it here.

The memory of the burned man—of Olave—had been flashing through his mind without mercy. With a deep breath, he shoved those thoughts aside. "We—we have to find Rob. Rob escorted her," Tor said. "He is nowhere to be seen either. He never arrived here."

"We'll find Rob and we'll find Anne," Munro insisted. "But first we must gather our wits and make a plan."

Tor stood, feeling as if his emotions fell from his shoulders as his warrior's instinct took control. He felt better, stronger, even his embarrassment finding no place to roost.

"I . . . I am sorry," Tor said, feeling as if he needed to catch his breath. "I should not have—I—" The words caught in his throat. His heart felt as if it were twisting inside his chest.

"Ye love her; that is plain to see. Never apologize for that." Munro strode to a small table and reached for a belt to strap on his sword. "I understand what it is to love a woman more than ye love the sun. More than ye love . . ."

To Tor's surprise, Munro's own eyes filled with tears. He strode to the wall to yank his mantle off a peg, making no attempt to hide his emotions. "I know what it is to love a woman so much that it makes ye hurt." He brought a fist to his chest. "Hurt here. I love Elen that much," he said, gesturing toward his wife, who still lay on the bed in a draught-induced sleep.

Munro walked to Tor. "Now, if ye think ye are ready, go to the hall and call for men. We cannae spare many because our walls must be protected, but we will take some from here and some from Rancoff." He gripped Tor's shoulder. "We'll find her. Maybe she fell, lost her mount, and walks home. Perhaps she stopped in the village. There are a hundred possibilities beyond what ye are thinking."

Munro held Tor's gaze, and Tor was surprised to find that his father's steadiness gave him hope.

"Go," Munro ordered. "Let me see to Elen, and then we will ride."

Tor left the chamber as Munro walked to the bed. Elen rolled over as he sat down on the edge of the feather tick. He smoothed her cool brow.

Her eyelids fluttered and opened. "What is it? Did I hear voices?"

"Anne is missing," he said, knowing she would spot a lie in spite of her headache. He knew better than to insult her by glossing over the situation, yet still he tried. "But we will find her. Ye know our headstrong Anne. She is probably walking on the beach, or gone to a crofter's cottage to help someone who is ill."

Elen's eyes were only half-open. She smiled faintly. "I will help. Give me but a—"

"Shhh," Munro soothed. "Ye will help by remaining here and seeing to your head so that it is clear on the morrow. Ye rest and I will find her."

She nodded and closed her eyes.

Munro leaned over to kiss her brow, thinking she had gone back to sleep, but when he got up to go, she grabbed his hand.

"Munro . . ."

"Go to sleep."

"Nay." She opened her eyes again and he knew by the pained look on her lovely face that it took great effort. "Listen to me. I heard what ye said about me." To his surprise, tears gathered in the corners of her eyes.

Munro groaned internally. In truth, he was concerned about Anne. He needed to go. But he could not leave Elen when she was obviously distressed. "Tell me," he murmured, stroking her head.

"I have been foolish these last months. A shrew."

He almost laughed. "What are ye talking about?"

"I was jealous of Tor's and Anne's romance." She closed her eyes and opened them again. "Nay, not jealous, only envious. And . . . Finn. In truth, I liked his attention. I—"

"Elen. 'Tis the sleeping draught. Ye nae know what ye are saying."

She squeezed his hand. "I may be light-headed,

but I ken what I say. I was afraid we had lost what we had when we first met, but I know now that I was being foolish." She lifted her lashes. "Our love is different now, stronger."

Munro sighed, feeling a constriction in his throat. Heaven above, he loved her so much. He knew things between them had been rocky these past few months, but he hadn't known why. "I am sorry," he whispered, leaning to kiss her again. "I hear ye now, but I suppose I wasnae listening before. I just—"

She shook her head. "Ye need nae apologize to me. I . . . I heard snatches of your conversation with Tor just now. At first I thought I dreamed, but I heard what ye said to Tor . . ." She smiled sleepily, gazing into his eyes. "And what ye said is enough for me to carry for a lifetime. I love ye, Munro Forrest . . ."

He pressed his lips to hers, wondering what he had done to deserve such a wonderful woman. What he had done to deserve her love. "I love ye, Elen."

She squeezed his hand again and then released it. "Now go bring my Anne home 'afore I get out of bed and find her myself."

Munro left the chamber, knowing he would come back with Anne or die trying.

"What do ye mean ye have never laid eyes upon him?" Rosalyn demanded.

Anne sat on the floor in the far corner of the room, her hands tied behind her back. Her feet were out in front of her and tied at her ankles. She had lost one shoe. Her head hurt so badly that she could barely think. The dark room seemed to be spinning around her, objects coming in and out of focus. She heard the woman speak, but she sounded as if she was a long distance from Anne.

Her captors were the man she had met in the north woods and a madwoman. He called her Rosalyn. She called him Finley.

Anne had heard Elen and Munro's sad tale more than once. The idea seemed preposterous, and yet how many Rosalyns and Finleys could there be in the Highlands? This Finley had been Elen's steward before Anne had come to live with them, the steward who had betrayed them. And this woman who was interrogating her right now had to be Elen's sister. Anne had no idea how Rosalyn could have escaped the nunnery where she'd been kept, or how Finley had been released from the prison for the insane, but here they were.

"Did ye hear me?" Rosalyn shrieked.

Anne winced as Rosalyn kicked her leg.

Anne tried to focus on the woman's voice. Finally, the room had ceased to spin.

"If he is your father, how could ye never have met him?"

Anne met Rosalyn's gaze with defiance. At last, she could see clearly, and though her head was still pounding, she felt as if she was in control of herself again. "I am a bastard," she spat. "Do ye really think a bastard girl child would warrant supper with the king?" She took a deep breath. "Now where is my mon who escorted me?"

"Dinnae take that tone with me," Rosalyn shouted.

Anne tried to duck as the woman struck out at her. She avoided the brunt of the slap, but Roslyn caught her chin with her hand.

Poor Rob, Anne thought. She knew he was probably dead, left in the woods to die, but maybe not. Maybe he had made it home or someone had found him. Maybe Tor was looking for her this very moment.

"Let her be," Finley called from the hearth.

Anne thought she was underground somewhere. It looked to be the cellar kitchens of some old castle. There was only one abandoned castle in the vicinity of Dunblane and Rancoff, so she had a good idea where she was. If she could escape this room, she knew which way to run. Of course, tied as she was, she would go nowhere.

"Listen to ye," Rosalyn said, turning on Finley. She walked away from Anne. "Tell the truth. Ye want to lie with her. Ye think she is pretty."

The black-haired man flinched as Rosalyn drew closer. "I dinnae want to lie with her."

"Ye think she is pretty. Say it! Ye think she is prettier than I am."

"I think she is ugly," Finley answered. "No one could compare to ye, my fair Rose."

"I should just kill her now," Rosalyn ranted, pacing back and forth in front of the hearth.

Finley turned a hare on a spit over the coals and picked at something on his forearm. " 'Twould make little sense," he said quietly. "If ye want ransom money, ye must have something to ransom."

"Dinnae tell me what to do!"

The woman's voice pierced Anne's brain, and she wiggled backward a little, drawing up her knees, trying to get farther away.

As the argument continued, Anne surveyed her surroundings, only half listening to the two of them. As far as she could tell, it was Elen's sister who was mad, not Finley.

Anne could see no entrance to the tumbledown kitchen. At the hearth, the ceiling was completely intact, but there were other places where parts of it had fallen in. Where Anne sat on the dirt floor, the ceiling was only three or four feet above her, slanted toward the back where where it had caved in. The room was dark, lit by only the fireplace and two burning candles. She could only guess the direction to run if she had a chance.

She glanced back at Finley and Rosalyn. They were still fighting. Finley appeared to be Anne's best chance at getting away. He did not seem as keen on holding her here, or ransoming her. He acted as if he just wanted to get away. If Anne could speak alone with him, maybe she could convince him to let her go. Of course, he also acted as if he loved Rosalyn. Would he kill for her? Anne surmised he would. It seemed obvious from the killings in the area recently that he had done it for her before.

"Tell me one reason why I should let her live," Rosalyn challenged. "Tell me."

Tor and six men rode the path two by two. So far, they had found no sign of Anne or Rob, or of their mounts.

Tor slowed, peering into the darkness beyond the light cast by torches the clansmen behind him carried to light the way. "We cross west here, go around the abandoned castle, and head north and around to meet Munro," he explained.

"And ye've checked here," Banoff said, indicating the ruins.

Only a week before, Tor and Munro had dismounted and walked the perimeter of the fallen castle for a second time. It had been attacked by the English and burned to the ground when Munro was a boy. What was left of the walls had caved into the cellars, and little still stood but waist-high walls and blackened timber.

"Twice," Tor said. "There is naught left standing to hide in."

"Good, no need to dismount," Banoff grumbled. "Some say that by night she is haunted with the souls of the dead."

Tor frowned. He didn't have the time to hear of crofters' superstitions. He had to find Anne and he had to find her quickly. "She's got to be here somewhere," he said gruffly as they approached the ruins.

"She couldnae disappear into the air," Banoff agreed.

Tor's chest felt so tight that he could barely breathe. Was he a fool to think she was still living? Was he a fool to think he would have stopped breathing if she had? He was so crazy with worry that he no longer knew what he thought about anything.

Still riding at the head of the search party, Tor silently passed the ruined castle, urging his mount through the underbrush and around a fallen wall.

If he were a murderer hiding out, where would he hide? Twice he glanced over his shoulder at the ruins, seeing nothing but shadows of destruction, hearing nothing but his instincts screaming at him. But the old keep was nothing but a tall pile of rubbish. He had walked the perimeter himself and dug his boot into the ashes. Slowly, the search party rode past the fallen stone structure, each man searching with a keen-eyed gaze honed in battle, for anything amiss. Tor wondered if perhaps they should be looking beyond the obvious.

"Tell the truth, 'tis her hair," Rosalyn shrieked at Finley. "That is why ye want to lie with her, because she has hair and I have this." Rosalyn yanked a cap off her head to reveal her short, bristly blond hair.

"Nay, ye are wrong." Finley rose from the hearth. Anne was scared. Rosalyn and Finley's argument was growing louder and uglier. Apparently, it had been Rosalyn's idea to kidnap her and ransom her. Now she was accusing Finley of being attracted to Anne. Wanting her. Anne had managed to inch close to a broken stool, hoping she could set herself free. Perhaps she could use a piece of the broken stool to cut away at the rope tying her hands.

That could take hours.

"What if she had no hair?" Rosalyn started for Anne.

Anne tried to shrink farther back beneath the fallen roof. Maybe she could roll away.

"Leave her be."

Rosalyn reached out and grabbed a hank of Anne's hair.

Anne cried out in pain.

Rosalyn pulled a knife from her belt and, before Anne could react, sliced off the handful of hair at chin level.

Anne cried out, more out of fear of the knife than for the loss of her hair.

Rosalyn threw the hair at Finley and it hit him in the chest. Strands floated to the floor, and Anne could not take her gaze from the falling red-blond hair.

It was just hair. But something deep in the pit of Anne's stomach told her Rosalyn would not stop there.

"I said leave her alone," Finley grunted, seeming to surprise Rosalyn. "There is no reason for ye to be jealous of her. I love ye. I have always loved ye, and I could never love another." He reached out to her. "We are meant to be together forever, Rosalyn. Do ye nae see that?"

Rosalyn turned up her lip in a sneer. "Meant to

be together forever?" she snarled. "Ye never truly believed that, did ye?"

Anne did not like the sound of Rosalyn's laughter. Behind her back, she began to yank as hard as she could, praying the rope would loosen.

Finley stared at Rosalyn; the two were standing just in front of Anne. His face was awash with pain, disappointment . . . and a flush of anger.

"Ye said ye loved me," he accused. "I did those things, those terrible things because ye said ye loved me. I did them for *ye!*" His last word was so harsh that spittle flew from his mouth.

"Ye did those things because ye loved me?" Rosalyn sneered. "So prove it." She got into his face, offering the blade. "Kill her now."

Anne's first impulse was to scream, but she suppressed the sound so that it came out of her throat as nothing but a squeak. She didn't want to draw attention to herself. She began to struggle with her hands again. The rope seemed to be loosening, but maybe that was only her imagination. All she could think of was Tor and their baby. She could not die here. She would not.

"No more killing," Finley snapped back. "No more killing for ye."

"Fine. Then I will do it myself."

This time, Anne made no attempt to stifle her cry. She screamed as loud as she could as Rosalyn whipped around, the knife's blade gleaming in the candlelight.

CHAPTER
TWENTY-NINE

"Did ye hear that?" Tor pulled his mount to a halt and turned his head to listen over his shoulder. They had just passed the castle ruins.

"Hear what?

"Voices . . ." Tor said. The night forest was filled with sounds: rustling leaves, animals large and small pushing through the brush, insects chirping, the fluttering of the wings of night birds.

But there should be no sound of human voices. Not here. Not at night. The nearest crofter's cottage was half a mile away.

For the first time, Tor thought he smelled smoke on the air. It was faint, but definitely smoke. Someone was cooking. Was someone cooking in the ruins?

It made no sense, of course. Tor had been here. He had seen with his own eyes by the light of the day that nothing was here. No one.

By the light of the day, but not by the light of the moon . . . .

Tor dug his heels into his horse's flanks and rode hard for the castle ruins.

"Where are ye going?" Banoff shouted. "Munro expects us to be at the meeting place. Tor!"

Tor rounded the corner of the ruins. It was very dark tonight; the moon was shadowed by clouds. He strained to filter out the night sounds and hear sounds that did not belong here.

Voices, and then a scream.

Tor wasn't sure which way to go. He relied on instinct now. He prayed the woman's scream had not been Anne's. He prayed it was. Now, if only he could reach her in time. If it wasn't too late.

Tor did not know if it was his forefathers' gods who were with him, or Anne's Jesus, but in a stroke of luck that could be seen as nothing but a miracle, he spotted a pinprick of light coming from the darkness of the ruins.

He jumped from his horse's back, grabbing his leather-handled broadsword. "Anne!" he shouted into the night. "Anne, I'm coming."

He ran straight into the pile of rubble, into an alcove where the crumbled wall was only chest-high. He ran blindly, blocking out all of the possibilities of what he might find.

Anne could not be dead. His child could not be dead.

Tor prayed to his wife's God as he searched for an opening in the rubble and forced himself to think . . . logically . . . rationally.

The light came from directly beyond this point.

The cellars. Munro had said the stone walls had caved into the cellars years ago, but there had to be something left. Some space beneath the rubble. That was where the light had to be coming from. That was where his Anne had to be.

"Tor!" Banoff called from behind him. "What in the blessed hell are ye doing."

Tor pitched forward, yet found solid stone beneath his feet as he stumbled down the stone steps. There had been no steps here before, just a pile of blackened beams. Beams a man could place in front of an entrance to block it from view.

"Anne," he shouted. "Hold on."

Tor came to an abrupt halt at an entrance that smelled of burned wood, damp stone, and rat droppings. He met with the solid wood of a door, and when he could not immediately find a handle, he took a step back and crashed through it.

The sound of splintering wood filled his head as he burst into a chamber that was dimly lit. An old kitchen.

Tor heard a sound and turned in that direction. There were three bodies in a heap; it was too dim in the low-ceilinged room to see who they were. He thought he saw a glimpse of Anne's slippers.

"Anne!"

The body beneath the other two moved. The slippers moved.

"T-Tor."

He shoved a man's body aside and then a woman's, then fell to his knees before the third person.

It was his Anne, his sweet, defiant Anne.

The bodice of her gown was stained dark. Blood? Tor pulled her into his arms and she hugged him tightly.

"I got my hands free, but I couldn't move fast enough to stop him." The words tumbled from her mouth. "I tried, but I couldn't stop him. And Rob . . . oh, heaven above, I think they killed him, Tor."

Tor didn't understand what she was saying. He

didn't care. All that he cared about was that she was alive.

"Are ye all right?" He pulled back to run his hand over her bloodstained bodice. "Are ye hurt?"

She shook her head. "Their blood." She glanced at the two bodies Tor had pushed aside. "Nae mine. Get me up." Anne waved her hands frantically. "Get them away from me."

He grabbed her arms to lift her, ducking because the ceiling was so low where she sat; but she could not walk.

"My feet. They tied my feet."

Rather than sit her on the dirt floor again, he lifted her in his arms and carried her to a bench. As he pulled out a dirk to cut the ropes that bound her ankles, Banoff and two other men bounded down the steps, swords drawn.

"What the hell?" Banoff said. He looked at the bodies and swore beneath his breath, making a sign to ward off evil spirits. "It cannae be."

Tor threw down the ropes he cut from Anne's ankles. "Are ye sure ye are all right?" he repeated, peering into her face.

She managed a shaky smile and reached out to brush her hand across his cheek. "I am fine. The baby is fine."

Banoff leaned over the two bodies. "Finley and Rosalyn," he breathed.

"Ye know them?" Tor turned to Elen's clansman.

"Know 'em? I lived with 'em half my life." He used his boot to give one and then the other a gingerly push.

The man made no response. The woman groaned.

"Finley and Rosalyn," Anne said. "Elen's old steward and her sister."

"Ye killed them?" Banoff asked Anne with disbelief

as he rolled Rosalyn onto her back and crouched to get a better look.

"Nae me, though if I could have reached a dirk, I would have. They killed Rob." She wiped at her tears.

"She is still alive, but barely," Banoff said.

Tor looked from Banoff to Anne. "What happened? How did they get here? I thought Munro said they were locked away safe for the rest of their days."

"I dinnae know." She rose shakily, using Tor's arm for support "Somehow they escaped. They were the ones doing the slaughtering. He was doing it for her." She spat in disgust.

"I still nae understand," Tor said. "Both are wounded. He looks to be dead already."

She pressed her hand to her forehead. "They got into a fight. I dinnae know which was madder. He loved her and did it all for her. She didn't love him. They meant to ransom me, to gain coin from my father, but then they got into this argument. She wanted him to kill me; then she said she would do it."

Tor's heart still pounded in his chest. It was a good thing Rosalyn and Finley were dead—or nearly dead—or he would have killed them himself now.

"So how, by God's brittle bones, did they both end up stabbed?" Banoff glanced at the bloody knife lying in the dirt near the bodies.

"She tried to kill me. He stopped her. She said she didn't love him, that she never did. He said that if he couldn't have her, no one could." Anne's voice caught in her throat, but she went on. "Then he just stabbed her and slit his own throat."

Tor grabbed Anne and pulled her to his chest, wishing he could take that memory away from her that he knew would be embedded in her mind forever.

"Rosalyn's still alive," Banoff told Tor. He sounded as if he wished she weren't. "Willnae last long, but we'd best get her to Dunblane."

Tor stroked the back of Anne's head. He didn't want to let go of her, not even for a moment. His entire body was still trembling. "Can ye ride?"

She lifted her lashes and tilted her head so that he could lower his mouth to hers. "Of course I can ride," she said against his lips.

"Rosalyn, can ye hear me?" Elen wiped her sister's face of the dried blood. There was nothing she could do about the gut wound. Finley's knife had cut too deeply, and no matter how Elen tried to staunch the blood, she could not stop the dark stain on Rosalyn's stomach from spreading. Rosalyn's eyelids fluttered.

"Rosalyn," Elen repeated. " 'Tis me. 'Tis your sister."

At last, Rosalyn opened her eyes. "Elen?" Her voice was barely a whisper. "What are ye doing here?"

"Ye are home." Elen stroked her sister's damp forehead. All these years Elen had struggled with a mixture of emotions she felt for Rosalyn. Rosalyn had betrayed her, tried to kill her. She had betrayed their father and all that the Clan Burnard stood for. But the anger that bordered on hatred was long gone now. All that mattered were these last few minutes they had left together.

"Home?" Rosalyn's eyelids slipped. "Dunblane?"

Elen had a million questions. How had she escaped? How had Finley escaped? Why had they come here and why had they committed such atrocities? But Elen knew her questions were pointless. Finley was dead, and Rosalyn would not likely live until the bell tolled midnight. The two would take their sordid secrets to the grave and, Elen feared, on to everlasting, burning hell.

"I dinnae want to be here," Rosalyn said, rolling her head one way and then the other. "Get away from me. I hate ye. I hate all of ye, Burnard and Forrest alike."

Elen wanted to think that a fever made her sister speak this way. But in truth, Elen knew some things never changed. Rosalyn could not change, not even on her deathbed.

"Shhhh," Elen soothed, dipping the bloody rag in the pan of warm water.

"Where . . ." Rosalyn winced as she took a deep breath. "Where is Finley?"

Elen would not lie. "Dead."

"The king's daughter did it." Despite her mortal injury, Rosalyn managed to sneer.

"Nay, he died by his own hand," Elen answered softly.

"Good riddance, I say," Rosalyn spat. "May his flesh rot in hell."

Elen sighed. Her heart ached for her sister, for all Rosalyn could have been. But Elen did not hold herself or her parents responsible for this creature Rosalyn had become. What Rosalyn had done had been by free choice.

"Ye should lie still," Elen said, shifting on the edge of the bed.

"I cannae believe he cut me. I cannae believe he did it," Rosalyn mumbled. "I wish I had thought to kill him first." Rosalyn opened her mouth to say something else, but it went slack. Her chest fell and did not rise again.

She was gone.

Her last words had not been ones of regret. She had not asked for a priest or begged forgiveness for the sins she had committed.

Elen pressed her sister's eyelids shut and closed her own eyes in prayer. She did not know what good it would do Rosalyn now, but she prayed to God for mercy on her sister's soul anyway.

Behind Elen, the door opened.

It was Munro. She got up from the bed. He met her halfway across the chamber. She didn't have to say a word. Her beloved Munro took her in his arms and let her cry.

"Ye dinnae have to do this," Anne argued.

Tor had already removed her clothes and sponged-bathed the blood from her body, and now he lowered a clean sleeping gown over her head.

"I do not, but let me. I need to do this."

"Ye are sure Rob is all right?"

"We found him just where ye thought he might be," Tor explained. They had dragged him into the forest to let him die. Elen will see to his wound. He will live."

Anne pushed the folds of the gown down, took Tor's hand, and gently laid it on her abdomen. It was just beginning to swell, but already Anne could imagine the son or daughter she would give birth to. "I can already feel the baby flutter," she said. "At least I think I can."

Tor slid into the bed bedside her and laid his cheek on her belly. "I love ye," he murmured, pressing his mouth to her belly. "And I love your mother. Do ye hear me, wee one?"

Anne looked at him. "What did ye say?"

Tor lifted his head to glance up. "I told our child that I loved him . . . or her."

She shook her head. She was still reeling from all that had happened tonight, but for the moment, she was able to push it all aside. All that mattered right now was the two of them. "Nay, after that. What did ye say?"

He slid up in the bed until they were nose to nose, facing each other. He seemed hesitant. "I told the bairn that I love ye."

She frowned. "Ye do?"

"Of course I do." He sounded surprised. "Why else would I have married ye, Anne?"

"Ye mean ye love me now, now that ye realize something could have happened to me." She ran her hand over her belly. "To your child."

"Nay. I have always loved ye. I've loved ye since the day I first laid eyes upon ye."

She gave a little laugh that was almost a sob. "So why did ye never tell me so?" she asked, her heart suddenly hammering in her chest.

He stared blankly. "I did."

She pushed up in the bed a little. "When?"

"The night on the beach. When we made love. Do ye nae remember? Ye asked me what I said and I told ye in English. I told ye then that I loved ye."

"I . . . I suppose I thought ye were just saying that because we had just . . . ye know."

He studied her eyes carefully. "Ye didnae know I loved ye Anne?" He sounded shocked.

"Tor, ye have to tell a woman when ye love her."

"I *did*. I assumed ye did not feel the same way, but I hoped ye would come to love me someday."

This time her laugh was genuine. If she had had something to hit him with, she would have. "I nae knew. Ye must tell a woman ye love her *more* than once."

"Must I?"

She felt almost giddy inside. He loved her. Tor loved her. He said he had always loved her, and the look on his face was as convincing as any words could possibly be. "Aye, ye must tell me. Ye must tell me that ye love me every day," she said.

He nodded. "I nae knew. Ye are my first wife." He grinned. "My first love."

Anne threw her arms around Tor. She still did not know what path her marriage with this Norseman would take, but she knew she would be happy. They would be happy.

"I love ye, Tor Henneson, son of Munro Forrest," she said.

"And I love ye, Anne de Bruc, daughter of a king."

"Say it again," she whispered.

"I love ye, Anne."

"Again."

"I love ye."

EPILOGUE

Eight months later

Ellen stuck her head in Anne's bedchamber door. "Are ye ready?" she called. "Munro says the priest has finally arrived."

Anne glanced over her shoulder as she lifted her daughter onto her shoulder. "I'm coming." She shifted the baby to one arm so she could tighten her bodice with the other hand. "Will ye take her? I swear, I think I could use three or four arms these days."

Laughing, Elen came into the room, her arms spread. "Come to me, my little poppet."

The baby waved her arms and giggled, her Nordic blue eyes bright with laughter.

"Where is Tor?" Her gown drawn respectably shut, Anne hurried to the tiny mirror on the wall to pat her hair. They were going to Dunblane's kirk for the baby's baptism and then a celebration in the hall.

"Downstairs, waiting for us."

"Anne!" Tor's footsteps echoed in the stairwell as he came up the steps.

"I'm coming. I'm coming." She fluttered her hands.

Her handsome husband stepped in the doorway. "Ye must come now."

Anne's brow furrowed.

Elen turned to Tor in surprise, his daughter balanced on her hip.

"Is something wrong?" Anne asked.

"There's someone here to see ye. To see the baby."

"I dinnae understand. Who—"

Tor grabbed his wife's arm. "Come to the hall." He glanced at Elen as he led Anne out the door. "I think ye will want to come, too."

"I cannae understand who would come today," Anne said as Tor led her down the stairs toward Rancoff's Hall.

"You'll see."

"Why are ye being so secretive? I swear by all that's holy, Tor, ye—"

Anne halted in midsentence as Tor stepped back and allowed Anne to pass through the door to the great hall. There was another man there—a man dressed like a king.

Anne could not lift a foot to take another step. Slowly, she raised her hand to her mouth. There was no need for introductions. She knew who this man was.

"Look who has come and brought a gift," Munro said, grinning.

Anne just stood there and stared. She did not know if she was angry, or thrilled, or a combination of both. She just stood in the doorway, staring at the red-haired man.

After all this time, he had come.

"Anne . . ." The king spoke, and she was surprised by the sound of his voice. It was a gentle voice. A warm voice. Was this truly a man who had led his soldiers to defeat the greatest army in all of Christendom? Was this really her father?

Tor gently gave Anne a push toward Robert the Bruce, and whispered in her ear, "There isnae much time. He only passes through."

Anne fell into a deep curtsy. "Your Grace," she said.

He came forward and took her hand, smiling broadly. "Ye are more beautiful than Munro described ye." He looked at Munro. "Why did ye nae tell me I had such a beautiful daughter?"

A lump rose in Anne's throat. For years, she had practiced what she would say if she ever met this man face to face, and now her mind was without thought. All she could do was stare at him.

The Bruce lowered his head and pressed his lips to her hand. "I brought a gift for your daughter." He smiled. "My granddaughter. I cannae stay. I only wanted to"—he did not finish his sentence, but met Anne's gaze head-on—"to see ye just this once."

She could not tear her gaze from his.

He spoke quietly, honestly, as if she were his equal. As if she were someone to be treasured. "I am sorry that I havenae written. That I didnae come to see ye."

"But ye've a kingdom to attend to," she said, surprised that there was no sarcasm in her voice.

"But I wanted to protect ye," he said, still holding fast to her hand. "I knew ye would be safe and happy here." He glanced at Munro. "I have trusted Forrest with my life, and I trusted him with your life."

His explanation was so simple. Anne did not know

if that explanation could heal all of the pain she had felt all these years, but suddenly the past seemed of little import. She was so happy here at Rancoff with Tor and her new baby. All the aches of her younger days seemed only a distant memory now.

"We are honored that ye have come, Your Grace," she managed. "Ye are certain ye cannae stay for Lizzy's baptism?"

"Anne, I have many enemies. On this shore and others." He kissed her hand again. "I cannae stay. I wanted only to bring my gift and to tell ye how often I have thought of ye over the years. Of your mother."

Anne swallowed against the lump in her throat, still holding on to her father's hand. "Ye have met my husband, Tor?"

Robert glanced over her shoulder at Tor, who stood behind her. "We had occasion to meet last year. If he is half the man his father is, ye couldnae have chosen a better husband."

His wording did not get by her. *She* could not have chosen a better husband, her father had said.

Anne covered her father's hand with her other hand. "I wish that ye could stay," she said, tears gathering in her eyes.

"I wish, too, that I could stay." He pointed to the table. "Your daughter's gift. A land grant for property near Aberdeen."

Land? For a girl child? The idea was almost unheard of. Elen was the only woman Anne had ever known who owned her own property.

"Well, whilst we are giving gifts, I have one as well," Munro spoke up. "Tor."

Anne glanced over her shoulder at her husband. Tor had been here a year and a half. He had worked his father's land and fulfilled all of the duties Munro handed to him. Tor had ridden into this keep to take what coin he could from his father, and then return to his mother's homeland. Now, he was just thankful to live beneath this roof and be loved.

"Elen and I have talked. Robert and I have talked. Elen and I will have no more children." He reached out and took Elen's hand and smiled at her. "And between the two of us, we have plenty of property to pass on to our children—all three of them. So, with permission from Robert the Bruce, I grant ye this keep to hold in the Clan Forrest name, if ye will have it. If ye will have us."

Anne pulled her hand from her father's and turned to throw her arms around Tor. "God speed husband, and God help ye." She looked into his eyes, unashamed of her tears. " 'Tis official, ye are a Forrest until ye die and then some."

Tor stood holding Anne and staring at Munro, who had just taken the baby into his arms. "I . . . I . . ."

"Just say ye accept," Munro laughed. "And let us get to the kirk so the celebration can begin."

Tor lowered his head in respect. "I would be honored to accept your gift, my lord." He lifted his gaze. "Father."

"Well, I am glad that I could come and settle this matter," Robert said. "And now I must go." He opened his arms to Anne. "So give me a kiss, daughter. Let me hold my granddaughter, and then we must all be on our way."

Anne released Tor and walked into her father's embrace, all of the pain and resentment slipping away as the older man's arms wrapped around her. Wiping the tears from her eyes, she took the baby from Munro and pressed her into the king's arms.

As Robert lifted the blond-haired baby into the air and she giggled, Anne stepped back into Tor's arms.

"Say it again," she said, leaning against his broad chest as he wrapped his arms around her waist.

"I love ye," he whispered in her ear.